Siberia

Siberia

Ann Halam

Seed corn must not be ground
Goethe

Orion
Children's Books

First published in Great Britain in 2005
by Orion Children's Books
a division of the Orion Publishing Group Ltd
Orion House
5 Upper St Martin's Lane
London WC2H 9EA

10 9 8 7 6 5 4 3 2

A catalogue record for this book is
available from the British Library

Typeset by Deltatype Ltd,
Birkenhead, Merseyside

Printed in Great Britain by
Clays Ltd, St Ives plc

ISBN 1 84255 129 9

www.orionbooks.co.uk

For Jacinta Elizabeth Jones

Arriving . . .

The little girl and her mother get off the train at a deserted platform in the middle of nowhere. The men in uniform who have looked after them all the way, never leaving Mama's side for a moment, get down too. There's a small hut, with a notice on the door that is half-hidden by a splash of frozen mud. A tractor waits beside it, with an open metal cart hooked up behind. The railway line stitches a scar that trails away to the horizon. There's nothing else to be seen except the snow, the wide sky, and a distant border of darkness in every direction, which the little girl knows is 'forest', though she isn't sure what a 'forest' is. The men help Mama and the little girl into the cart, and put their bags in after them, then turn away without a word.

'Goodbye!' calls the little girl. 'Thank you, and safe home!'

The nicest of the four men looks back, and smiles sadly.

The tractor starts to move. There's nowhere to sit except on their bags, or on the dirty metal floor. The little girl thinks this is strange, but everything has been strange since Dadda went away; she's getting used to it. The cart bumps and rattles over the frozen ground, and the little girl soon

1

becomes fascinated by the whole experience. The tractor is like a giant toy, there are no tractors in the city except in toyshops. The flat open space all around is unbelievably *huge*. She lies on her back on the floor, and the jolts and jumps are like a funhouse ride. The sky is so empty it seems to be roaring silently. 'Rosita!' Mama's voice comes. 'Rosita, sit up. Your coat is getting dirty.' The little girl sits up, and carefully brushes the dirt from her cherry-red coat, which she loves, with her mittened hands. The journey goes on, for what seems a very long time. *I am hungry, I am thirsty*, thinks Rosita, but she doesn't complain, this isn't the time for complaining. She nestles by her mother's side. The emptiness of the cold land is like magic, so wide, so wild. It catches at the little girl's heart, and fills her with a longing she can't express.

At last black marks appear on the endless white, and grow until they are huddled, bow-shouldered huts like the one at the station platform. There are tracks leading from one hut to another, dirty and deep-gouged between walls of snow; larger buildings can be seen in the background. The border of forest is where it was, neither nearer nor farther. The tractor stops. There are people waiting, but nobody is in uniform. It seems wrong that there are no guards: it must be very dangerous to be on an adventure so far outside the city.

Rosita speaks, for the first time in hours. 'Where are the guards, Mama?'

The mother looks at the little girl, with a sad smile that reminds Rosita of the nice man at the train station. 'Guards aren't needed here.'

'That's *good*,' says the little girl, because she thinks Mama needs cheering up.

Someone's lifting out the bags. In a moment it will be

Rosita's turn. She peers over the edge of the cart, looking down at the rumpled, ice-packed surface onto which she'll be lowered, like a package. Midwinter is a dry season here: there'll be no new falls until spring is on the way. The snow is old, but Rosita doesn't know about that. She looks at her feet, her red shoes. She can feel how thin the soles are. Suddenly she knows how it will feel to walk on that icy snow. It will be as if she had no shoes at all! A shock runs through her. She wants to say something: Mama, you made a mistake, we can't stay here ... She doesn't speak. She doesn't want to upset her Mama, who has been so sad since Dadda went away. She only *looks.*

The mother takes the child in her arms. She's a small woman and the long, cold journey has made her stiff and clumsy, but she manages to get out of the cart without any help. The people standing round are fat bundles of grubby clothes with hollow faces, they don't look like people at all, more like ugly toys. Is this Toyland? Is this where bad toys go? Rosita hides her face. Mama carries her, along a track and into one of the huts, and sets her down.

1

The little girl was me, Sloe. I was Rosita. I had to give up my name; I'll explain why when I get to that part. That tractor ride is my oldest memory. I think about it often and I treasure all the details, because I can't remember anything from the time before. I have been told things, and I've seen photographs, but I can't remember my father's face. It's as if my life began that day, under the wide blank roaring sky, with the nice guard who smiled, the coldness; my cherry-red coat. The strangest thing is remembering that I didn't know there was anything wrong. When I realised that my shoes were too thin for the snow, I was frightened because my Mama had made a mistake – and Mama never made mistakes! I didn't know what had happened to us, I didn't know what was going on at all.

I didn't know anything: I was only four.

I don't remember what I saw when my mother put me down, but I know how our hut must have looked when it was empty. I know that Rosita saw a rather long, thin room (I thought it was big, until I knew it was our whole house), with a concrete floor. At one end there was a dark green enamel stove, with a chimney going up the wall. Beside the stove there were wooden sliding doors shutting off an alcove in the wall, that turned out to hold the bed that Mama and Rosita shared. Along the edge of the cupboard-bed the floor was covered by a kind of raft of wooden planks, gratefully warm to your feet compared with the concrete (which was like walking on grey ice, winter and summer). On the other side of the room there was a dark green sink, with a strange kind of spout standing by it and no taps. The walls were dusty bare planks, in places cracked so you could see the earth-bricks behind them. There was no ceiling, just the naked beams of the rooftree, and a shelf going all around, where the roof and the walls met.

Half way down the room was a partition, with sliding doors like the bed-cupboard, but dark green and shining like the stove and the sink. Through there, Rosita would find the workshop where her Mama was going to spend hours and hours, every day, turning out nails from scrap metal. The nails were to be used in the making of huts like ours, and furniture for huts like ours, in prison Settlements all over the wilderness: but the little girl didn't know that. She didn't know what the red light on the wall in the workshop meant, either. She thought the machines were more ugly toys, and she hated it when Mama insisted on playing with them. All she wanted to do was to get out into snow, into the wild emptiness ... But if she had to stay in, why wouldn't Mama play with her?

When we arrived our hut had nothing, not even a mattress for the boards in the cupboard-bed. Mama had a wad of start-up vouchers, better than the normal paper-money of the Settlements, (which was called scrip, and which would hardly buy anything, as we found out later). We went to one of the big buildings with our wealth, and bought a mattress, a table and two chairs, an oil lamp and some lamp oil. There was enough to pay for delivery of the table and chairs. Mama dragged our mattress home herself on a sled, with me sitting up on top in my thin little babyshoes; then she returned the sled to the store. We had to go to another building for food supplies and kitchen things. We didn't have to buy fuel for the stove: The heat came through pipes, from a smoky, stinky brown-coal power station. We didn't have to buy water, either. It came out of the spout by our sink when you pumped the handle . . . except in the worst part of winter, when we had to melt snow and boil it.

We thought we'd done well on that first shopping trip. In fact it was weeks before we had everything we needed. Mama didn't know how to live like this. She didn't know that you needed chemicals to drop down the hole in the earth-closet, to keep it from smelling bad. She didn't know what a tin-opener was. We didn't know we needed vegetable seeds; or a sack of grit, to keep in the bin by our door. There was nobody to tell us these things. No neighbours came round to help us. We didn't have any friends until much later.

There were no warm clothes or thick-soled shoes for a little girl in the store that month, and there was only one clothing store, so I had to stay indoors. Mama spared an hour a day teaching me to read and to play with numbers. The rest of the time I was very bored, and I sulked a lot. I spent hours pressed against the workshop partition, crying for her to come out. But the nights were cosy. I loved being tucked up with my Mama, under our new rough blankets, between our new, scratchy sheets. On one of those nights (this is my second true memory, the second treasure) I woke feeling cold, and Mama wasn't with me. I sat up and dug out my socks, which I'd kicked off in my sleep (we slept in our socks, for extra cosiness). I pulled them on and got down onto the raft of planks. The workshop partition

6

was open a crack: I could see a moving shadow. Mama was playing in there, in the middle of the night. The stove was burning low. I went padding over, with the icy cold piercing through my socks and my little pyjamas, and peered through. My Mama was at work but the machinery was silent. She was crouched down on the floor, *under* the bench. In front of her she had a round white case; it was open. I could see tubes and droppers in a rack, and a row of glass dishes, all very small, like glassware for a doll's house. As soon as I saw these things, I wanted to play with them. They were so neat, so small, so perfect: and I loved the way Mama looked like a child, a little girl like me, playing down there on her knees, under the grown-up things. She had a strip of white gauzy stuff over her nose and mouth, and her fingers glimmered, as if they were coated in magic. I saw her take the droppers, and drop something liquid into each of the dishes . . .

I was shivering until my teeth rattled. I had to clamp them shut or Mama would have heard me: but I was incredibly excited. I was sure my Mama was doing magic. I was frightened, and so thrilled. I was sure something dreadful or wonderful was going to happen. I watched, my eyes popping out of my face, until each of the dishes had a drop of dark goo, and a shaking of pale powder from the little tubes. Then I couldn't bear it any longer. I tiptoed back to the bed-cupboard as fast as I could, and hid my head under the covers, my heart beating fast.

Next morning nothing had changed. I didn't say a word to my mother about what I had seen. Wild horses couldn't have dragged it out of me: I was scared to death of having a Mama who could do magic. It was as if I'd seen her turn into a swan, or a wolf, or a witch: and yet it only made me love her more. But I was so little that I forgot. By bedtime, the whole thing had gone out of my head like a dream. I didn't think of the magic again until Nivvy appeared.

You wouldn't have known it in the winter, but our huts were built on concrete pillars. If they hadn't been, the heat from our stoves would have made them sink into the boggy ground in summer. When you looked out of the front door you were at the top of a flight of steps, buried in the winter snow. We sprinkled them every morning with grit, (wise people put extra salt in it) to make them less slippery. Mama had given me this job. It was the nearest I could get to being outdoors until I had boots, so I made it last. A few days after that strange night, I was on my knees on our doormat, patting the grit and spreading it with my mittened hands. It tasted of salt, when I tried licking it. I was getting my mittens filthy, but Mama didn't say anything. We both knew those city mittens weren't going to last. Suddenly, I saw something move (and this is the third treasure). A tiny animal, with brown fur and bright eyes, was sitting on the doormat beside me. I didn't dare breathe. I had never seen a wild animal, or heard of such a pretty one, except in a fairytale.

'Mama!' I squealed. 'Look!'

I stared at him. He stared right back, fearlessly. Then he jumped at my mitten and *bit* me, with teeth like tiny, white-hot needles. Instinctively, I grabbed him.

'Mama!' I ran into the hut, hugging him to my chest, blood dripping from me. 'Mama! I've found a wild amnimnal, I've found a wild amnimnal!' (I couldn't say *animal*-) 'Can I keep him? Can I keep him, oh please say I can keep him!'

'Ooh, I don't know if we're allowed pets,' said Mama doubtfully. 'Where on earth did he come from? Did you see where he came from?'

'I think he came from a tunnel in the snow. Mama, let me keep him! I can play with my amnimnal, and then I'll leave you in peace!'

'Animal,' said my mother. 'He's an *animal*, Rosita. Well, yes, you can keep him, unless somebody tells us no. Put him down, let's see what he does.'

'He'll run away,' I protested. I didn't know much about animals, but I knew what *I* would do. If I were captive, I would always run away.

'No he won't,' said Mama. 'He's a wise little thing. He has sharp eyes, and looks before he leaps. Let him make this hut his territory, and he'll never leave it.'

So I set him down. He looked carefully around him, then made for cover in the heap of toys: my toys, that Mama had brought from the city, which I had refused to play with. 'Stay still,' said Mama. We knelt there, me hardly breathing, until his tiny head appeared from the window of a toy car. Gradually, rippling his slender body around and around, he made the toy heap his own, checking out every crevice. Then he sat up, with his chocolate nose quivering, and made a dart for me. He jumped onto my knees, grabbed my fingertip, (not the bitten finger, I was hiding that hand!) and looked up with bright attention. 'I'm your friend,' I whispered. My animal nuzzled and licked my fingertip, but he didn't bite. He made a chirring noise in his throat and curled himself up, settling in my hand as if it was his nest.

Then something I can't explain happened. Or at least, I can partly explain it. You see, I knew that Nivvy had not really come from a tunnel in the snow. I hadn't seen him until he was sitting by me on the doormat, but I knew he must have come from inside our hut. He was like something from a fairytale, and I had seen my Mama doing

9

magic. I looked from her to the warm little creature in my hand, and felt dizzy.

'Mama, did you *make* him?'

Mama looked at me as if she were seeing me for the first time. (This is the bit I can't explain, how it felt to have Mama gaze at me then: so carefully, so solemnly). 'No,' she said. 'Life made him, the same as Life made you and me. But you have asked an important question, and I'm going to start telling you the answer—'

I must have looked frightened, because she smiled, and kissed me.

'Not now, but in a little while. Don't worry, Rosita, it's a nice answer.'

That was how Nivvy came into our lives (I'll explain how he got his name soon). Before long he chose a home for himself, a small grain jar with a narrow neck, that we kept on its side up on the roof shelf; but I was always his preferred territory. He'd spend whole days climbing over me, or sleeping in my pocket. I got bitten hard from time to time, but I didn't care. He grew, quickly, until he was a little more than the length of Mama's hand, with a slim, sinuous body and a furry tail. He played with me, he watched over me, he guarded me while I slept: and just as I'd promised Mama, he kept me happy, so she could work. Nobody except Mama and me knew about him. He never left the hut, and nobody came to visit us in those days except Mr Nail Collector.

Once we got caught by Mr Nail Collector. At first I'd been respectful of this man because he wore a uniform, like Mr Security who stood in the hall of our apartment block in the city, and was always nice to us. But Mr Nail Collector's 'uniform' was just a tattered collar with a number on it, stitched onto a jacket made from old hairy blankets, and though he didn't scowl as fiercely as the uniformed ladies at the stores he was rude to Mama. He came to visit us often in that first month, even though we never invited him (and I thought this was rude, too). The first time, he threw the boxes Mama had filled with nails all over the floor of the workshop, and shouted at her that she didn't know how to work, and he would report her. It got better, but he'd always find something wrong with at least one box.

Usually he came to the door at the workshop end of our hut, and I would stay out of sight, although I peeked through the partition, to see what was going on. The time he saw Nivvy we were taken by surprise, because his motor sledge pulled up at our front steps. He talked to Mama there and they both came indoors. I knew that Mama was upset to have him in our living room, though she was smiling. I thought, oh no, he's going to throw her nails on the floor again. I decided I would run over his foot with my toy tractor, which had quite sharp wheels.

Then I remembered Nivvy.

I could *feel* that Mama was afraid. It was as if there was a wire connecting me to her, and it was pulled too tight . . . I stayed on the floor, among my toys, and didn't look up as I felt the Nail Collector's eyes on me. Out of the corner of my eye I could glimpse Nivvy, up on the roof-shelf. He'd been playing there: looking into things, sniffing around, making sure there was nothing new. The Nail Collector sat down, and Mama gave him a cup of tea. He asked in a wheedling voice did she have something sweet, maybe a little jam?

'Not this time,' said my Mama, with a smile in her voice, and deadly fear behind the smile. 'We're rather short of extras—'

'That's because you don't know how to work,' said the Nail Collector. I felt him looking at me, and he gave a cough. 'You could sell the child's toys.'

'That's a *good* idea,' said Mama. 'I'll have to see about that.'

I wasn't angry. I didn't care about any old toys, I only wanted to keep my Nivvy safe. I was trying to watch him without looking up, and I knew Mama was trying to watch him too. I prayed he would be scared and stay out of sight. But Nivvy had no fear. He was never, never afraid. He came to the edge of the shelf, by his grain-jar. I saw him peering curiously at the top of the Nail Collector's head, and had to bite the inside of my mouth to keep from gasping with horror. I knew what Nivvy could see. He could see a big furry thing – the top of the Nail Collector's hat – moving gently up and down as the Nail Collector sipped his tea. I knew what would happen next. Nivvy couldn't possibly resist. He could never resist pouncing on anything that moved! He would have to attack the hat.

Nivvy jumped. I could see the hat jerk, and I knew he was twisting around up there, biting fiercely and gripping the enemy with his claws. I prayed harder, to all my Mama's magic . . . It was no use. The Nail Collector got a very puzzled expression, he set down his cup, reached up and took his hat off. His head was round as a ball and smeared with black streaks of hair. He held the hat, his eyebrows coming together in a frown; his face, seamed with dirt in the creases, screwed up in amazement. Although I was terrified I had to bite my mouth harder, to stop myself from laughing. I *prayed* that Nivvy would not attack those tempting fat bare fingers—

Nivvy stared back at the man for two seconds, no fear in

his bright eyes, and then he vanished: a streak of brown too fast for eyes to follow.

'What the devil was that—?' exclaimed the Nail Collector.

Mama was perfectly calm. 'I don't know. Some kind of rat that lives in the walls. Don't all the huts have them?' She shrugged, as if this subject was completely boring. 'I think it keeps the bugs down.' There were a lot of big, mean bugs in our hut. They bit us when we were asleep, and the bug-poison you could get from the store was useless.

'I could get you rat bait,' said the Nail Collector, shrugging the same way, and putting his hat back on. 'It would cost you, but good product, real poison, not like the store stuff. Only, we keep it quiet.'

Mama smiled again. 'Thank you. Maybe next month.'

When he had gone, taking her boxes of nails, Mama came and sat with me on the planks by the bed, with her knees tucked up: there was just enough room for the two of us, on the warm wooden shore beside the icy concrete sea. The smell of the Nail Collector lingered, almost stronger than the smell of an excited Nivvy. Mama put my princess-doll's tiara on my head, and pulled a funny face at me.

'Are you frightened of the Nail Collector?' I asked her.

'No,' said Mama, putting my red dressing-up cloak around her own shoulders, and fastening the jewelled clasp, which would just about fasten around her neck, 'He doesn't mean us any harm, Rosita. This is the safest place in the world.'

I knew she had been terribly scared, but I didn't blame her for lying.

'What does *increase your quota* mean?'

I had heard the Nail Collector say that. He would increase Mama's quota.

'It means I have to make more nails, and I get more scrip. It's kind of him to offer. But it's not true that it would help us to buy extra jam; the jam is rationed.'

I nodded, as if I knew what *rationed* meant. My mother put princess-bracelets on her arms, looking at them carefully as she fastened them. Her wrists were thicker than mine, but the bracelets fitted. I thought she looked very beautiful. She raised her eyes, which were clear and dark like mine. 'Toys and books,' she sighed, 'toys and books. I brought what I thought was precious, and nothing that we needed. I didn't know, I didn't think . . . You have a very silly Mama, Rosita.'

'The guards were in a hurry,' I said. 'They didn't give you much time.'

Nivvy came bouncing up and skipped onto my knee. I could tell he knew he'd been naughty, so I told him off. 'No biting hats! Don't bite hats!' I said, shaking my finger at him. This was a dangerous thing to do (I think I was trying to distract Mama from her thoughts); but Nivvy was not in a biting mood. He grabbed my finger and wound himself around it, licking and purring and tickling with his whiskers.

'Mama,' I asked, 'Why did we call him Nivvy? Did I think of that?'

'No, it's his proper name,' said Mama. She touched my darling Nivvy's sleek nose with her fingertip, and he purred louder. He loved my mother. 'His whole true name is *Mustela Nivalis Vulgaris*, it means he's the king of the snow.'

'But he must never tell anyone his true name,' I whispered. 'Except us.' I knew, from the fairytales Mama used to tell me at bedtime, that true names are magic.

14

'That's right. He must never tell, and neither must you, Rosita.'

That night, or maybe the night after (I know it was before I had my boots), Mama woke me up long after I had gone to sleep: and this is the fourth treasure. She made me put on my coat over my pyjamas, took a blanket from our bed and carried me into the dark workshop. She set me on the floor, wrapped in the blanket.

'Now,' she said. 'Remember how you asked me if I had made Nivvy? I'm going to show you. Are you ready, Rosita?'

Sometimes Nivvy slept with me, but he was sleeping in his grain jar that night.

'Are you going to hurt him?' I whispered.

Really, I was sure my Mama would never hurt Nivvy, but I was frightened.

'Of course not. You stay there.'

Mama went and fetched our oil-lamp and set it by me on the floor, turned low. Then she reached under the workshop bench, and pulled out a nailbox from under the other battered boxes that were piled there. It looked like all the rest. When she opened it I saw the round white shining case.

I didn't say a word. I was shivering in awe. Mama looked at me and nodded, so I knew I should keep quiet. She did something to the case and it unfolded, making a flat, white shining flower. Mama started taking things from inside, showing them to me and setting them out on the spread petals. There was an envelope, which was full of slim white packets that had a clean sort of smell. I got an odd feeling from that smell, like a memory trying to be born: about another time, another place, my Mama and my Dadda ... Then came the doll's house droppers and tubes and dishes, in a little rack just the right size for them, and last of all a small box shaped like a wrinkled nut, a nut big enough to fit snugly in the palm of my Mama's hand.

The other things were city things that brought fuzzy memories of our old home. I was so little, everything before our tractor ride was already dim and long ago. But I *knew* the nutshell was magic. It was exactly like something in a fairytale.

There was a thin dark line around the middle of it. Mama ran her fingertips around there: the nut came open in two halves and inside, snuggled in a nest of silky stuff, I saw tiny, furry living creatures. They looked up at me, with eyes no bigger than pin-heads. The boldest stood on its hind legs and reached up its miniature paws, whiskers that you could hardly see quivering with excitement.

They were so tiny, like pets for a dolls' house! They couldn't get out, there was a clear barrier in the way. But I wanted to touch them. I wanted to hold them, and I *knew* they wanted me to stroke them, with the tiniest tip of my finger—

I stared, my heart beating hard with longing—

'Do you like them?' came my Mama's voice.

'I *love* them.'

'Good,' she said. 'It's good that you love them.'

'What are they?'

'That's what I'm going to tell you. But first you have to know that one day you might be their guardian. I'm their guardian now, one day it might be you.'

She closed the nutshell, and set it down. I was terribly disappointed, but I trusted my Mama. I knew she wouldn't tease me. She would let me touch those little fairy-pets soon, if I was good and kept quiet and listened.

'Now,' she said. 'Do you know why there are hardly any wild animals?'

Of course there were no wild animals in the city: it was all indoors. But I had been told there were no nice ones in the wilderness either. There were only *vermin*, and *muties*: nasty names of nasty things. I had heard about them at my crèche.

'Is it because of the *vermin and muties*?'

Muties were horrible creatures, ugly monsters that would eat you or give you diseases. I had never seen one. I'd never seen a rat or a cat or a gull (these were the vermin), in the city either: but I was scared of them.

'No, though that's a good guess. You're a very clever little girl, Rosita. It's because of the cold, and because of other things that people did, a while ago, that took away all the places where wild animals could live freely. The only animals that thrive now are the ones that can survive on our garbage. But the spring will come again; the true spring. The little creatures in the incubator – that's the case I just showed you – are like seeds. They are the seeds of all the wild animals that once lived in our land.'

I nodded solemnly, although I didn't understand.

'We must look after them, and tend them, until it's the season for their return. They're safe here for the moment. One day, maybe quite soon, or maybe years and years from now, when you are grown-up, it will be time to take them to the city ... Not our city, another city; where the sun always shines. It's a long journey, hundreds of miles to the north and west, through the wilderness and the forest, through the forests to the sea, and across the ice to the other side—'

I was overjoyed. There was nothing I wanted more than

to go running into the roaring silence of the wilderness. Then my heart sank.

'Oh . . . But we can't walk that far, Mama.'

'We won't have to walk, Rosy. The country out there looks empty, but it isn't. There are many people living in it, and some of them will help us.'

I was doubtful about this. I believed that the only people who lived in the wilderness were the ugly Toytown people in these huts.

'Will the ice on the sea be strong enough?'

'There's always ice on that strait. In the summer, special ships can sometimes get through it. But we wouldn't get tickets. If we cross in winter, the ice will be safe.'

'When can we go? Tomorrow?'

'Not tomorrow. I don't know how long.' She smiled at me. 'But I'm going to teach you how to look after the Lindquist kits, that's what we call the seed-creatures. Only you must promise never to tell anyone else. You must never, never talk about these things to anyone except me. You understand that, don't you?'

I nodded firmly. 'I won't tell.'

'Good girl.' She looked at me, with that solemn, magical expression again, the same as when I had asked her did she make Nivvy. Then she raised her hands, and opened the collar of her nightgown (shrugging aside her coat, which she was wearing over her nightclothes, the same as me). 'Look here, Rosita.'

I got up and looked, holding onto my blanket, and I saw a pattern, marked on her white skin by the base of her throat. There was a pretty circlet of green feathery leaves, spoiled by a black cross.

'That's the Chervil Ring tattoo,' said my Mama. 'Chervil is the herb that old-time people used to plant first in the spring, or when they came to live somewhere new. It's the sign of life. It means that I'm from the Institute, a place for people who have vowed to learn about life, and serve and protect all living things.'

'What is the black crossing-out for?'

'It's not for anything,' said Mama. 'It's to show that I don't belong there any more.' She spoke so calmly that the loss in her voice didn't worry me.

'Can I have the life mark?'

Mama smiled. 'Maybe, one day, who knows ... Remember to keep secret the things that are secret, Rosita, and we can live here. I think no one means to hurt us, not even the Nail Collector. We'll have to be careful, and no one must know about Nivvy, but I will quietly teach you what you need to learn, and all will be well.'

When I had my boots and I could play outdoors, I didn't mention Nivvy to the other children I met, and I never spoke of Mama's magic. There are things small children understand better than most grown-ups think. I didn't know why we had come to live here, but I knew we were in hostile territory, my Mama and I. And though I was not naturally a good little girl (I was often very naughty, I couldn't help it), I knew that a promise is a promise.

Nivvy was my best friend and dear companion. I would wake up on the coldest nights, when the heat was so low it barely made a thread of red on the stove's dial, with a warm silken weight in the hollow of my collarbone, and it would be Nivvy, snuggled tight. He made tunnels behind the planks of our walls and I would chase him, tapping and whispering 'Where's Nivvy?'; until I pretended to give up. 'Oh well,' I'd say, in a mournful voice, 'Nivvy's gone! Bye bye Nivvy—'. Immediately his head would pop out of one of the cracks. He'd laugh at me with his chirring noise, come jumping across the room and bounce into my hand – and curl up there, cuddling my finger and purring like a kitten.

The months passed, with no incident except for the supply trucks that arrived with troops of armed guards and brought food and goods to our stores, and visits from Nicolai the Nail Collector, who was our 'Brigade Chief', and the nearest thing our Settlement had to a prison officer. The spring blizzards came, and at last the thaw; and again I couldn't go outdoors, because the mud made our street into a disgusting oozy river. I cried because the beautiful snow had gone, and then I was *astonished* to see the blank emptiness grow green, and dance with the flowers of a wilderness spring. We had gardens in the city, but I had thought it was always winter outside. Nicolai the Nail Collector gave Mama and me a vegetable plot, out on the edge of the Settlement where people were allowed to grow extra food. We didn't have much success, not that first year, but we tried. Then in a few weeks summer was over, and another long, hungry winter began.

The little king of the snows lived with us in secret for a year and a half, then he got old and died. Mama had given me several lessons in magic by then. She tried to tell me that Nivvy, the real Nivvy, was NOT gone forever, no more than a plant is gone forever when it sets its seed and withers at the end of the growing season. But I cried and cried, and wouldn't listen. It was summertime. Mama wrapped the poor little remains in one of my city mittens, and we buried him among the dwarf willows, out by the vegetable patches. And life went on, day after day: a hard, empty and hungry life, but the only one I knew.

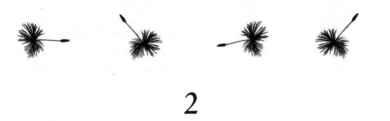

2

The year after Nivvy died, at the end of the summer, I had to go to school. I didn't want to. Mama told me it would be like my crêche, but I'd forgotten all about the city, and I *knew* the Settlement children would pick on me. I got on with them all right playing in the street, but that was because I could run home when they started calling me names. But Mama had kept me at home as long as she dared. I was six, and I must be schooled. When she told me she would get into trouble if I stayed at home, I had to give in. If a grown-up 'got into trouble', Nicolai the Nail Collector would make a call on his radio. Guards would come and take the person away, and they would never be seen again . . .

It turned out that the children weren't so bad. They would say, *You're not so special, now, are you snottyboots?*, because I had lived in the city, and hit me, or spoil my work, or steal my food. But I had friends as well as enemies. I was small, but I didn't mind hitting back if I had to, and I could run like the wind. The worst thing was Miss Malik, the teacher of the junior class. She was tall and thin and dried-up looking, she had bushy black hair and she wore red lipstick, which made her different from most of the women in the Settlement, but didn't make her any prettier. I *hated* her. She didn't know anything. She didn't know the earth went round the sun, she didn't know there had once been dinosaurs. She was stupid as mud, and she knew I despised her so she punished me whenever she had the chance. She had a metal ruler, called *the rule*, which was her favourite weapon. She would call you out, and you had to stand with your hand spread, so she could whack you on the palm. If you'd been really naughty, it was both palms.

I trudged back to our hut after one of my tussles with Miss, feeling very bitter. It was the beginning of winter, a fairy time: everything ugly hidden under a cloak of new snow. The smoke from the power station turned the murky air of the afternoon into a mysterious gloom, in which our few, yellow streetlights were hovering globes of gold ... I didn't care. I was only wondering how I could bear another day with Miss Malik. I couldn't understand why my Mama wouldn't stick up for me, why she was on Miss Malik's side. One day, I thought, I'll be big enough and I'll run away—

Mama was working, as always. I knew she couldn't stop to come and greet me. She had to be where the red light could see her, all through her working hours, or we got no scrip, even if she had filled her quota. I still couldn't forgive her. I opened the sliding doors of our bed and sat there staring at the cold, miserable, lonely room, until the blood all rushed to my head.

'I HATE THIS PLACE!' I screamed, as loud as I could, and flopped down and howled, kicking at the wall at the back of the bed until the planks rattled.

'I WANT NIVVY! I want my Nivvy, I want to go, go, *go away*!'

Mama came out of the workshop. When I opened my eyes, which were screwed up tight in misery, she was standing there with her dirty apron wrapped round her, and her greasy work gloves on her hands. I had broken two of my big promises, (the one that said I wouldn't be naughty when she had to work, and the one where I would never, never talk about Nivvy so people could hear). But she didn't look angry, at least not with me.

I sat up, ashamed of myself.

'Mama,' I said, 'I'm sorry I screamed his name, but *please* make Nivvy come back. I can't bear it here without him.'

She sat on the bed, and pulled off her gloves. 'I can't, Rosita. I can't let another kit grow. We got away with it once, but remember when Nicolai saw him? What if people thought we had a mutie in our hut?'

Mama had explained why muties were so feared, although I'd still never seen one. Things that were once tame animals were grown in factories now, for food and other important things like wool and fur and leather. They'd been changed so much, to make them easy to use, that if they escaped and bred with the wild animals that were left, the result would be a plague of monsters. That's why nobody was allowed to take the factory-animals out of their factories, or buy and sell them. There were special police, called the Fitness Police, who patrolled the wilderness, making sure everybody kept the law, and killing any muties they found.

I was afraid of the Fitness Police, because everybody was. I was afraid of vermin too. The rats and gulls and feral cats that haunted the stores and the tip where we piled our rubbish would not attack humans – except at the end of winter when they were starving – ; but they were dirty and savage. I was also afraid of *dogs*, a kind of tame vermin-animal that I'd never seen except in pictures. There were *dogs* at the fur-farm, which was a wilderness factory and the nearest human habitation to our Settlement. We could smell the stink of it sometimes, in the summer: and the guard dogs featured largely in stories told by Settlement children. They had fiery eyes, huge teeth and stinking breath, and they would eat a child like me on sight.

But except for summer midges and the horrible bugs, and the rats and gulls and cats, I'd never seen any animal or bird out here, apart from Nivvy. 'I don't believe there *are* any muties. It's just a story to scare us.'

Mama peeled off her gloves and held me warm and tight, resting her chin on my hair. 'Ssh, Rosita, don't talk like that. We have to believe in muties, that's the law of the Settlements Commission. And people tell tales, you know.'

I knew by this time that the Settlement we lived in was a prison without walls. I knew that the red light in the wall that spied on Mama, making sure she was always at work, was part of her punishment. Of course I believed we had been sent here by mistake, and one day the police would realise the truth, and come and rescue us. I pitied the children I knew, because their mothers really were wicked: they had been married to murderers or robbers ... But there were other people who didn't seem to belong, besides me and Mama. There was Madame Imrat, who lived on our alley and had once been an ambassador, there were teachers (who didn't teach) and there was a very proud gentleman who had been a Chief Surgeon. It was all very puzzling, and it got more puzzling as I grew older, and noticed things more.

I sighed and picked at a hole in my jumper. It was a scratchy, ugly jumper, the colour of dirt. I'd grown out of all my city clothes long ago. No more little red shoes: I was onto my third pair of Settlement-store boots. They looked thick and tough, but they weren't. They hurt my feet and the soles were worn through. Unfortunately, we couldn't afford a new pair this winter.

'One day we're going to run away, aren't we Mama? Why doesn't *everyone* run away? I don't understand it.'

Mama laughed a little, wryly. 'Where would they run to, Rosita? It's hundreds of miles to the nearest city, and the cities are closed: no one from outside can get in. If they tried, they would be shot down without mercy. The people of the wilderness have their own way of living, they wouldn't support a prisoners' revolt. Some do run away, and some of them even survive. But most of us just endure it. We have food and heat, we have work. We're better off than many "free" people out here.'

'But you and Dadda didn't do anything wrong!'

'Didn't we?' said my Mama, talking to me but really talking to herself, as she sometimes did, and it gave me shivers. 'All the time that we were living inside, where it's warm and bright, with good clothes and plenty to eat—'

'And hot water,' I murmured, 'and proper soap, and no bugs—'

'Yes. We knew about the Settlements, and the many, many innocent people who lived outside: all the children who were hungry and dirty and cold, and dying of diseases. We thought we were *good*, Rosita, but we did nothing.'

She hugged me again, and then let me go. 'Let's not talk about it anymore. Look, it's dark, and my quota time is over. Let's have a magic lesson.'

We went into the workshop, and got down on the floor with the lamp turned low. Mama took out the secret nailbox, and the white case. She opened the case into its white flower shape. The nutshell was smaller now, it had shrunk because there were no tiny animals inside it. The seed-stuff that would grow into animals was kept in the little glass tubes, each of them with a coloured cap.

Each of these tubes had a strange name, which I had to remember (I knew how to read quite well, but nothing about the magic was written down). *Insectivora . . . Lagomorpha . . . Rodentia . . . Artiodactyla . . . Carnivora . . . Chiroptera . . .*

'Tell me about them, Rosita,' said my mother.

'Inti-sectivore is most often small and her fur is like velvet,' I said, feeling very important. 'You will know her by her long nose and her poor eyes. She eats bugs; she has the best sense of smell. I call her Nosey, is that all right, Mama?'

'It suits her. And *Lagomorpha*?'

'Lagomorph is very few, there are only two kinds. I call him "Ears" because he has big ears. He has big back legs so he can kick and run. One of them lives in burrows, one of them has no home but the open ground, and he turns white in winter.'

I picked up the third tube, carefully. 'This one is the Rodents, they never stop gnawing with their teeth, and they multipulise very fast—'

'Multiply,' said Mama. 'They multiply.'

'A lot. You get a lot of them, very, very quickly. I call her Toothy.'

The fourth tube was *Artiodactyla*, the word that gave me most trouble. I couldn't find my way to the end of it. I called her Article: she was big, and she went in herds. The fifth tube was my favourite, because *Carnivora* was Nivvy's Order. Carnivore means 'eats flesh', but I called this seed-tube Nivvy, of course.

Lastly there was the *Chiroptera . . .* a furry animal that

had wings and could fly. Which was thrilling, but frightening, because it sounded like a mutie-monster. I called that one Cheepy, because it could find its way in the dark by cheeping (I didn't understand how).

'Very good!' said Mama, when I had finished my roll-call.

Then we went through the drill that I must learn, although I wasn't old enough to do the real magic yet. You had to put a few drops of the dark liquid food (called *new-treat*) into six little dishes, sprinkle in a pinch of seed powder from each tube, wait until they began to grow, then put the dishes carefully into the incubator. The next time you looked, six tiny kits would be there. They were called *Lindquists*, another strange word I must remember. They would live, snuggled up together, and they would die, and curl up in their dishes again, and turn into cocoons (I knew furry animals didn't do that, caterpillars turning into butterflies made cocoons: but this was magic). Then you had to crumble the cocoons into powder, and put the powder into a new seed tube, with the right coloured cap.

When they were kits they all looked the same. When they grew they became different kinds of wild animals. Nivvy had been a full grown small Carnivore. You had to grow them to full size sometimes to make really sure the seeds were in good condition. But we didn't dare, so we had to hope for the best.

'Once there were Lindquists for all eight Orders,' said Mama. 'The two missing ones are *Cetecea* and *Pinnipedia*. But the marine mammals were lost.'

I nodded, not worried that I didn't understand. I knew I couldn't understand magic yet. But I could learn. 'How do you mean, lost?'

'They were taken.' Mama's mouth went tight and hard,

and her voice turned grim. 'And I think I know who took them—'

'It wasn't ... it *wasn't* my Dadda?' I quavered, frightened at her tone.

I had strange ideas about why Dadda had gone, now that I knew that other mothers were here because their husbands had been criminals.

'Oh no!' said Mama. 'It wasn't your Dadda! Don't think that, Rosita! When you're older, I will tell you the whole story. I'll explain a lot of things that I can't explain now.' She fell silent then, looking at me seriously, and then took my hands, her eyes very dark and sad. 'Listen, my baby. One day you may find yourself alone, with no one to help you to decide what to do. Then you must look deep inside yourself. Try to find the spirit of life, that lives everywhere and lives in your heart ... and try to do what it tells you. That's your only hope, Rosita. Your only hope.'

I thought she was talking about the magic lessons. Little children understand more than people think. I knew she had trusted me with her secrets, although I was just a baby; and she hoped she was doing right ... I wanted to say I would never, never betray her. But her solemn words reminded me of that day when the guards had come, a day that I couldn't remember, and my mind was filled with a scary, confusing blur—

I knew we couldn't go back to the city. You had to have a special voucher to ride the tractor to the station platform. Even if we could have got that far, and even if we had a cartload of scrip, we wouldn't be let on the train. We would not be allowed to have tickets. We were the people who were shut out, now. And what would be the use, if we managed to find our way back to the home that I didn't remember? Who would be there for us?

28

'Will we find my Dadda again?'

'I don't know,' said Mama, softly.

'Is he in another Settlement?'

'No,' she whispered. 'I don't think so. I don't know where he is. Go and put the kettle on, sweetheart.' She started to put everything away, not looking at me. I saw that her eyes had filled with tears. I saw in them a sorrow that I could never reach, never make better, and my heart burned. I vowed to myself that *one day* I would find my father, and I would bring him back to Mama, and she would be happy.

I was just a child. I was proud when I could remember the funny long words, and I loved to play with the doll's house tubes and dishes, but I didn't understand what Mama was teaching me at all. I didn't tell her, but I thought the 'incubator' really was a magic nutshell, like the one in the fairytale that the lost princess opens when she has nothing to wear for the ball, and there is a beautiful dress inside, folded up tiny and small ... Everything strange and magical entranced me. The puzzling, frightening things she sometimes said went right out of my head in a moment. But that night when we went to bed, I realised that I wanted to ask, *do you think he's dead?* I couldn't say it. Big sobs came heaving up from my chest, I couldn't stop them. The weight of what I couldn't understand, and things I barely remembered, fell on me, and I felt so lonely and helpless, like a baby left on a doorstep. *My Dadda, my Dadda* ... Mama held me in her arms, and rocked me until I was quiet.

We made an agreement that if I was good at school and did not cheek Miss Malik, I would have Mama-lessons more often, and if I was *very* good, we would grow the Lindquist kits again, as soon as it was my birthday at the end of winter. Sometimes I'd wake in the middle of the night and she'd be gone from our bed, and I'd know she was doing magic. I didn't get up and spy on her, but I'd watch and wonder, after these nights, and try to guess what she'd done, either for us, or for someone else. Maybe she'd caused a snowfall in midwinter, so the tracks were soft and pretty again, and Madame Imrat didn't have to be so terrified of slipping and falling. Maybe she'd cast a spell to make the Settlements Commission send an unexpected shipment of jam—

I was very muddled. Mama knew it, because I'd ask her about the good deeds that she had Ordered the Lindquists to perform. She didn't correct me. The important thing, I realise now, was that I was practising the skills I would need: practising every step of the Lindquist process, with my hands and eyes and mind, over and over, until I couldn't possibly forget.

After school, when she'd finished her quota for the day, and we'd eaten and done our housework, we'd have a magic lesson (not every night: Mama kept those lessons feeling special). Or she'd tell me about other exciting things. Then we'd go to bed, and she'd tell me stories about our great journey, north across the snowy wastes, through the forest, over the sea: taking our treasure to the beautiful city where the sun always shines. Not now, in a while, when I was grown . . . I would fall asleep to the murmur of her voice, and dream of Miss Malik, and fairy-tale animals, and the far adventure, on the other side of growing up.

Mama and I, alone and free in the wild, white emptiness.

*

The short summers and long winters passed. Supply trucks came across the hard-packed snow, with their guards (they never came in summer, because then the wilderness was a swamp and the roads were impassable for trucks). Sometimes the bandit families who ruled the wastelands ambushed our supplies, and we went hungry. It was impossible for us to grow enough to eat in the poor soil of our little plots. Rumours of change reached us, terrible stories of thousands upon thousands of 'rebels' taken out of the cities; taken to the middle of nowhere and left to freeze in their indoor clothes. But where we lived, nothing changed.

When I was nine I moved up to the senior class. I was very proud, though it only meant moving from one end of the schoolroom hut to the other. I took my two mushy, rag-paper exercise books, my pencils, my old bread that I used for an eraser, and my precious sharpener (one of the few relics of my city toybox). I walked away from the juniors' bench, overjoyed that I was leaving Miss Malik behind, and feeling the respectful gaze of the children. I walked past the narrow windows that would be icy on the inside in the winter, past the stove in the middle of the room, where the big teenagers spent the day in idleness, and up to the two rows of real desks of the senior class. The senior teacher's name was Mr Buryat: everyone called him Snory. He had a lung disease and couldn't speak without making a snoring noise in his throat. He was kind. He was writing something on the battered blackboard, so I went to the senior bookshelf, which I had often longed to examine. There was a coloured globe, beside the raggedy textbooks, that had my passionate admiration. I switched it on, and beamed in delight as all the cities lit up like stars.

Then Snory noticed me, and sent me to sit by Rose, a very pretty girl with yellow wavy hair and green eyes, who had previously been the youngest senior. I put the better of my exercise books onto the shelf under the desktop, with my extra pencil. Rose ignored me. She was cutting a new point to her pencil, with a blunt penknife. Shyly, I pushed my sharpener across the desk. Rose looked around, a gleam of malevolence in her green eyes. She smiled coldly and turned away, her back to me. But my pencil sharpener had disappeared. I never saw it again.

I liked the senior lessons. Mr Buryat couldn't breathe without snoring, and we laughed at him cruelly, but he was a good, patient teacher. My playtimes were lonely. The other senior girls followed Rose's lead, although she was the youngest, and the boys followed the girls. They treated me with complete contempt. I was too proud to go crawling back to the juniors, so when I'd eaten my lunch I had nothing to do but walk around the muddy schoolyard with my arms folded, my nose in the air, and one wet foot where my boot had a big hole in it.

I hoped the ice was melting when Rose came up to me.
'What's your name?'
'Rosita,' I said, shrugging, not to look too eager. 'Same as it was yesterday.'
She curled her lip. 'That's not a name,' she said, loudly. 'That's not a *name*.'

This must have been a signal, because the seniors gathered. All six of them got in a circle round me, and I was scared. The big teenagers (who were generally kind) weren't out in the yard. Snory never came outdoors, and I knew Miss Malik wouldn't protect me. The two top boys, Storm and Soldier, were twelve and thirteen, and looked enormous to me. Rope, who was older, was small, and slow in the head: but he could be violent. The two girls besides Rose were Aspen and Snow. They were both about twelve, tough and vicious in a ruck. Here we go, I thought, and braced myself. Maybe Snory would see through the windows and come out and break it up, if they all set on me at once.

'You can't keep your city name any more,' said Aspen. 'We won't let you, it's wrong.' She was a very thin girl (we were all horribly thin, except Rose), with a long, pale, yellowish face, and an irritable temper. I kept an eye on her hands, which were twisting and tugging at one of her pale braids.

'You have to have a plain name. You can't have a dressed up name,' said Snow, who was shorter, and had thick dark hair. Snow was very short-sighted. She peered at me from under her fringe, scowling.

'Rosita is a false name,' said Rose, smugly.

'Who says I'm not allowed? Rosita's only the same as "Rose" . . . It's not as pretty as Rose,' I added, in a hurry. 'It's less fancy, it's *junior* to Rose.'

The boys murmured, as if they were half ready to let this thing go. But the girls glared at them, so they stayed in the circle. Storm said, quite kindly, 'You can't be Rose. *She's* called Rose. Pick another name. How about Sugar?'

This was meant for a compliment, and I should have seen that he was trying to help me. But I didn't have any sense.

'I don't want to change. It's the name my Mama and Dadda gave me, and I'll never see my Dadda again. Make me do something else. What else can I do? I'll give you my lunch, every other day—'

They looked at each other. 'Her Mama,' muttered Rose, rolling her eyes. 'Mrs Bighead the peepee. Her Dadda, not too good to be hung.'

'They act like they're better than us,' said Snow. 'When

33

they came they were rich. They could have given us things, but they sold their fancy stuff to the bandits.'

Mama had given my toys and books to the school, but they had disappeared, *like my pencil sharpener*. If they'd ended up with the bandits, that wasn't our fault.

I didn't say anything. I set my teeth and waited for the thumps.

'Think it over,' said Soldier, and they drifted away.

I asked Mama what it all meant. She said the children of the Settlements knew this was their world, the only world they were going to get, and they wanted to make rules for belonging, the way any tribe or nation will. That's where the craze for 'plain names' came from. She said people who'd been sent here when they were grown-up, whether they were ordinary criminals or exiles, didn't feel the same way.

'They've told me I have to have a name like theirs.'

'That's good,' said Mama. 'They're inviting you to belong. What are you going to choose?'

'I don't want a new name. They're not inviting me, they're picking on me because Rose makes them. She took my sharpener. She scribbles on my book, and pretends it was me. She's jealous, because I was moved up and I'm younger and I get higher marks than she does.'

'Why don't you let Rose get the high marks?' said Mama, frowning. 'If that would make her happy. What does it matter?'

'It matters to me.'

Mama was frowning because Rose's mother was one of the people who told tales. She and her daughter lived in a hut like the rest of us, and didn't wear a uniform, but they had nicer clothes, and better food that somebody import-ant sent to them, maybe a Settlements Commission official, maybe a bandit. Even Nicolai was polite to Rose's mother, and tried not to offend her. But I knew I was in the right.

'I could still call you Rosita at home.'

'I won't do it. I don't see why I should. It's not a school rule. Mama, what does *peepee* actually mean? It doesn't really mean wetting yourself, does it?'

'It means political prisoner.'

I knew that was bad, worse than being an armed robber. It didn't worry me. I'd learned that in the Settlements there was no point in being ashamed. 'That's what they call you. Are we *political prisoners*, you and me?'

My Mama was tired after rolling and heading nails all day: too tired to be bothered with me, I thought. She pulled off her torn work gloves, and rubbed her worn and dirty fingers. 'I've never been involved in politics,' she said. 'Your Dadda did something that the government didn't like, but he didn't know it was wrong, he thought it was his duty. Rosita, pick yourself a new name. You can't win this one. Don't insist on learning everything the hard way.'

Storm secretly passed me a note saying CH+NG YR NAME ITS F+R YR OW+N GD. I mean, secretly as in trying not to let Rose see. No one had to keep secrets from Snory. He was too harmless. I didn't answer it. I went on spending my playtimes walking around alone. I knew the thing about the plain name wasn't over, but the others didn't come near me, so I didn't know what to do. It was the worst season of our year. The whole Settlement, except for those who were too ill, had spent the brief summer weeks frantically tending and harvesting our potato patches (we grew anything that would grow, but mostly potatoes). Now the warm days had gone, the excitement was over and the tasty food was stored away. But we were still living in an unfrozen bog, and the insects were still biting. Everyone was longing for the frost to set in, and every day we hoped for the first snow.

About a week after they'd told me to change my name, we seniors were sent out into a sleety, freezing drizzle to eat our lunch. The juniors were allowed to stay indoors, with the big teenagers and the teachers. I walked up and down eating my meal: a piece of ryebread with a chewy dried tomato. The bread was rations from the stores, and nasty, but the tomato had been grown and dried by my Mama and me, and it was very nice. Then I went to get myself a drink of water. I was standing by the pump, sipping from the tin cup, which was attached to the pump handle by a chain, when I felt a creeping in my shoulder-blades.

I looked around, and there they were.

They made a circle round me.

The pump was near the schoolyard wall. I looked up at the crumbling bricks, and a reckless plan leapt into my mind. The schoolyard gates were kept locked, and the walls were high. But if I managed to escape and run home, what would happen? I had never heard of anyone doing that, so I didn't know. I could get expelled. Then I'd have to stay at home and help Mama ... That didn't sound too bad.

'We've decided,' said Snow, glowering from under her fringe. People said her father and her oldest brothers had been executed for several gruesome murders. That was why the mother and younger children had been sent here. It was the law: if someone in your family was guilty, you were guilty too. 'You have defied us and must be punished, but we are merciful. Give us your lunch every day for three

36

weeks, and give Storm a kiss right now, and we'll let you be called Sugar. Is that a deal?'

'I don't want to kiss anyone,' I said. 'And I can't give you my lunch every day, I'll get sick. I'm only nine.'

'You're in the senior class,' explained Rose. (I was sure this was all her idea.) 'That makes you a teenager. You have to be tough when you're one of us.'

I knew they would do it. They'd steal my food. I wasn't sure about the kiss, but I couldn't look at Storm, and I had started shaking.

'I'll t-tell Snory what you just said. *You'll* be in trouble, not me.'

They laughed. 'Oooh, she'll tell Snory!'

Rose bent down and scooped up a handful of mud. She never got herself dirty, so that caught me off guard and the first gob hit me in the chest. I ducked the next one. I dodged another gob, and they let me run. I ran around the yard, getting mud flung at me, and horrible names, and stones too. I didn't cry, I didn't scream for help. I galloped around, ducking and diving, sleet stinging my face: it was almost fun. I could take it. Maybe if I showed them I could take it, they'd decide they liked me ... But I had my plan in mind. When I saw my chance, I made a break. I leapt at the wall in the corner of the yard, and scrambled up, bracing myself between the two sides. Then I was on the top, standing on the slippery coping stones, waving my arms to keep my balance. It was a longer drop on the other side. Suddenly I wasn't so sure this was a good idea. I knew Mama would hate it if I was expelled—

Miss Malik's tall, thin form appeared at the door of the school hut. She came marching over, through the sleet, in her indoor shoes, without her hat or coat—

37

'*Rosita!* Get down! You're going to get a whipping for this!'

'They were throwing mud at me,' I was going to get whipped whatever I said. I was just putting it off. 'They said horrible things.'

'GET DOWN!'

Her mouth, red as blood, seemed to gape at me, her hands were like claws. I was so scared I lost my balance and fell, my right leg doubled under me.

'Get up! Right now! Back into the classroom, this minute, all of you!'

My head was ringing. I managed to stand without crying, but my leg hurt very badly. But I wouldn't beg. I tried to walk, with my head up—

'Stop favouring that leg, you little show-off. *March*, and be quick about it.'

I got myself across the yard and into the school. I remember seeing poor old Snory, a glowing image far away, standing by our miserable scuffed blackboard, shuffling a stub of chalk from hand to hand. Miss Malik fetched the rule.

'Hold out your hands!'

I saw her furious face, looming down, and the loose skin on her throat all wrinkled like skin on porridge. I felt the first stroke, but not the second. I heard someone say *Rosita*, I don't know who it was, and the world faded into nothing.

When I opened my eyes again I was in a bed.

My leg hurt, but everything was far, far away. There was a fat woman sitting by me, with a hard square face. She had a uniform, and a nurse's cap on her head, so I knew I was in the hospital. 'Mama?' I said. 'Where's my mama?'

'Yourmamawillbeallowedtovisityouatvisitingtime,' said the

38

fat woman, in a grumbling, monotonous voice, all the words running together.

'When is visiting time?'

'Next week.'

I found out later that Mama had tried to rescue me. But I had been taken to the hospital from school, on Nicolai's tractor, before she knew what had happened, and afterwards she didn't have a chance of getting me out. My kneebone was cracked, and my shinbone too. They weren't bad breaks, they were what is called greenstick fractures, but the doctor didn't treat them properly. He wrapped my whole leg in thick plaster, and made me stay in bed for weeks. He gave me medicine that made me sleepy and weak; and Mama had to increase her quota to pay towards my treatment.

Nobody trusted the Settlements Commission doctors, who travelled around the wilderness, visiting the useless Prison Settlements hospitals that were supposed to be a sign of how good the government was. Anyone who was really sick or hurt did their best to stay at home. There were women among the ordinary prisoners who knew about herbal medicines. In our Settlement there was also Mama, and Madame Imrat, and the proud gentleman who had been a surgeon: who would give good advice, at least. But I didn't get any of that. I don't expect the hospital doctor meant to cripple me. He just didn't know much.

I was in a room with four beds, called Children's Orthopaedic Ward. I could read the notice from my bed, and spent hours wondering about that strange long word. Most of the time I was alone. It was very cold, as winter came on, much colder than in the cupboard-bed I shared with my Mama. I lay and watched the snow fall, and thought of the wilderness that stretched forever out there, like an endless dream. What about the great journey that Mama had planned? How could I walk hundreds of miles? How could I cross the wilderness?

It would never happen now.

The end-of-winter blizzards were blowing when they let me go home. I could get about by then, though I had to use my ugly crutches. My right leg was like a thin white stick, with a strange bend in it. Mama helped me to practice, and soon I could walk fairly well. In March, on my birthday, I limped out to the potato-patches on my own. It was tough, but I made it.

I sat among the dwarf willows, by the place where we had buried Nivvy. I thought about never being able to run, ever again. I was ten years old, but I felt a million years older. If only I had listened, when Mama told me to let Rose get the high marks. If only I hadn't been so proud. I saw my life stretching ahead of me, into the dim desert of being a big teenager, and I knew that Mama and I would never run away, that was just a daydream. I would live in the Settlement, in the dirt and cold, for ever and ever. And now I was a cripple too.

The blackthorn hedge, that someone had planted out here for a windbreak, was half buried in spring snow: but there were flowers opening on some of the thorny twigs. Mama had told me that blackthorn is one of the trees that remember. It tries to live the way it did before the winters were so cold and so long. I thought of the sour little plums, called sloes, that people gathered to flavour their home-made liquor. That suits me, I thought. Stupid flowers that try to grow in winter. Bitter fruit.

I went back to school. My leg dragged, but nobody laughed at me as I limped to the seniors' end. When I sat down, Storm reached across from the desk he shared with Soldier, and shoved a package of furry, exercise-book paper into my hand. There was a piece of real chocolate inside; I don't know where he'd got it from.

The smell was amazing.

'What do I have to do for this?' I asked, not looking at him.

'Nothing,' muttered Storm, not looking at me. 'It's ... free.'

'I'm going to change my name,' I said, still not looking at him, or at Rose, silent on the other side of me. 'You can tell the others, I'm going call myself *Sloe*.'

I had no trouble in school after that. Not from Rose, or anyone else. I had become one of them, and they knew it. I had the same weight on my soul, the same hardness inside, that comes from living without hope.

Snory had sent my lessons to me, and visited me in the hospital when he was allowed, so I hadn't fallen behind. I was always top of the class. Nobody minded after I came back with my crooked leg. Before the summer break that year, we seniors had to take a test. This was a new idea; nobody had tested Settlement children before. You had to stay in school until you were fourteen or fifteen, whether you were learning anything or not. Then if you were a girl you got a quota and started making nails, or you were sent to labour camp if you were a boy. That was the way it had been: but not any more, apparently. No one told us what the test was about. Snory checked our papers before he sent them off to the Examining Board, and he got very excited.

He said Rose and I were the best students he'd ever taught, and we were a credit to the Settlements Commission.

I wasn't excited, but it hurt my feelings when Mama wasn't proud of me for coming top. I heard her muttering about it with Madame Imrat, the old lady who had been an ambassador, who sometimes came to spend the evening with us. They were sighing as if I'd done something wrong, and looking at me with pity. But Mama didn't say anything, and no one at school explained. The first thing I knew about what it meant was when Mama got a letter.

We hadn't had a letter in six years. The outside world had been as if it didn't exist (really the *inside* world. We were the ones outside, shut out from city comforts). I was with Mama when Nicolai, acting as Brigade Chief and not Nail Collector (he had several official positions), handed over the envelope. It was dirty and crumpled from travelling inside his clothes, but it had the Settlements Commission stamp on it. Mama's face went completely white. Then she tore it open.

Dadda, I thought. *My Dadda—*

I thought the letter would tell us that Dadda had died, in some other prison far away . . . But it was about me. I had to go away to school, a *real* school, specially for the brightest and best of the Prison Settlements children. It was hundreds of miles away. I would have to leave my Mama. I wouldn't be allowed to come home, except for the long summer break.

3

One warm, still day at the end of that summer, Mama made a picnic. We walked out beyond the potato-patches, slowly because of my leg, into the marshy green plain which always looked wrong to me, as if snow and winter were the only clothes the wilderness should wear. Forest rimmed the edges of the sky; the sun was already lower than it had been. It was the farthest Mama had been from her workshop since the day we arrived. For six years her life had revolved entirely around our hut, the stores, and the potato–patches.

Nicolai had graciously allowed Mama this holiday, because I was going away. I knew he'd also fined her many days' pay. (That's what our Brigade Chief was like. He was quite kind in his own way, but if he did you a favour it cost you plenty.) I tried to be happy, to make the expense worthwhile: I kept chatting about the birds and the flowers, and the sweet, fresh air. Mama was very quiet. We found some boulders, lost in the seeding grasses and rattling reeds, and settled there. There were midges, but we were used to that. She took out our picnic, I limped off looking for berries. When I came back she'd spread a napkin, and poured cold fruit-tea into our beakers. I arranged cloudberries in a circle round the chunk of rye-loaf, the pieces of concentrate 'cheese', the tomatoes and the small, luxurious pot of jam. Far away in the distance a bird was calling, one note over and over, clear over the droning of insects.

'Does your leg hurt you?'

'No, it's fine. It feels great.' (I was lying, a bit.) 'Don't worry, Mama. Kolya will put it on the records that you were allowed to have the day off. He wouldn't take our scrip and then do nothing.' 'Kolya' was short for Nicolai. I didn't *really* trust him, nobody official could be trusted – but I wanted to cheer Mama up.

Mama gazed around, opening her eyes wide, as if she was bathing them in the light and air. I saw that my beautiful Mama looked older, and that hurt me. 'It doesn't matter, sweetheart. I won't get into trouble. The red light is only there to keep us frightened. These days nobody cares if we make nails or not … Our world is changing, Rosita. The supply trucks need more guards, and the supplies are getting very poor. Things nobody would have dared to say, just a few years ago, are being whispered: so that rumours even reach us here. I can't tell if the changes will be good or bad, but maybe life won't go on the same for much longer.'

Mama was the only person who called me Rosita now. I nodded. She'll explain what she means later, I thought. When I'm older.

Then we ate our picnic, and talked as happily as we could about my new school, and how we'd get me the things I would need. Underwear without holes in it, said my Mama, wistfully. I wish I could send you away with underwear that didn't have holes in it … I would have loved a new pencil sharpener. The light grew pearly and the air grew chill. We knew we should be getting back, but we lingered on, our cheerful talk falling into silence.

At last Mama said, 'My sweetheart, do you understand

44

that if I'm not here when you come back, *you are the guardian*?'

'I'm coming back next summer,' I whispered.

I had been getting excited, as the summer went by. I wanted to go to a real school, away from these mud huts, and have a chance in life. But oh, I didn't want to leave her. I wanted never to leave her, I wanted my Nivvy back, I wanted everything. My eyes started stinging, my mouth trembled, I blundered into her arms. We sat there rocking each other, heartbroken.

'It won't happen,' said Mama. 'It *won't* . . . But if you come back and I'm not here, you must do exactly what I've taught you. Keep the Lindquists safe, grow them and harvest them, keep the seed refreshed, and live quietly in our hut until—'

'Until you come back?'

Mama went on hugging me. 'Of course, yes. Until I come back to fetch you.'

'And then we'll take the Lindquists to the city where the sun always shines?'

'They say it's a wonderful place,' said Mama. 'There are green parks and fountains, and indoor farms like beautiful gardens. We could be so happy there.'

I had forgotten my first home, and I'd stopped believing that cities were wonderful. I thought of a huge Settlement with a roof of some kind over it: full of people like Rose and Rose's mother, living in luxury on their ill-gotten gains while the rest of us starved. It was Mama herself who'd made me realise that the way the privileged people 'inside' behaved was wrong . . . But I could hear the longing in her voice, so I said nothing. For Mama, getting back to the city still meant everything.

'But if by any chance I can't come back,' persisted

Mama, 'I will try to send someone to help you, so you won't have to make the journey alone. Remember, you have to travel in winter. No one can travel in the summer—'

'North,' I said. 'Across the wilderness, through the forest to the sea.'

We packed up our meagre picnic and walked back, each of us pretending hard to believe the fairytale, each of us saying only the things the other wanted to hear.

Late that night we went into the workshop for my last magic lesson.

It was past time to grow the Lindquists again. Mama had planned to grow them the winter before, but I'd been ill in the hospital and then getting better at home. And then it had been spring and summer, which were the wrong seasons for sowing these strange seeds. My hands were bigger than they had been: I could put on the clinging, glimmery gloves that were folded up in the white envelopes, though they were still over-large. I could put one of the gauze masks over my nose and mouth—

Mama watched carefully as I prepared the dishes of new-treat all on my own, and added the seed powder. I watched for the signs of life, then I fitted the six tiny dishes into their places in the bottom half of the nutshell, and stretched the barrier my Mama called 'the incubator membrane' over them. When the shell was closed and sealed, we put everything away and I repeated my roll-call, glowing inside because I knew I'd done everything exactly right. I repeated the strange names of the Orders; I dsecribed the different kinds of animals . . .

'The nutshell will grow as the kits grow,' I said.

'*Incubator*—' murmured my Mama.

'I should look at them often, and I should handle them when I have learned to handle them safely. If you're friendly to them that helps them to grow, and it will remind them that I am the guardian, so they'll trust me. They get enough food from the new-treat to grow into kits, but if you're growing a kit into a full-grown animal, you have to feed it extra. When the nut – er, incubator – is about as big as an apple, the Lindquists will get sleepy. One day I'll look inside and find they've shrunk and curled up in their dishes again, and turned into cocoons. They can't make a mistake. They know which dish is theirs, because it has traces of them in it. Then I powder up the cocoons, and put them in fresh tubes, with the right coloured caps. But I don't throw the old tubes away until I've tested the new seed, by letting a Lindquist kit of each kind go through its full expression.'

There was a store of extra tubes in the base of the white case, with the packs of extra gloves and new-treat, and the cleaning powders.

'You can't tell how long—' prompted my Mama.

'You can't tell how long it will take for the kits to live and die, or to go into second stage, which is a real wild animal like Nivvy. It depends on many factors.'

'When you test them to the second stage you must be careful—'

'Not to distress them, because if you do they will express everything. They have instructions packed inside them, although they are so small, for making lots of different kinds of animals. You ought to check that they're all there, to make sure the Lindquist is working properly. But we can't do it because we are in hiding. It wouldn't be safe ... That's why we didn't distress Nivvy. He was always happy. Why wouldn't it be safe, Mama?'

'Ah,' said Mama. 'Well, strange things, marvellously strange things, happen to the Lindquists at full expression

. . . Artiodactyla is big, but Nivvy is a special case. Be *very* careful about distressing the Carnivora kit, should you ever second-stage him.'

'I'm not going to second-stage them,' I said, uneasily. 'I'm going to school. Next summer I'll come home, and you will be here, and you'll teach me lots more.' 'Yes,' said Mama. 'That's how it's going to be. But *suppose* I wasn't here, you do understand everything, don't you Rosita? You know what the Lindquists are, and what you have to do, and why they are so important?'

'Of course I do.'

I said it to please her. My mind wasn't really on the kits at all . . . I was thinking about the heartbreak of leaving Mama, and the excitement of my new school. But I put everything away while she watched me, and I did it all exactly right. The next night we opened the nutshell, and six tiny creatures stared up at me, already clad in brown fur, with shining pinhead eyes and quivering almost-invisible whiskers. The delight came back to me then. I felt all-powerful, and full of love.

'Well done,' said Mama. 'I'll harvest them for you this time. Next time we grow them you'll be a great big teenager, and do it all yourself.'

My Lindquists were still alive, sleek and playful in their miniature kingdom, when it was time for me to leave. Mama had tried to get a voucher for the tractor ride so she could come with me to the train platform, but Nicolai had told her it wasn't allowed, because she was a *peepee*. I sat in the metal cart by myself, with the bag that held my clean and mended clothes, and as much extra food as Mama had been able to put together. I waved until she was out of sight: then I crouched there and stared, as Nicolai's tractor jolted me through the ruts and the mud of summer's end, until all sign of our Settlement had vanished over the horizon.

The New Dawn Rehabilitation College stood on the edge of a town that was just another Prison Settlement, much bigger than ours, and not so remote. I had travelled there over four days, with the guards who had been waiting for me at the train platform, sleeping in station huts and on hard railway carriage benches. I never found out what the town was like, I only glimpsed it on the way from the station.

New Dawn had formerly been a hospital. The buildings were low and grey, and surrounded by a very tall fence. The corridors smelled of disinfectant and the wardens, who were in charge of us except for lessons, wore nurses' uniforms. Mama needn't have worried about my under-wear. Everything I'd brought with me, including my extra food, was taken away as soon as I arrived. I was scrubbed, de-loused, my hair was cropped and I was given my junior school uniform: a dull red dress and a round cap, grey scratchy drawers to below my knees, grey socks, indoor shoes, outdoor shoes, grey underwear. Then I was taken to my dormitory by a white-coated warden, with a clanking chain of keys, who kept unlocking doors ahead, and locking them behind. I was given a bed, and I was told some of the most important rules, which all started DON'T, or IT IS FORBIDDEN.

Before the end of the first day I wished with all my heart that I had failed the stupid test, so I could have stayed with Mama. We weren't allowed to use the word 'prison', or say we were at prison-school. We were being rehabilitated now. But New Dawn felt more like a prison than the Settlement ever had.

The idea of having a school for Settlement children was quite new, but this wasn't the first year of New Dawn. It was just that remote areas, like the place where Mama and I lived, had taken a while to catch up. There were already seniors who looked down on the juniors, and traditions and special words that you had to learn quickly, if you knew what was good for you. Juniors were Bugs, in red and grey. If you were over fourteen, you were a Rat and your uniform was brown. The teachers were Gulls, the guards were Dogs and the wardens were Cats. I'd been afraid people would pick on me, because of my crooked leg, but about the only good thing I found out in the first few days was that lots of Juniors – and Seniors – had something wrong with them, and I was far from being the worst off. I was assigned to a physiotherapy class. They screwed a brace onto my leg, to straighten it where the front shin bone had knit badly (there was nothing they could do about my knee); and put me on vitamin pills, because I was undersized and my teeth wobbled. I also had to join the line for malt extract, a disgusting brew that the dormitory Cat spooned into us weakling girls, night and morning.

At mealtime hundreds of new Bugs with stick-thin grey legs poured into the junior canteen and sat down in roaring confusion, to eat the food that had been dumped on our plates by the dinner-Cats. When I saw the fibrous brown stuff on my plate, I rammed it into my mouth without a thought: everyone else was doing it. Too late, I found my mouth was full of tough, slimy string. Or tree bark, mixed with glue. I chewed and I chewed, and nothing changed. I didn't mind the taste (most food was nasty, in my

50

experience; except for what you grew yourself). But I couldn't swallow! The wardens were patrolling, and I knew you had to clear your plate or you were in serious trouble. My panic must have shown in my bulging face.

'It's *meat*,' said the boy beside me, softly. 'Stick it in your cheek, and bite off little lumps. That's the way to do it.'

'It isn't real,' I muttered, when I'd managed to reduce the wad. We weren't supposed to talk at meals. 'I've tasted meat, and it tastes nothing like this.'

'I'd never seen meat in my life,' said the boy, 'until I got here. What d'you mean, it isn't real? It's not imaginary.'

'I mean real meat, like, from an animal.'

The boy laughed. 'Eat up, joker girl. This is the best food you can have for getting strong, and you'll need your muscle, with that crippled leg.'

I looked at him properly then. He was dead white in the face, his hair was furry-short and dark, and his eyes were rain-coloured, with thick black lashes. He was skinny as a string bean, and he looked about my age (he was a year older).

'You sound sensible,' I said. 'What's your name?'

'They call me Rain. What's yours?'

'Sloe.'

He choked on his mouthful, and spluttered, 'You're a real joker, you are.'

'It's S-l-o-e, not S-l-o-w. It's the fruit of a wild blossom-tree, people put it in the vodka where I come from. But I did choose it for the double meaning. I reckoned, if I have to have a bad leg, I might as well get some fun out of it.'

'No blossom trees around, where I come from,' said Rain, grinning. 'It's desert. Never rains. You got any friends in this dump, Sloe?'

'I don't want friends,' I said, determined to sound tough. My only friend was Mama, and I missed her terribly, but I wasn't going to tell a stranger that. 'Friends are fake. I know what happens in school. If you have anything good, a bigger kid takes it. If you get good marks everyone hates you, and copies your work and scribbles on it. Nobody stands up for anyone else, and only tell-tales have power.'

'You're dead right.'

Then we didn't dare talk any more, because the hall had gone quiet, and the white-coated Cats were prowling. When dinner was over I dodged the girls' warden and followed Rain's line, hidden in the surging crowd. I didn't want him to see that I was interested, but I wanted to know where he'd gone ... At last I saw his trail of boy-Bugs disappear through a door. Their warden swept after them and locked it behind her. I was left stranded, far from the corridors I knew.

'What are you doing, Bug?' said a passing senior. 'This is the boys' side.'

'My friend went through there. What's through there?'

The big teenager looked at the notice on the door, and looked at me.

'That says PERMANENT BOARDERS, kid. Can't you read? That's where they keep the lost souls who don't have homes to go to. They live here all the year round, until they die and get rendered down for stew and fertiliser.'

'I can read,' I said. 'I didn't know what it meant.'

'Are *you* Permanent?'

I shook my head.

'Then you can't have a Permanent for a friend. We don't do that.'

But I was already backing away, horrified. Never to go

home! I didn't want to know anyone in who was in such terrible trouble. Trouble rubs off . . .

I made friends with Rain, later, when everything had changed

The first week was very, very hard. The days were bad enough, but the nights were terrible. I had to lie in my cold narrow bed, surrounded by strangers; I wanted my Mama desperately but I *must not cry*. Anyone could tell that if you showed your feelings in a place like this, you would be done for.

I didn't know if I could survive. Then, after a week, Rose turned up, and was put into my class. She'd been staying in the town with her mother, and her mother's important friend, having a shopping spree. Her uniform was made to measure. Her underwear was out of this world compared to what the rest of us had to wear. She'd also got herself kitted out with mouth-watering pencils, and coloured pens, and a geometry set. I was surprised she wanted to be friends with me, but I wasn't too proud to go along with it. Better the devil you know, I thought. Rose can't pull any surprises.

And it got better. In ways the fact that we had no contact with our families made the loneliness easier to bear. You concentrated on the present. I joined the running club for the disabled, because I was allowed to take my brace off when I went running. The physiotherapy teacher said it would do me good. I didn't think so at first, but then I could *feel* myself getting stronger. At night I'd lie in my dormitory bed, which was so narrow you had to be careful about turning over, and tell myself, *Mama is all right, she's sleeping now, cosy and warm in our cupboard bed* . . . If I was feeling strong, I would write imaginary letters to her in my head.

I'm all right Mama. I'm going to be good and do well and make you proud. Until next summer. I love you . . .

Winter closed in, more quickly than at home. Snow poured out of the sky, until the pillars that supported the buildings were buried. The dormitory was freezing at night, and the night-warden would patrol, stripping back the blankets suddenly, to make sure we weren't cuddling with each other, or sleeping in our nice thick uniforms (both of which were strictly forbidden). By the 'midwinter break' – when none of us left school, we just had boring activities instead of lessons – I could run twice round the snow-packed playing fields before I collapsed. I didn't look good, but I could cover the ground. We were allowed to stop for a breather near the main gates, and I noticed, while jumping on the spot to keep warm, that I could see a tree: one skinny, crooked tree, away down the road towards the town. It was bare and iced-up now, but it would have buds. It would have leaves, unfurling in the sun: and when those skinny branches were hidden by a green cloud, it would be time for me to go home.

One day in February my class had a science class, in the laboratories. This was a privilege that we'd been waiting for, but the laboratory was a disappointment. It already looked run down; there was no electricity, and there were broken hospital-notices that no one had removed. I was still excited, because I knew my Mama and my Dadda had been scientists, when we lived in the city. She'd taught me interesting scientific things (I didn't count the Lindquists, which I thought were purely magic); and I was looking forward to showing off my knowledge.

I felt important. No other Bug had a *right* to be in here, but I did!

We were divided into groups, one group to each bench. I was with Rose, and our friends: Tottie – a girl so small she only came up to my elbow, but she had a fierce temper – , a boy called Ifrahim (not everybody had plain names, it was about half and half), a boy called Lavrenty, a girl called Bird, who had homemade tattoos all over her face, Bird's friend Miriam, and a girl who wasn't one of us, who'd been dumped on us by the teacher. We had a tray of different materials. We were supposed to write whether we predicted they would burn, and then wait for our turn to use the bunsen burner and try and burn them. We set ourselves up, with our goggles, and our beaker, and our spatula and our notebook, and I wrote down what we thought would happen.

Wood would burn, and a stone wouldn't burn.

Water wouldn't burn, and metal wouldn't burn.

I felt all this was beneath me. I said that *anything* would burn if you made it hot enough, even rock or steel, but nobody agreed. Bird said I was daft. I suppose she was right: a bunsen burner isn't a volcano . . . It wasn't like one of Mr Snory's lessons. Nobody messed around in class, at New Dawn. The punishments they gave you were too horrible. But the science teacher didn't mind us talking, if it was about our work.

Tottie said that earth would cook, like meat.

'But cooking is the opposite of burning,' protested Lavrenty. 'Cooking is so you can eat things. If something's burned, you can't eat it.'

'Burning is when you cook something too much,' said

the girl we didn't know. 'How can it be too much, *and* the opposite?'

'Smartypants,' said Tottie. 'Sloe, you write down what I said.'

Ifrahim sniffed the earth sample. 'You know what? I bet this is the meat. This is school dinner meat before they cook it.'

The meat was supposed to be a luxury. It wasn't too bad once you knew to bite and swallow, never try to chew: but it *worried* us. Some people said it was dead bodies. You died here, you got minced and served in slices. Others believed it was our poo, collected from the toilets and processed in a big vat.

'Nah,' said Laventry. 'All meat comes from factories.'

'Meat products didn't always come from factories,' I announced. 'They were once made from raw animal flesh.'

'Eeeughgh!'

'You mean, vermin like rats and cats?'

'Only bigger. They were called cows, pigs, sheep. I used to have toy ones.'

'You're lying,' said the girl who wasn't one of us, looking sick. 'That's disgusting, imagine eating a rat—'

She must have come from a very easy Settlement . . . Bird jeered at her. 'Ho, softie. You'd eat a rat if you were hungry. And you'd like it.'

'People ate wild animals too,' I said, getting carried away. 'That's the reason why they're extinct, besides habitat loss. My mama told me, and she's a scientist—'

'Oh, you big liar. You don't even know what those fancy words mean.'

'Nyah,' said Bird, 'Your mam's not a *scientist*. You're the same as us, and your mam's a convict and your dad was hung.'

It was an ordinary New Dawn insult, but I wasn't as tough as I pretended. I was stabbed by the thought of Dadda, whose face I could not remember, and the noose going round his neck. I dared not show my pain, so I looked as proud as I knew how. 'She's a convict *now*. She got sent down because Dadda did something against the government. But she's still a scientist; it doesn't go away. She taught me about the earth going round the sun, and dinosaurs, and—'

I noticed they'd gone quiet. I looked around, and our teacher was standing there. He was looking at me with a very shocked expression. I felt confused. What had I said? Had I been saying something rude, or cheeky?

'Hello Mr Pachenko,' said Rose brightly. 'Sloe was telling us about her mother, who taught her about the earth going round the sun, and—'

'Stop chattering and get on with your work,' snapped Mr Pachenko.

He went away. I saw the flash of disappointment in Rose's green eyes, and felt I'd scored a point. I would have bet she'd seen Mr Pachenko coming over, and hadn't warned me because she'd hoped I was going to get into trouble. Rose was like that: she had a mean streak a mile wide. But this time she'd failed.

A week later I was called out of class and taken to the Principal's Office.

I was terrified. I couldn't think what I had done, but I knew it made no difference. Once you were taken to the Principal's Office you were going to get punished: and it would be something horrific. I was afraid I'd get The Box. Stronger children than me had been known to die after they'd spent a day or a night in The Box. The warden walked ahead, her keys jangling. Behind me walked two guards with guns in the holsters at their waists, which was really, really scary. What could I possibly have done that was *so bad*, without knowing it? The hairs on the back of my neck stood up. I imagined those men dragging me, kicking and screaming, to the coffin of cold darkness, and locking me in for hours, for a whole day. I was so afraid I thought of running: so they'd have to shoot me and get it over with.

The warden opened a door, took my arm and pushed me forward.

There was a thick, patterned rug on the floor, that went all the way into the corners. The room was warm and there was a bright lamp, dispelling the gloom of a murky February afternoon. All I could see was the pattern on the rug. I *couldn't* raise my eyes. The warden gave me another push, and I stumbled forwards.

'So this is Sloe.'

'Look at Madam Principal,' said the warden sternly. 'Stand up straight!'

I stood up straight. I saw a tall, slim woman in a tailored uniform. I had seen the Principal only once before – a far away figure, across a sea of heads in student caps, at the Winter Break General Assembly. I'd never expected to get any closer. Smiling, she came from behind her desk and led me, by the hand, to a stool in front of an easy chair near the stove. I wondered what on earth was going on. A warden, in a smarter white coat from the one who'd brought me, set a tray on a little table.

I could feel the armed guards behind me.

'Now, Sloe, don't be afraid. You aren't going to be punished, you haven't done anything wrong. I'd like to talk to you about your mother.'

I nodded.

'Say "Yes Madam Principal",' snapped the warden who'd brought me.

'Yes Madam Principal,' I whispered, reeling with shock and fear, trying not to let my voice shake, trying not to show any feelings. What had happened to my Mama? The red light on the wall behind Madam Principal's desk meant everything in here was being recorded. I stared at the tray, which held a glass of milk, a plate of yellow slices of cake, and a glass dish heaped with glistening purple jam. What were the treats for, if I was here to be given bad news? It made no sense.

'It's been reported that you have confessed to your playmates that your mother taught science, when you were living with her in the Settlements. Is that true, Sloe?'

Nothing had happened. Mama was safe. I almost fainted with relief.

'Do you like cake?' suggested the Principal. 'A little jam wouldn't go amiss?'

The deal was clear. I must talk about Mama or I would get nothing. I had been hungry every day of my life, for as long as I could remember. I was hungry now. They could have stabbed me with red hot pokers, and I would never, *never* have told anyone about the Lindquists, but I thought hard, and I could see no harm in what the Principal was asking. Of course Mama had taught me. There was nothing wrong in that. She'd only taught me things everybody at New Dawn was learning—

'What kind of things did she teach?' coaxed the kindly voice.

My hand reached out. 'Well, she didn't teach anyone but me, but she told me oh, lots of things. About the planets, and the moon and tides, and how the winters got so cold, and how once there were dinosaurs—'

'Yes, yes—' said the Principal, smiling sadly.

I didn't understand. Mama had always said she would explain things when I was older. She had never told me why we were in the Settlement. I didn't know that what Dadda had done wrong had anything to do with science. I'd never thought about it, never put two and two together ... I was just a little girl, and I believed New Dawn was different, in spite of the guards and the wardens. I really believed I was being given a chance. Mama had taught me to respect teachers, even Miss Malik. I never suspected that a Head Teacher would get a little girl to betray her own mother.

I ate two pieces of cake, with a big spoonful of jam spread on each. I couldn't believe how good it tasted. I drank my milk, and I answered the questions. Then I was escorted to my next class and sent to my desk. My friends and enemies stared as much as they dared, their brains frying with curiosity, amazed that I'd come back alive. Rose and Bird and Tottie jumped on me, the first moment they had a chance.

'What happened!' Rose gasped.

'We thought you were a goner. We thought we'd next see you on a plate—'

I shrugged. 'Nothing much. We chatted. I think she used to know my Mama.'

I didn't understand.

News of my experience spread: I was famous. Some Bugs thought I would be taken to the city next, and have expensive treatment to fix my knee. Some were saying the Principal wanted to adopt me. Suddenly I had a crowd of friends, wanting to get close to me, in the hope that my luck would rub off. Bird and Ifrahim and Tottie weren't so sure. Nor was I. A visit to the Principal's office could not be good news.

But I seemed to have got away with it, whatever 'it' was.

March began, and I had my eleventh birthday. I didn't tell anyone; nobody celebrated birthdays. My trip to the Principal's office faded from my mind, except for a strange, nagging uneasiness . . . Then there was a blizzard that went on for days. The running club was suspended. When we had to cross between the buildings we were lost in a world without outlines, where the air you breathed was made of snow. If there were buds on the branches of my tree, I would not have been able to see them. One evening in the blizzard we walked from the study-hall to our dormitory, the night-warden swinging her keys behind us. When we got into the room, I saw that my bed was stripped. My things had been turned out of my locker and put on the mattress. A strange warden, with different flashes on the collar of her white coat, was folding up a sheet. The other girls looked at each other, and went very quietly to their own beds.

I heard someone murmur, *Is she really going to the city?*
Someone else muttered, *Ssh!*

The strange warden set down the folded sheet, stacked my things on it and briskly tied the small bundle. She handed it to me.

'You take that with you to Permanent Boarders, Sloe.'
'Permanent Boarders? W-why do I have to go there?'
'Because you're a Permanent Boarder.'
'But why am I suddenly a Permanent Boarder?' I quavered, tears beginning to start in my eyes. I had never cried at school, but I had such a sense of utter doom—

The warden's mouth was a hard line. I could see she was one of the soft ones. Some of them were like that: they had to be on their guard, or they'd have been tempted to protest at the harsh way we were treated. Trouble rubs off, and you can't be too careful. They were always the worst kind.

'It's not my business, and it's not yours, but I believe it's something to do with your mother. She's been practicing her profession, although she was disgraced: and that's forbidden. She's been taken away. There's no home for you to go to, and you're a Permanent Boarder. Get a move on, I haven't got all night.'

In dead silence I limped out of the dormitory, clutching my bundle. My Mama had been taken away, like my Dadda. She was gone.

I suppose days went by, and nights passed. I suppose I went to lessons, sat in the canteen, finished my food. I know I was taken to the Principal's office a second time, and told officially that I was now a Permanent Boarder, because my mother had taught me science, and they had a recording of me saying so, so there was no way Mama could deny it. It was a grave crime, *an act of criminal insanity*, for someone sentenced to exile in the Settlements to teach science. What if she had taught dangerous rebels how to make a bomb? But it was all right, it was over now, and my Mama was getting the appropriate treatment.

The Principal said I mustn't worry, I was not in trouble. New Dawn was proud to be teaching the daughter of such distinguished scientists, even though my Mama and my Dadda had fallen into wicked error. I could have a shining future, and make up for their unfortunate crimes. I could be Rehabilitated-Settlement-Child-Number-One. I suppose I said thank you ... You have to say thank you. It isn't enough to nod and look at the floor. You can't keep anything for yourself, not even your anger. They want it all. They want everything.

She didn't tell me where my mother was. I didn't ask.

She's been taken away—

She's been taken away—

Taken away like my Dadda, and hung, or shot—

And I knew who was to blame. Not the police, or the Settlements Commission, or Madam Principal: it was me. I was eleven years old, and I had killed my mother. She was dead for two pieces of cake, and a taste of fake berry-jam.

At the end of March there was a day of blue skies. The town's waste tips, which you could see through the mesh of the main gates, were smudged with brown where smouldering rubbish had melted through the snow. Scavenger gulls were on patrol, screaming to each other in harsh, alien language. I huddled in the place where the running club stopped for a breather. My leg had stiffened badly since I'd given up running. Today the physiotherapy teacher had ordered me out with the others, but he hadn't forced me to keep up . . . I could see my tree, but I couldn't make out if there were buds on its scrawny branches. I tucked my cold hands up into the sleeves of my uniform coat, and pressed my face against the icy mesh.

I wondered what I would have to do to get myself shot.

'Better off staying here,' said a gravelly deep voice behind me.

It was one of the guards. They all looked the same in their grey uniforms: heads shaved to stubble, big shoulders, hard faces; but I thought I hadn't seen this particular man around before. He was tall. A pair of deep lines pinched the flesh between his arched brows, his nose was long and straight. He looked quite old for a guard. He had his rifle slung on his back, a gun in the holster at his waist, and a bottle tucked under his arm. His uniform tunic was open, as if he didn't feel the cold. The shirt under it was very dingy.

'You're called Sloe,' he said, with a grin. 'From Wilderness Settlement 267, Third Brigade, East Sector?'

'What if I am?'

He slipped the bottle from under his arm, popped the cork out with his thumb and took a big swallow. Then he handed it to me.

'Yagin's the name. You look as if you're planning a break-out, that's all, and I'm saying you'd be better off staying here.'

'What's it to you?'

'Oh, nothing. But think about it. Forget the lessons. Think about three meals a day, a dormitory bed, vitamin pills. There's the physio, too. You know it's done you a lot of good. My advice is, stay put until you're grown. You won't be ready for the trek before then, and where could you live better? Back in 267 you'd starve. You wouldn't last a winter, without her to support you.'

I shrugged. I was too deadened to be surprised. The smell of liquor stung my nose: I wondered what I was supposed to do with the bottle.

'You don't know if you can trust me,' said the strange guard. 'I know. So let me put it this way. Spring's a dangerous time for little animals. Worse than the winter, in many ways. The safe blanket of snow is melting away, and all your enemies are hungry. But things aren't as bad as they seem. *It's not as bad as you think, little girl.* You hang on; you'll see. Hang on, and lie low.' He tapped me on the head with his hard fingertip (he wasn't wearing gloves).

'And I'll be here. Look around, any time, and I'll be watching over you.'

I took a swig from the bottle, handed it back and started to limp off towards the school buildings. I heard him laughing, deep and strong, behind me.

I didn't know what to make of this strange meeting. But later, as the day went wearily by, I realised that somewhere inside me the flame of hope had started to glow.

4

After they took my Mama away, I gave up the idea of getting an education and having a chance in life. I kept the hope that Yagin had given me, but I hid it deep in my heart, and tried never to think about it. One day I'd be old enough to leave this dump, and I would go and search for my Mama. Meanwhile I was here for the three meals a day, the warm clothes, the vitamin pills, and whatever else was going.

Rose went on being friends with me, when I was a Permanent Boarder, and I went on being friends with her. There wasn't a school rule keeping Permanents and Termers apart – it was something the students had decided themselves – but my self-appointed guardian didn't like it. Once he found me sharing a weed (that's a prison cigarette) with Rose, behind the kitchen rubbish bins. He took great pains to catch me alone after that, and told me Rose was bad company, and she would do me harm.

I knew Rose wasn't to be trusted. It was the spice of danger that made her interesting. 'I'm bad company myself,' I said. 'Warn Rose.'

Yagin watched me, as he'd promised. He had an annoying way of looking – as if he knew every naughty thing I'd ever done, but he would always forgive me. It gave me the creeps. But there wasn't much he could do about me being friends with Rose. He couldn't hang around near the students without getting into serious trouble. I often avoided seeing him for weeks at a time.

My tree down the road put out its leaves. It was never much of a green cloud, but made the best show it could manage. I went to the gates to look at it sometimes: until the summer faded. New girls moved into the dormitories. After they'd been issued with their uniforms, we old Bugs took anything worth having, substituting our own worn-out stuff. We threw shoes at them when they cried at night, and warned them they would be killed if they complained ... Deep inside, where my hope was buried, maybe the person that I used to be survived. But I had betrayed my mother, and the only way I could live with that was to become hard and hateful; so I just let it happen. At least, as the winter went on, the crying stopped. It was a relief not to have to be cruel any more. On very cold nights I wrapped my stolen extra blankets tightly around me, hid my head under the pillow and dreamed I was in the snowy forest. Mama, I whispered in my heart. I'll come and find you.

I knew she was probably dead; but you have to believe in something.

I knew I wasn't the little girl she had loved anymore, but I couldn't help that.

The winter passed. By March my tree emerged from the blizzards, looking more sickly than ever, but at least it was alive. So now I was twelve.

It was during my second year that we started the real stealing. I don't know what Yagin would have done if he'd found out: but he didn't. Maybe he was fooled by the way I still worked at my lessons and got high marks (which I did, because it was easy and it was good cover). Or maybe it was because it happened very gradually.

First we were taking things from the new Bugs, same as the year before: a nasty game, but it kept us warm and fed. Then Rose talked to one of the town people, one of those bad lots who hung around the New Dawn College gates in the hopes of some kind of pickings, and set up a regular trade. That's what she told us, anyway. Maybe it was really something to do with that friend of her mother's: I never knew. I left that side of it to Rose.

My job was to organise the stealing. We Permanents had chores, around the kitchen and the housekeeping stores, and we weren't too well supervised. I recruited Rain, and a couple of other Permanents. Later there were more people involved: Bird and Lavrenty, Tottie and Ifrahim. We'd recruit anyone useful. It grew to be an empire. On my thirteenth birthday I didn't go to look at my tree: I'd forgotten all about it. We'd just traded a stack of blankets and a box of canned food over the fence: I sneaked out of the dormitory (we had a lockpick in our gang by then) after lights out, and celebrated with my thieving friends, on vodka and plenty of greasy chocolate.

The third summer break was endless. We got short rations when the Termers had gone home, on the grounds that we weren't doing brain-work. But the Cats liked us to be exhausted, because it made us easy to handle, so they didn't cut our chores. Hours of scrubbing floors that didn't need scrubbing, and not even a full stomach to look forward to. It was awful. And we didn't steal during the 'holidays', not even food for ourselves. It wasn't safe. There were only a few students, which meant the Cats could watch you every minute ... Also Rain was ill, and they took him to the school clinic. I tried not to think about it, but I missed him, and I worried about him.

It was a big relief when the Termers came back and Rain was let out of the clinic. I was tempted to concentrate on my school work for a while just to relax. I was getting bored with being a criminal. But this was the fat time of year, with a new crop of Bugs to be fleeced, and kitchen opportunities it would have been a shame to miss. I told myself I would quit once the harvest was over.

One of our meeting places was a disused watchtower, north of the Dogs' barracks. (The wardens were still 'Cats', and the guards were still 'Dogs'). It was out of the way, but near enough to the school buildings so we didn't look suspicious heading in that direction; and we weren't afraid of the guards. They wouldn't do anything except under orders. It was the wardens we feared: they *enjoyed* being nasty ... Our safeguard was that the stairs to this tower had been taken apart, to stop anyone from doing what we were doing. You had to climb the metalwork of the struts, and get in through the open trapdoor in the floor of the tower. It was a challenge, especially for me: and you were a long way off the ground when you got to the most awkward bit. But that added to our security.

I met Rose there, after lights out, to discuss what to do with our plenty. The watchtower was heaped with stolen blankets, plus a big stash of canned stew, and fat jars of pickles. We wrapped blankets around us, opened one of the cans, which was full of 'con' – our favourite, protein concentrate – stewed in savoury gravy, and sat there, with our dark lantern, slurping stew and gnawing on pickled cucumbers. Rose counted the blankets with an expert eye. She didn't even need to touch them.

'You sure there's no fleas or lice?'

'College issue, just fumigated. The same blankets that we sleep in ourselves. What d'you think you can get? Chocolate? I can get unbelievable prices for chocolate from my Permanent customers. New shoes, pens, really good stuff.'

She narrowed her eyes impressively. 'Maybe I can get chocolate. I'll consult my associates.' I never asked her who these 'associates' were. It was better not to know. She grinned suddenly. 'Hey, Sloe, I've got an idea. We've got all this stuff. We're doing so well. Why don't we throw a party up here?'

'What, you mean at night?'

'Yeah. After lights out, with cards and liquor. No strangers, just the gang.'

I said, 'No one would hear us. It's that time of year: the dorms will be full of screamers, sobbing like strangled cats.'

We both laughed. I savoured a lump of cheesy, delicious concentrate—

'I never cried,' said Rose.

'Nor did I. Not even when they made me a Permanent Boarder.'

Rose gave me a brooding look. She leaned over to fish for another pickle. 'D'you remember the day you were moved up to the Seniors, back at home?'

I shrugged. 'Maybe I do. So what?'

'You walked up from the babies' end as if you owned the place, and you went straight to the globe. That light-up globe on the bookshelf?' Her eyes caught cruel yellow gleams from our shaded candle. 'Not even the big teenagers dared to *touch* it without special permission. You went over and casually started pushing the buttons. You were so far above us. We could tell you'd had lots of things like that, when you lived in the city. You and your Mama . . . I wanted to *be* you, back then. Or I wanted you to be me. Maybe I still do, and that's why I told the warden—'

'I wanted to be *you*,' I broke in, quickly. 'I still do. I want yellow hair.'

I had realised, long ago that it must have been Rose who got me my invitation to the Principal's Office and caused me to betray my mother. Teachers didn't report students for crimes against the Settlements Commission, like boasting that your mother had taught you science. They'd be too scared of being questioned themselves ... Wardens did things like that. But how would a Cat have got to know about something that only happened in a school lesson? Somebody must have told tales. Rose had been there, she'd seen Mr Pachenko looking shocked. She must have realised she could get me into bad trouble, and she wouldn't have been able to resist an opportunity like that.

I knew, but I didn't want her to confess. I didn't want to be told for sure. I didn't want to have to do anything about it—

How can I explain about Rose? I think she truly liked me, but she hated me too. She hated me because I *belonged* in the city. I had been born there, and nothing could take that away from me. But Rose had been born in the Settlements, and it didn't matter how many pretty things she had, she could never be like me ... And I knew she hated me, but I never tried to get away. I suppose I thought if I could handle the danger of being friends with Rose, it proved I was tough enough to survive ... Yet I sort of really liked her, too. Life gets very twisted, in a prison.

'We're a team,' I said. 'A mutual admiration society.'

Rose hiccuped, giggled, and put her hand over her mouth. Her hands were soft and pretty: somehow Rose managed never to be the one scrubbing floors. Her nails gleamed, like little pink claws, in the candlelight.

We called the party our Annual General Meeting, and held it on a night when the moon was dark. We'd been out of the dorms together before. It wasn't too dangerous when you knew the wardens' routine; if you had a skeleton key. Ifrahim was clever like that. He could make a key out of a pin or a paperclip, and he'd taught us all how to pick simple locks. In third year, top juniors, they didn't patrol the dorms through the night the way they did with the younger Bugs. They locked us in, and came around to look through the glass of the door at intervals. They trusted in the red lights to keep us behaving ourselves: but we knew how to avoid the camera eyes.

Rain, Amur (another Permanent I'd recruited for his criminal skills) and I left our beds stuffed with blankets. We sneaked out of the Permanent Boarders block and met the Termers up in the tower. There we feasted among our spoils, wrapped like savages in stolen New Dawn blankets, in the smoky, smelly light of stolen New Dawn candles; playing cards while we passed the bottle round. Someone drunkenly called for a speech. I stood up, arm in arm with Rose, and explained how much I'd learned at New Dawn College, and how rehabitu-witulated I was,—

'Here's to a life of crime!' cried Rose.

We were getting dangerously loud. We didn't hear the lookout scrabbling down from the roof, until he catapulted into the room, head first. It was Amur, and he was scared. 'Out of here!' he gasped. 'The guards are coming, a bunch of them, out of the main gates guardhouse. They must have had a tip-off!'

'How d'you know they're coming here?' cried Rose.

'Where else? Come on! Come on—!'

'But all our stuff!' groaned Bird.

'Don't be stupid,' I hissed. 'There's always more.'

The candles in the dark lanterns were doused, all but one. Amur was already shooting down the struts: Rose and Bird, Lavrenty and Ifrahim followed. Tottie grabbed a last spoon of stew, stuffed it in her mouth and dived wildly through the trapdoor. We heard her gasp and choke as the metal bar on the other side of the gap connected with her midriff, then she was gone into the dark. Rain and I looked at each other. We were the weaklings, the ones doomed to think too much.

'What if they get us by our fingerprints?' whispered Rain.

'They haven't got the things they'd need. They're not trained police. They're idiots, guarding a lot of half-starved children. *They* don't care—'

'Why did we get into this, Sloe? Why did we go to the bad? It's crazy. It was a privilege to come to school, and we've wasted it. Why were we such fools—?'

'It's not a privilege. You finish your course, then you end up back in the Settlements. Oh, I don't know. It's a rotten world, we were desperate. *Go on*, Rain.'

Rain put out the last candle. 'You first.'

I flung myself through empty space, grabbing ahead of me for that cold metal. I was flying, I was falling, then my hands hit the bar and locked onto it. I couldn't see them, but I could hear the guards coming. The tramp of their boots was like thunder. I was always scared of that gap; and Rain was more scared than me, but I knew he'd jump now I'd done it. I scrambled down, slipping through several handholds once, and wrenching my weak leg.

I dropped to the ground.

'Rain!'

'I'm right behind you—'

I could see him moving. He was high up, but he'd made the leap. I thought he was safe so I hobbled and stumbled for cover. I was in the undercroft of the Dogs' own barracks when they hit the watchtower, surrounding it, flashing their torches, letting off rifles. When they started barking and yelling in triumph, I knew they'd got Rain.

There was nothing I could do. I sneaked into my dorm again, before they really began hunting for the rest of us. I found out next morning that everyone else had got safely away too. But we'd lost all our stuff, and Rain was in deep, deep trouble.

A General Assembly was called in the great gymnasium hall, with the teachers up on stage. Madam Principal was at her rostrum, her most trusted stooges, the chief wardens, in a half-circle behind her, and all of us Bugs lined up below. Permanents on the left, Termers on the right. She said how shocked and appalled she was that a Bug (she said a Junior, of course), a mere child, had been involved in the crime ring that had been uncovered. She said the ringleaders had corrupted his innocence, and deserved no mistaken loyalty from us. Any Bug who gave information would be treated firmly but kindly, and she was sure somebody knew something . . . I didn't listen, any more than I'd listened at Midwinter Break, when she was telling us what a wonderful place New Dawn was. I looked at Rain, who was standing on the stage between two guards. His uniform had been taken away, because he was in disgrace. He was wearing a dirt-coloured T-shirt and patched, knee-length trousers that must have been in his baggage when he first arrived. They were far too small for him.

Rain didn't look at anyone. When he was sentenced to thirty six hours in The Box, his expression didn't change. When he was told he would be given time to think it over, he went on gazing out over our heads. The guards brought him down, and led him through the gap between our ranks. He was walking on his own, his chin high, but I don't think he saw us. His eyes were bruises. You could see bruises and weals on his white throat, and his arms, too.

And we kept silent. Rose and I, Amur and Tottie, Ifrahim and Bird and Lavrenty and Miriam, and everyone else who might have spoken. We couldn't have done anything to save Rain. He was going into The Box whether he talked or not: we knew that. But we could have shared his fate; and we didn't. We hadn't had a chance to talk to each other, but we all probably had the same idea. Obviously whoever had tipped off the guards had mentioned no names. Madam Principal was convinced that it must have been seniors who were stealing on such a large scale, and Rain had been just their errand boy. We knew that Rain had TB, and The Box might kill him. But Madam Principal knew that, too, and she didn't care . . . If he didn't break, and if we all kept our mouths shut, there was a *chance* that we'd get through this,—

When the prisoner and his escort had passed, we faced about and waited our turn to march away. There was a moment when I was looking straight at Rose, across the space between Permanents and Termers, and I *knew* she was the one who had informed on us. Why had she done it? Maybe she'd seen that the racket couldn't go on much longer: I don't know. Rose was just like that.

Hail and farewell, Rose, I thought. I'll never speak to you again. We could never speak to each other again, none of us. We'd taken care not to act like friends when we were running our empire, except in secret. It would be real now. Each of us was on our own.

Rain went into The Box. It was a cold, wet day when they put him in. When he came out he had to be carried, and they took him straight to the clinic. He died there, about two weeks later. Nobody told us, officially. One of the clinic Cats let it slip, and the news went round the school in a wildfire of whispers.

I don't remember what I did, after I heard. It's a gap in my life, like my baby years in the city, like the time after I found out that I had betrayed my Mama. One day I got beaten up by the wardens on the dormitory, after I'd done something very cheeky: I didn't remember what it was ... Yagin the guard found me, the evening after my beating, huddled in my favourite lurk by the main gates. He had a bottle of home-made vodka with him. It was raining, cold and small. The big man hunched himself down beside me, – his rifle clattering, his uniformed bum in the mud.

'Drink up,' he told me. 'It's good for you.'

'It's a rotten world,' I said. 'We were desperate.'

'A little girl who takes a knife from the canteen, and tries to stab a night-warden, must be desperate. You know, you didn't even break her skin. You're lucky they pitied you, and dealt with it themselves—'

So that's what I did. 'I'm a fool. I'll sharpen it next time.'

'I think you will, my chicken. Drink up.'

I was in deep trouble already; why not have a drink? I knocked back the liquor and soon the world went all swaying and vague. Maybe he's drugging me, I thought. Maybe this is poison. But I hadn't eaten anything that day, so I suppose it was easy to get me tipsy. My tree down the road, my little crooked tree, it had no leaves ... Yagin looked into my face with that creepy expression of love and pity in his eyes. He took my chin between his hard, dirty finger and his thumb.

'Seed corn must not be ground,' he murmured.

I blacked out.

I was found in one of the boys' dorms, dead drunk. That's not the kind of offence that gets a girl sent to The Box. That's low and disgusting, and it gets you dumped out of the whole world.

I was expelled, of course.

I never considered trying to explain what Yagin had done. I couldn't care less if I got expelled or not: I was too far gone even to be glad I was getting out of New Dawn. But I was disgusted with my so-called guardian. Why had he set me up? Why would anyone do something like that? What harm had I ever done to him? It was a while before I realised that Yagin and his vodka had probably saved my life.

5

The Settlements Commission had arranged for Nicolai to pick me up at the railway platform with his tractor. I don't know what I'd have done otherwise, I suppose I'd have had to walk, even though it was about twenty miles. I parted, silently, from my last lot of guards, threw my knapsack into the cart and climbed after it: very stiff and sore after the long, long journey. The snows hadn't yet begun here and the road was horrible, a mess of mud and potholes. We left the platform behind; the guards still standing there, growing smaller in the distance. Our Brigade Chief looked over his shoulder. The glass in the back of the tractor's cab had been broken for a long time.

'Your mother left you something?' he remarked, hopefully.

'No,' I said. 'She had nothing to leave me.'

I thought of little Rosita in her cherry-red coat. It must have been Nicolai who was driving the tractor that day too. I didn't remember if he'd spoken to us. He grunted at my reply, and turned back to the road. Nothing more was said, until we reached the potato-patches on the outskirts of the Settlement. The tractor stopped, and Nicolai got down. He pulled out my bag and dumped it in the mud.

'You get out here. I have work to do.'

The huts were still a mile or more away, and I was very

tired. I could have pleaded my weak leg, or tried wheedling, but I couldn't be bothered. I shrugged and got down. Nicolai stood rubbing the bristly stubble on his upper lip.

'Your mother *did* leave you something. Everybody knows.'

I was looking at him eye to eye. I had grown tall while I was away. Nicolai the Nail Collector, controller of our lives, feared by all, was a small, smelly man with shifty eyes, who was getting old and had bad teeth. That gave me a strange feeling—

'Everybody's wrong. Mama left me nothing. She had nothing.'

He fished inside his layers of ripe clothing. 'You're a little girl, you must trust someone. What about the Mafia, eh?' (We called the ruling bandit families 'Mafia' in the Settlements, from an old tradition.) 'They'll want their cut. You can't bargain with them for yourself. You let old Kolya do the business for you, Kolya will see you right. Here, a little something—' He shoved a paper-wrapped jar into my hands, and clambered back into his cab. 'When you remember what it is she left you, you tell me. I'll look after everything.'

He had given me a small jar of berry-jam.

The potato-patches were stripped and bare. A few straw-coloured, mildewed tomato vines straggled in the mud. There wasn't a sloe left on the blackthorn hedge; yellow leaves rattled on the dwarf willows like teeth chattering. If I'd been a good girl at New Dawn College, I might have come back to this desolation – or somewhere like it – as a teacher. That was what they meant when they said they'd give you a chance in life. I could have become someone like Miss Malik, getting old and dried up and nasty: remembering the glory of learning and knowledge, but forever shut out. I thought of her life, how cruel I had been to her, how she must have hated us. At least I hadn't lost much by messing up my school career. I shouldered my knapsack and trudged, limping, towards my old home.

Our hut was standing empty. I'd been told I could live in it and take on Mama's nail-making quota. I was supposed to be grateful for this . . . and I was. I didn't have any other ideas. It must have been empty since Mama had been taken, it was very damp and cold inside. Our furniture was long gone, of course: our table, our chairs, our kettle; everything we'd owned. Except the narrow-necked grain jar that had been Nivvy's home, which lay on its side, empty, on the roof shelf. There were many boot-prints trodden onto the dirty concrete, and places where boards had been shifted, pulled away from the earth walls. The hut had been searched, but all the signs looked old, which was reassuring.

I had no food, nothing to cook with, no blankets. A very thin wad of start-up vouchers stood between me and starvation right now, and the coming winter was going to be a rough one. I stood just inside the door, thinking of my mother. How she must have felt, arriving here from the fabulous warmth and luxury of the city, with a tiny little girl. How brave she had been . . . I opened the bed-cupboard, and there was still a mattress on the boards. I tried the water pump; it was working, and the stove had started to get warm. Kolya must have done that, when he knew I was on my way. It was almost like a welcome home. I sat on the floor with my back against the warmth, and ate berry-jam with my fingers. If you only have one meal there's no use in trying to ration it.

While I was waiting for dark someone tapped on the door. It was one of our neighbours, a herbalist called

Katerina who had been friendly with me and Mama in the old days. She thrust a paper sack into my arms.

'For you, Maria's daughter. We made a collection.'

The sack was full of food. There was a bag of fruit tea, another bag of herb medicines; dried tomatoes, dried peppers, dried mushrooms, a collection of bread-ends, a kilo tin of 'con' stew, and a big chunk of that hard, dry, white kind of 'con' we called cheese, though it had nothing to do with a cow. There were a few sticky, dingy candles too, a slim jar of oil, and best of all a pack of paper matches.

I knew you don't give something for nothing. I knew my neighbours had hopes, like Kolya, of getting a share of my 'legacy'. I still felt like crying.

'I'll pay you back,' I promised. 'As soon as I can.'

'It's no matter,' she said. 'Everyone had a good harvest … It was a great comfort to us. No, it was an honour, to have your Mama living here.'

I nodded, feeling puzzled: I didn't remember us being honoured. I remembered the other kids saying Mama was a 'peepee', and throwing stones at me. Katerina took a good look around, noticing how little I'd brought back with me, from my great chance. 'What did you do, that you were sent home from the school?'

'I got drunk and I was with a boy.'

'Ah. Well, you are young. What do they expect? What good is too much book-learning anyway, it only corrupts the heart.'

'Who took her away? Where did they take her? What did they say?'

Katerina gave me a reproachful look, and shook her head.

'It was a long time ago now. No use in thinking about it.'

I was embarrassed. You don't ask those kind of

questions in the Settlements. When somebody is taken, it's understood that *nobody knows anything, nobody saw anything*. It's dangerous to get involved. I don't think Katerina blamed me. She stayed a while, talking to me kindly in the Settlement way: a few simple words, a lot of silence. She said she would come with me to the store, to help me spend my vouchers and see I didn't get cheated.

When she had left I went into the workshop, where the red light still glowed from the wall like a one-eyed rat. I found a screw-top lid, a bent nail and a hank of string, and made myself a makeshift oil lamp. I had to cut the string for my wick with my teeth, I didn't have anything like a knife. I wasn't afraid of the red eye. I was pretty sure it meant nothing at all, but I thought I'd better not take chances. I waited until it was fully dark before I crawled back and groped under the bench.

Under the heap of empty nailboxes there was one that felt heavy. I opened it, groped through the crumpled paper inside and touched the smooth, segmented dome of the Lindquists' case. Whoever had searched our hut hadn't looked in here. I could feel some canned food hidden under the bench, too, but I left investigating that for later. Back in the other half of the hut, I knelt by the stove and lit my lamp. The white case was roughly wrapped in shabby brown corrugated paper; the packing from a batch of scrap-metal for nail-making. When I unwrapped it, a folded paper slipped out, and something small with a round dial. I thought it was a watch, but it wasn't. It was a compass, and the paper was a printed map.

I set the compass down on the concrete. The needle shivered and rocked, and settled pointing to the corner of our hut.

North. What other direction could there be?

I had never seen a printed map before. They were absolutely forbidden in the Settlements. You could have a light-up globe, but not a map. Even at New Dawn, maps of our own country had been forbidden. Mama must've had hiding places I didn't know about, because I'd never seen these things before. I unfolded the paper and peered at it, fascinated, tracing the fabled landmarks of my world, places I had mostly never seen: the fur farm, the forest, the railway line, all converted into symbols on paper.

I felt dizzy as I realised my mother must have left this map for me.

She had really meant for me to make that impossible journey—

There was no note. When I'd searched and found not a word from her, not one scrawled word, I cried, at last. I couldn't stop myself from trying to picture what had happened. Did they come for her by night or by day? Did she have any warning, did she try to get away? Did she defend herself with brave, wise words? Did they hit her? I saw my Mama tied up and put into something like The Box, before she was taken out and shot. Or they might have beaten her up, with heavy fists and leather straps— But Katerina was right: it was over, no use thinking about it. My Mama had been taken from this hut before I was eleven. Now I was thirteen, and a different person. I'd been a thief, and betrayed my friend and let him die ... I'd turned into a person my Mama would not even recognise.

I cried, and then I wiped my eyes. I could not undo what had happened at New Dawn, I could not know if Mama was alive or dead. All I had was the mysterious words of Yagin the guard, whom I didn't trust at all. But I could find out, right now, whether the treasure I was supposed to guard still existed.

I opened the case, so it unfolded like a flower, and set everything out neatly. I put on my gloves and mask, and the glimmering cloak of my mother's magic wrapped itself around me. Before I began my work I prayed, some kind of prayer without words, to the spirit of life. I don't know if I believed in this spirit – I was out of the habit of believing in anything – but I think she had my mother's face. It was a short prayer, because I needed to move fast. My oil lamp's 'reservoir' wasn't very deep: if I had to replenish the oil, I'd have to start all over again with fresh gloves. My mind was trembling, but my hands remembered everything. They took me, sure and swift, through the Lindquist process.

When I knew that the seed-powders had begun to grow, I set the dishes safely in the magic nutshell, and sealed everything up. I hid the nailbox in the locker under the cupboard-bed, and piled the food that Katerina had given me in front of it. Then I put out my lamp and lay down to rest, leaving the cupboard doors open. I wasn't used to sleeping shut-up, it made me think of The Box.

I had no blankets, nor pillow, but I was still wearing my school uniform. The wardens had let me keep it, as there was no way I could fit back into the clothes I'd worn when I was ten. I didn't like the idea of going around dressed as an expelled schoolgirl, but I knew I'd soon be thankful for the thick, warm clothes. I just hoped I'd stopped growing. I kept my boots on for warmth, pulled my socks over my knees, and lay with my arms wrapped around my head, dormitory style.

It must have been neighbours who searched the hut, I thought. If it had been the people who came to take Mama, they'd have found everything ... Our neighbours had searched the hut, but they'd been afraid of the red light in the workshop. Now I was back they'd see I didn't have anything extra, and they'd forget about my 'legacy'. If Nicolai only lets me have our old vegetable plot, I thought, I'll be all right. Then one day when I'm grown up, if she hasn't come home, I will take the map and the compass and set off for the city where the sun always shines . . . The old life folded round me: the old promise as distant as ever, a hope that I could live on for years. My sleeves smelled of cold and dust, and coal-smoke, and dirt. I'd been travelling for five days, in frowsty train carriages. I closed my eyes. I was rocking on a 'hard class' wooden seat again, falling asleep while the guards sat and watched me—

The bugs in the bed-walls came out to bite, but I was too tired to notice them much. When I woke the room was dark and cold, but I could tell that the night was rising towards morning. I jumped off the bed. I'd left everything where I could find it by touch. As soon as I had my lamp alight I opened the locker, shoved everything aside and hauled out the nailbox. I lifted out the case, and opened it. I didn't need gloves: the kits couldn't be harmed by contamination now—

Maybe I should leave it for longer. But I had to find out—

If they had survived. If the seeds had not died. It was the difference between having nothing, and having a reason to live—

I ran my fingertips around the seam of the nutshell: it opened. The kits were alive. They looked up at me, through the clear shield, with their pinhead eyes.

I took the nut back into the cupboard-bed, set my lamp on the little shelf on the inner wall, and sat cross-legged in the warm hollow my sleeping body had made, staring at the living treasure. How tiny they were! Six identical miniature animals, each no bigger than my thumbnail. They scrambled over each other, trying to get a better look at me. How miraculous and strange, the way they grew from seed-powder and new-treat, and tumbled about and seemed perfectly happy in their little home. I tried to look at them properly, checking them for signs of damage and deterioration, but they kept climbing over each other and confusing me. I'd have to take them out and examine them one by one.

I was nervous about doing this. I knew how to handle the kits: but they were so *tiny*. I told myself there was plenty of the seed-powder, so I could always start the process again. Mama had never had to do that, but she'd told me it would sometimes happen. Not all of the seed would be sound . . . I opened the membrane by running my fingertips around it. But I hadn't had enough practice at this part! While I was picking out one kit, the other five bubbled up, and they were free—

For a moment I panicked. I visualised them vanishing into the cracks in the walls, my big hand crushing them, breaking their tiny bones as I tried to catch them—

But the Lindquists didn't run away. They tumbled out of the nutshell, fell off the edge of my skirt, and dived into a bundle on the lumpy mattress, their almost invisible whiskers quivering madly, ten tiny berry eyes shining.

My heart welled up with love and tenderness.

'It's all right,' I whispered. 'I'm here. I'm your guardian now.'

Mama had said I should talk to them. They would hear my voice as a distant booming, but they would feel – by magic, I supposed – that I was telling them things, and they would like that. It worked. The kits slowly dared to unbundle, and began to creep around: making tiny forays, and scuttling back to huddle again—

I had not remembered how sweet they were. They were *lovely*. They had whiskery snouts and tiny pink noses, black eyes and round ears set close to their heads. Their limbs stood out at the shoulders and the hips, so they scurried like bugs, not slinking or striding like a dog or a cat, but there was nothing disgusting about them. Their tiny tails were covered with fur, not naked like rats' tails. Their coats were bright brown, with minute bars of darker brown across their backs, and running down their arms—

I felt a tickling on the palm of my hand. I opened my fingers and saw the sixth Lindquist, busy licking up a smear of berry jam from my finger. Its tiny claws caught on the white raised lines which were the marks of Nivvy's love-bites of long ago. Without a thought, I reached for the jar Nicolai had given to me, which was on the shelf beside the lamp. I dug out a fingertipful, and offered it. The little creature grabbed onto my giant finger with its doll's house paws, and licked with its doll's house tongue.

A tingling shock ran through me.

I was sure this *special* kit, the kit I had chosen without realising it, must be Nivvy. It was Nivvy come again. My Mama's magic had caused me to pick him out, and caused me to feed him so he would start to grow into the second stage. He would be my dear companion. I held my cupped hand close to the lamplight – very careful not to get too near the flame – and examined my new friend carefully, while its brothers and sisters continued their miniature adventures. I wasn't afraid any more that they would run away. I knew they would always stay close—

Suddenly a different shock swept over me, a shock like waking up from a dream. I was not little Rosita any more. I was thirteen. How could I believe in this fairytale? I had done all the practical things, I'd started the Lindquist process without a slip, but I had been sleep-walking. I couldn't make sense of what I knew. It was all in pieces, a muddle of childish ideas and bewildering explanations that wouldn't fit together. My head started spinning in wild confusion.

What *are* these things? Is this really *magic*?

How did my mother get hold of them? What does it all mean?

The kits got into a very tight huddle. That was the first time I found out how easily they could read my feelings: I'd frightened them. I put the kit that had eaten back with the rest, because my hands were shaking too much for me to hold it, and set the open nut down beside them. Eagerly, obediently, they all climbed in.

'Go to sleep,' I whispered. 'We'll play again in the morning.'

I sealed them into their home, with my shaking hands. I got the oil and topped up my lamp, and went through everything again. My heart was beating so it drummed in my ears. There *must be* a message! A few words, anything, anything that would explain what was going on . . . I took out the extra tubes, the tightly packed envelopes, the new-treat and cleaning powders from the base of the white case. There was something else in there, tucked in at the bottom. I pulled it out. I was holding a small photograph: head and shoulders of a man. I'd never seen it before. I thought it couldn't have been kept in the case when I was a child: Mama must have put it here while I was away. It had been a colour photo, but the colours had faded to shades of yellow and brown, and the surface was all cracked. A man with a long straight nose, arched eyebrows, a short dark beard; wearing glasses—

There was no name, no date, nothing written on the back. I could only guess that this might be my father. There was a lump in my throat as I tried hard to see the person through the cracks and the fading. When had this picture been taken? What would this man look like now? If Mama had left me a picture of my Dadda, what did that mean? But maybe she had not 'left me' anything. Maybe she'd had warning that they were coming for her. She'd put all her treasures together, getting ready to escape, but then—

I heard the noise of a motor engine.

A car, not a tractor, was snarling as it struggled up our horrible track. I quickly shoved everything back into the box, shoved it into the bed locker and put out my lamp. The room didn't go dark. There was light outside, which I hadn't noticed before: and I could tell it wasn't the dawn. I tiptoed to our hut's only window, which was small and grimy. I could make out a group of people standing on the corner of our 'street' of mud and rocks and holes, carrying flickering rag-and-oil torches. They looked like big teenagers, or very young men. They were obviously waiting for the snarling vehicle, which was getting closer.

There were no vehicles in our Settlement except the 'Community Tractor', which was Nicolai's prize possession. The only people in the wilderness who had their own transport were the bandits, who had no fixed towns or villages; they lived in great caravans, continually on the move. Only the Mafia had actual private cars. I watched as a powerful brute of a car came lumbering out of the darkness, its headlights cutting swathes of yellow light. I saw the figures on the corner waving their torches, and the men getting out when the car stopped: the kind who have guns. I knew straight away that this had something to do with me—

It was mostly women and children who were sent to Settlements like ours: the families guilty of being related to criminals. The few men were either old, or broken in some way – like Snory the senior teacher with his lung disease – or they were small-time officials like Nicolai. Boys who grew up here got taken off to labour camp when they were about sixteen, if they didn't run away first. The figures out there, waiting to show the gangsters where I lived, were probably boys I'd gone to school with, boys only a year or two older than me. I didn't expect that to make any difference.

Mafia—

I backed away from the window. *They're crazy*, I muttered.

What did they think I had in here? Gold and jewels?

I found my knapsack, put the Lindquists' box in the bottom of it, then piled in the food Katerina had brought. Better not leave anything: I stuffed the makings of my lamp and my hank of string into the outer pocket, and added Nivvy's grain jar. I did all this without pausing for breath, thinking only: I've got to get out of here!

Our hut had been searched long ago, but the Mafia have long memories. Someone must have tipped them off that the city woman's daughter was coming back today. They believed in my mother's legacy, and they thought I could be made to talk ... I tiptoed into the workshop, heading for the back door, not caring about the red light. But where could I go? I couldn't knock on anybody's door. If there was any neighbour brave enough to take me in, I couldn't do that to them. It wouldn't save me, it'd just mean they suffered the same fate. I'd have to spend the night outdoors, hiding while the bandits ransacked my house. At this season I'd survive, but was there anything I could use to cover me? Yes! There was the tarpaulin that covered the nail machine.

I dragged it off, bundled it up and slipped out into the night. It was darker and colder than I'd expected. I could hear the men hammering at the door of our hut. All else was silent. The people who had collected their spare food for Maria's daughter weren't going to help me now. I wished I could still run like the wind – except there was nowhere to run . . . My knees got weak, I was so afraid. All I could do was crouch down in the pillar-space, under the hut at the corner of our back alley, with the tarp pulled over me like a stiff, thick cloak. The bolt on the door of my Mama's hut gave way soon. I heard them breaking in, and wondered how long it would take them to realise there was nothing to find.

I could see a swathe of the potholed track, and the big black car, all plastered with mud. A look-out, wearing a cap with earflaps, was walking up and down, holding a rifle. I didn't see how I could get by him. Terrible crashing sounds came from inside the hut. They must be breaking up the concrete floor! *What do you think I've got?* I muttered, hiding my face . . . I don't know what happened after that. Maybe someone was careless with one of the rag-and-oil torches. Maybe the bandits set fire to Mama's hut on purpose, out of frustration. All I know is that there was a lot of yelling. Shots were fired, figures burst out of the open door. When I dared to look again, flames were leaping into the sky.

The men jumped back into the car and it thundered away. My neighbours came leaping from their huts, shouting and carrying buckets. They had to put out the blaze, to save their own homes. For me, there was nothing left to be saved. I straightened my stiff limbs and limped away, in a daze, still under my tarp. No one noticed me.

By the time I'd left the last huts behind it had started to rain: the hard, biting rain that comes before the first snows. Sleety drops rattled on my carapace. Once I stumbled into a pothole that sent water spilling down inside my boots. I kept going until I reached the potato-patches. I had remembered the blackthorn hedge: the only shelter I could think of, between here and the distant forest, where I would not be turned away. I burrowed under the branches, my stiff cloak protecting me from the thorns. I tugged a fold of it between me and the wet ground, and it made a good bivvy. I longed to make sure the Lindquists were safe, but I was afraid to get them out, in case something else suddenly happened ... so I just cuddled the knapsack in my arms. Soon I was even warm.

I must have dozed, listening to the machine-gun rattle of the rain. I didn't notice when it softened into a gentle, catspaw pattering. When I roused myself and looked out, it was full daylight and everything had changed. The sordid mud and withered litter had vanished, the ground was pure, smooth white. I sat under in my snail-shell tarp, and thought about my options.

I was afraid to go back to the Settlement. I had nothing left there: nowhere to live, no work; nobody who would take me in, and the Mafia would be back, looking for me. They knew I hadn't been in the hut when they torched it. What would they do when they caught me, or when my neighbours handed me over? Maybe this is it, I thought. Time to lie down and die.

But I was too proud to die right there.

It came over me that there was only one thing left to do.

A journey of a thousand miles begins with a single step . . . I had the Lindquists, I had the map and compass. I had a bit of food. I had everything of value I possessed, right here in my arms. Obviously, I must go north. North to the forest, through the forest to the sea. I had thought of waiting until I was grown up, but there would never be a better time. I would take my Mama's mysterious treasure to the city where the sun always shines, and maybe, who knows, she would come and find me there.

It was a plan, anyway: better than having no plan at all. I took out my hunk of 'con' cheese, broke off a fragment, and ate it while I thought about how to start.

The first thing was to get right away from the Settlement, before anyone came looking for me. Then I'd need somewhere to regroup, and collect supplies. I couldn't start on a journey of hundreds of miles with just a few scraps of food. When Mama and I had planned our trek we'd imagined saving up for years, putting together stocks of cans, rope, lamp oil, all the things we might need . . . I couldn't do that, but I knew where I should head for, though the thought of it scared me.

I didn't mind being on foot for a while. I had a limp, and I was certainly slow: but I was strong, after the years at New Dawn. The snow was more of a problem. Every step I took I'd be leaving a trail visible for miles. My tarp was another poser. Though it had kept me warm, it was completely sodden: but I was determined to take it with me. I crawled out from under the hedge. There was no one in sight, and there'd be no reason for anybody to come to the potato-patches this morning, so I felt reasonably safe. I spread my sodden house and folded it into the neatest bundle I could manage, which I tied to my knapsack with the string.

I'd hardly started walking, trying to keep to puddles and stones where I'd leave less of a trail, when I heard the tractor. I ran for cover, dodged down behind the nearest heap of boulders, and looked back. I could soon see that the driver wasn't Nicolai. It was a boy, a teenager: someone I recognised. I ducked out of sight, and looked up into the grey sky. There would be more snow. My trail would be covered: but I would be out in it, without a coat, a wet mountain of tarpaulin on my back. Just getting as far as my boulders had shown me what it would be like trying to tramp across this country before it was frozen . . .

I made up my mind and set out at a trot, cutting across the next bend. Then I stood and waited, the bundled tarp in my arms. The tractor stopped, and Storm looked down from the cab.

It was four years since he'd tried to help me over the plain-names business, when I was a conceited kid. He must be sixteen now: I wondered why he hadn't run away. Wasn't he afraid of being taken to labour camp? I couldn't tell anything from his expression. In the Settlements we don't show our feelings very much.

'I heard you were back,' he said, dryly. 'Word got around.'

I nodded. 'What's my mother's house look like this morning?'

'Like a hole in the ground,' said Storm. 'You're in trouble, girl. They all think you've got some big secret stash. Have you any plans?'

'Yes . . . I have a plan. What are you doing, driving Nicolai's tractor?'

'Delivery run.' Storm glanced over his shoulder, and grinned. The cart was half-full of bulging sacks. No more need be said: we both knew how our world worked. He was part of an empire like the one Rose and I had made, involving an unofficial trade in Settlements Commission supplies.

'Will you give me a lift?'

'Where to?'

'I want to get to the railway.'

He shook his head, joggling the ear-flaps of his fleecy cap. 'Can't do that, Sloe. I'm not going that way: and if I was, you should stay away from there. They'd never let you on a train, and that's the first place anyone'll look for you—'

'I don't want you to take me to the platform. I know that's no good. I want you to take me to the cutting where the freight cars have to slow down, on the fur-farm spur. There'll be a train, probably, tomorrow or the next day, because it's the end of the month. I'm going to jump a ride.'

'Right, I get it.' He thought about it. 'You know there's guard dogs, don't you? They attack to kill.'

'I can look after myself,' I said. 'I'll be all right.'

'My mam would let you stay with us for a while.'

'Thanks, but I'd just be an extra mouth to feed until the police came to take me away. Unless the gangsters came around first, and *your* hut got torched.'

'All right then, up you get.'

It was warmer in the cab than outdoors, in spite of the broken window. I tried to spread my tarp out on the engine housing, so it might get a bit dry. Storm didn't talk and neither did I. After a few minutes he reached for a bundle of jerky sticks, stripped two off and handed me one. I chewed, and my mouth ran with saliva. Now *that* is meat, I thought. I knew I was chewing on a strip of salty, smoke-dried cat. Or maybe rat: I wasn't fussy. The tractor juddered on. I kept wanting to look over my shoulder: I felt as if the Mafia must be close behind. I looked at Storm's cap with the earflaps, and thought of the look-out on the corner, when my mother's hut was being trashed. Someone with a cap just like that . . . I wondered if I was a fool to trust him. But you can't tell somebody's loyalties by what they do for pay.

At last we reached the place where the fur-farm spur, heading north from the main railway line, ran in a cutting, no more than a half mile or so from the tractor track. I started bundling my sodden tarp: it wasn't any drier.

Storm shook his head. 'You don't want that crap. It's a liability.'

'I do. I left my coat in the hut. I don't have anything else to shelter in.'

He reached behind him, to the shelf under the broken window, and tugged out a spare jacket that must have belonged to him, not Nicolai, because it was fairly clean. It was brown, slick on the outside, and it had a fleecy lining.

'You can borrow this.'

He wanted me to get out first, and he would hand me my stuff, but I wasn't going to let anyone else touch the knapsack. I scrambled out, in my new jacket.

'Thanks for the loan, and the lift. I'll pay you back, soon as I can.'

'*Did* your mother leave you anything tasty, girl?'

'Nothing,' I said. 'Nothing but a few tins of food, which I had to leave behind. It was just one of those rumours that gets around.'

Storm looked at the knapsack, and shrugged. 'Well, if anyone asks, that's what I'll tell them.' He took his cap off, leaned down, and dumped it on my head, and then, as an afterthought, plonked the rest of the jerky strips into my hands. 'When you get where you're going, send me a postcard, eh?'

I nodded, and walked off into the snow.

I made my camp in a stand of tall dead reeds. I ate freely of my food, because food is like having a fire inside, and I had to keep warm. I also burned two of my candles, which kept my tarpaulin bivvy cosy at night. The Lindquists were all right in their nest. I opened the nut and talked to them often; but I didn't open the shield, so they didn't get cold. It was a great comfort having them there, even though I was scared the whole time that the bandits would turn up. I hoped that I'd see them coming, and have a chance to bury the nailbox (I had a place ready) under a cache of stones before they reached me. I would never tell them where.

No one came. I would never know who had tipped off the Mafia that I was coming home (I suspect it must have been old Nicolai). But it seemed Storm hadn't told tales. The sun was an orange split in the clouds, getting on towards setting on the third day, when the freight train turned up at last. I was waiting by the line, wishing I had some more jerky. My feet were blocks of ice: I didn't know if I *could* jump onto a freight car. I only knew that if I didn't make it I was probably done for. The engine came in sight, rose up like snorting, choking old dragon and hauled itself by. I'd broken out in a sweat despite the cold, but then the long trucks started crawling past me, groaning like old ladies with rheumatism, and it was no problem at all. The fourth truck had an open gap in the side. I threw my bundle of tarp and scrambled on board after it, onto some piles of old sacking.

I flopped down, incredibly relieved and triumphant. Sacking! What a luxury! And dry shelter! Maybe I could take my boots off, and get my feet dry ... Somebody coughed. I realised I was not alone. My eyes got accustomed to the darkness and I saw that the shadowy length of the empty goods truck was littered with bodies: tramps like me. Someone even had a little brazier going. I remembered what my Mama had said: the country looks empty, but it isn't. Some of the people will help us ... Already Storm had helped me, and my neighbours had given me food.

I'd been thrown out of school, burned out of my home. I was sore and filthy, cold and wet, and I knew I should be terrified of the vast journey ahead. But I had hope. It came to me that this was my mother's gift. It was because she gave people hope, because she *glowed* with it, that our neighbours had cared about her, and felt that she mattered. I didn't understand what the Lindquists meant, and I longed for peace and quiet so I could try to put together what I had learned as a child. But I felt that I was carrying that hope with me, like a burning flame.

The goods truck rattled on, slower than Nicolai's tractor. None of the other unofficial passengers took any notice of me. I unfastened my knapsack, and lifted the lid from the nailbox. The magic nutshell had grown, the wrinkles had filled out a little. When I opened it the kits looked up at me with identical pointed faces. Five of them were just slightly bigger. The sixth, the one who'd eaten the jam, was about as big as the first joint of my thumb. The last time I'd looked, this morning, it'd been only a little larger than the rest—

Oh, this isn't good, I told myself. Now I have a second-stage Lindquist to look after, and it's soon going to be too big for the nutshell. But really, I was delighted. I felt that my Mama had given me a faithful friend.

'Nivvy?' I whispered. 'Are you Nivvy, come back again—?'

No, this wasn't Nivvy, pressing tiny paws against the shield. It was a different animal, with a drooping nose, a pelt dark as ditchwater and a skinny hairless tail. Teeth glinted white, under the curling edge of its whiskered lips.

I opened the seal. Confidently, it hopped into my palm. The rest of the kits huddled down and didn't try to follow. I was holding what looked like a rat, a miniature rat with a drooping nose, and there was something wrong with its eyes, I didn't like its bleary little eyes—

'You're not Nivvy. But who are you—?'

The memories began to come back. The Orders, those strange long words—

There was a phlegmy, throat-clearing noise next to my ear. I jumped, and found an old man's face peering over my shoulder. I glared at him and closed my hand over the Lindquist. The tramp retreated, muttering, but I saw other faces turned towards me from the shadows: dark eyes, gap-toothed mouths. People were supposed to kill muties on sight. Would tramps do that? I slipped the creature back into the nest and sealed the nutshell again, trying not to let anyone see what I was doing.

My spine tingled. What kind of magic treasure is this?

6

Insectivora

The sacking was full of bugs. I dozed and scratched in misery, somehow never getting warmer. The thought of the miniature rat kept me awake. I was afraid something had gone wrong ... I'd made a mutie, instead of making Nivvy, and it was because I was a bad person, because of all the awful things I'd done at New Dawn. In the end I sat up. The tramps seemed to be asleep. I got the makings of my lamp out of the knapsack pocket, and took out the nutshell as quietly as possible. I lit my lamp, and opened the shell. The strange kit was awake, the others were snuggled down asleep. I opened the shield and picked it out. It peered at me with those dim, sunken eyes I didn't like. I checked it over and couldn't find anything wrong, except that it looked like a doll's house rat. 'It' was a she, a female ...

She liked to sniff and nuzzle, and like my Nivvy she had no fear. I let her investigate me a little. Instantly, she crept up my sleeve and found a louse: brought it out and sat on her haunches chomping neatly. 'Is that what you do?' I asked her, softly. 'You're a bug-eater?' Nivvy had never eaten bugs (in spite of what Mama had told Nicolai the Nail Collector once). He'd sometimes kill roaches, but never to eat: you could see they disgusted him. The new creature sniffed at me, that nose going up and down, as if it was nodding its head. I felt the presence of a little *person*, a living, animal person, trusting me to be its friend.

The 'magic lessons' were coming back to me, things I'd learned by heart before I was ten years old. It all sounded so different now. *Insectivore*, that was the long name for the bug-eater Lindquist. I'd shortened it to Nosey, when I was a child.

'You are *Nosey*,' I whispered. 'And you're all right, just not what I expected.'

I woke again with a shock. Something was clanging and banging. For a moment I didn't know what was happening or where I was: I couldn't remember going to sleep ... Then I remembered. My lamp had gone out, and Nosey was curled up in Storm's cap, beside my head. I nearly sat up, terribly shocked that I'd been so careless. Then I realised there was somebody walking through the truck. A man with a light was shaking the tramps by the shoulder, one by one. I tried to see what was happening. Were they giving him money? Could there be a ticket collector on a freight train? Did tramps have to show their papers? I saw the outline of a peaked cap, and knew that this 'ticket collector' was in uniform.

That decided me. I stuffed the lamp away, put my cap on my head with Nosey safe inside, grabbed my precious knapsack (I'd have to leave the tarp behind) and began to edge towards the opening in the side of the truck. I almost made it, I was ready to jump ... But I couldn't see what was out there. I hesitated too long. The light shone in my face, dazzling me. The man's words ran into each other, the way the fat nurse had talked in the clinic. 'Whatareyou-doingonthistrain?'

'I'm travelling north.'

'Youhavenobusinessonthistrain.'

I didn't have any money, prison scrip or any other kind. I didn't know what to say: I could hardly see the man's face. The light jerked at me. 'Up. Come.'

I had to follow him. At the end of the truck he threw the bolts in an iron plate, with a lot of clanging and banging, and it opened like a door. We had to step out into the night air to cross the coupling. I stood clinging to an iron ladder while he opened another plate in the back of the next truck. I thought of jumping: but wouldn't you know it, just then the train was rattling down an incline, faster than it had moved all night. I'd have been mashed to bits, and I wasn't as desperate as that. We went through another empty truck, which had closed sides and no tramps in it, and over two full ones, and so, by swaying ladders and rusty, greasy handholds, down to the fire cab, where the stoker was tending the orange cave of his furnace – and to the engine driver's swaying den.

It was a steam engine, burning brown coal. The driver's cab was very dirty, and choky with coalsmoke, but warm and dry. There was a tea kettle sizzling on a hot plate. The driver, a thickset man with black moustaches and rosy cheeks, turned from his dials and levers. My 'ticket collector' muttered something I couldn't make out, poured himself a mug of tea and settled on a metal seat bolted to the wall. He started to roll himself a cigarette. The driver looked me up and down.

'What are you doing on this train?'

'I'm travelling north.'

'Do you have money?'

'No.' I wrapped my arms around my knapsack and

glared, silently daring him to take it from me. Behind me, the 'ticket collector' laughed.

'You can't travel on this train,' said the driver.

'What about all those other people?' I demanded. 'Why can they ride?'

'You're a child,' said the driver. 'We have to turn you off, next stop. It's the law ... Give her a cup of tea.'

The ticket collector gave me a chipped, greasy mug of hot tea with sugar in it. I sat on the floor, my knapsack between my knees, sipping the delicious sweetness. The two men ignored me. Occasionally they'd say a few words to each other but mostly they sat in sleepy silence, while the train lumbered on. I started to get warm. My feet began to unfreeze, steam rose from my boots. I took Storm's cap off and held it on top of my knapsack, my hands inside so I could stroke Nosey. I knew where their next stop must be, and it was where I'd planned to get off, anyway.

Everyone helps me, I thought. I wondered if my Mama's magic worked on people who'd never known her.

Or were ordinary people just good by nature, if they had the chance?

The engine driver and his mate didn't do me any harm, they didn't try to rob me. They let me sit in their smoky haven, getting dry, and soon I knew we were coming to the fur-farm. I could smell the foulness that had sometimes drifted as far as our Settlement, when there was a strong wind in the summertime ... and I could hear the dogs. That was frightening. I dimly remembered pictures of 'dogs' in my baby books, but I'd never seen a real one. In the scary stories the kids in the Settlement used to tell, the fur-farm guard dogs were fed on human flesh, to make them savage. The flesh of runaway children, for preference, of course—

But the farm was the only place where I had a hope of finding supplies for my journey. I stood up, lifted my knapsack and put my cap on, with Nosey safe inside. By now the smell in the cab was appalling. I couldn't believe it was really from the farm, I thought the stoker must have tipped some rotten meat into his furnace—

'Thank you,' I said to my friends. 'I'd pay you if I could.'

The 'ticket collector' smiled crookedly, and took my knapsack. It happened before I could stop him. He helped me down, and got down himself. It was pitch dark, and the foul smell was even thicker outside the train. It made me gag, and the 'ticket collector' laughed at that. Further down the platform there was shouting and banging, as heavy containers were loaded or unloaded.

My plan had been to leave the train unofficially here and hide, and see what I could steal . . . but all I could do was follow the man who had my knapsack. We walked along to a small door in a big dark wall, with a dirty yellow light burning above it. The yammering and howling of the dogs got louder, as he handed my knapsack to the man who opened it.

'What's this?'

'Minor, child. Suspected runaway. No authority to travel.'

'Well, we don't want her.'

The 'ticket collector' pulled out a wadded handkerchief. He pressed it to his nose, and held it there while they argued. In the end he convinced the other man it was worth his while to take me in. I think some scrip changed hands: I wasn't paying attention, I was keeping my eyes fixed on my knapsack. The 'ticket collector' retreated, the fur farm man took hold of my arm. I was a captive.

Maybe ordinary people are good, as long as you stay away from the bad ones, but they're not as good as all that.

The fur farm man was wearing a big rough coat of brown and grey fur. I must get myself some furs, I thought (to keep my spirits up). We were in a long yard, lit by more yellow lamps, and grey with new snow. On one side there was a row of sheds, bigger than the Settlement supply stores. The other side was a pen of wire mesh, and that's where the dogs were. They flung themselves at the wire as we passed, snarling and yelping. I didn't get a clear impression: they were just a roiling mass of fur and teeth and lolling tongues. But I was very glad they were shut up.

The man pointed at them.

'That's what we do with runaway children. We feed them to the fur stock. Nice, gentle animals ... You don't want to meet the guard pack.'

The smell was terrible. It filled the air, seeming to coat my skin and clothes: rotting flesh, old blood, mouldy fat, oh, but more than that. It was unspeakable. We walked to the end of the yard, where there was a little clapboard building tucked between more of the store-sheds. A dirty, faded sign showed the number and sector of the farm. The man who held my knapsack knocked, and we went in.

I was taken through a bare outer room and into an office, where the smell was even worse because of the warmth of an enamel stove. The man in the fur coat reported that I was a runaway, to a short, dark-skinned man in uniform who was sitting behind a very messy desk. Fur-coat man tossed my knapsack onto the littered floor, so carelessly I nearly yelled ... and there was a sinister rush of scuttling, as if something alive moved among the dirty papers and cardboard boxes.

'Bugs,' growled the man behind the desk, 'I hate 'em.'
Fur-coat man laughed, and departed.

There were heaps of papers everywhere: cliffs of them
jutted from the drawers of a filing cabinet, layers of notices
hung from the dirty, yellow walls. The dark man pointed
to a chair. I read the nameplate that stood among grubby
mountains of more paperwork. Farm Manager: Osman
Ismail. There were charts on the wall behind him, with red
jaggy lines on them, and a calendar with a picture of a lady
in a silky, shining black fur coat, with boots and a jaunty
fur cap to match. But everything looked old.

I looked at the heaps of papers, and tried to think of a
plan.

'Are you Mr Ismail?' I asked. 'Is this your office?'

'Speak when you're spoken to, little girl. Take off your
coat.'

I took off Storm's jacket and handed it over. He sniffed
the fleece, and rubbed it the wrong way to feel the
thickness of the pile. 'Synthetic trash. Worthless. Here we
have real skins. Every worker has his own furs. What do
you have in that bag?'

'N-nothing much. My rations.'

Then Mr Ismail noticed my school uniform, and his
expression changed. 'Well, young lady,' he said, sitting up
straighter. 'Don't you know it's a serious crime, travelling
without a voucher? You have to answer some questions, I
have to write out a form, and do you think I have time for
this?'

'Nobody asked me for a travel voucher.'

'Huh. Do you have one? Why were you on the freight
train?'

It was just bad luck. The freight train crew had dumped
me because I was a child, maybe a runaway, and they didn't

want trouble. Now the farm manager had to do something, even if he didn't want to. My uniform would have been an advantage if I was grown-up, people in the Settlements are very careful how they deal with anyone in uniform: but now it was going to make things worse. He wouldn't dare to just rob me and let me go. I was going to end up back at New Dawn, if I wasn't careful.

I didn't dare look at my knapsack. Nosey was still inside my cap, and she'd stared to scrabble around. I took it off before Mr Ismail could notice anything strange, and put it on my knee, my hand inside so I could stroke her.

'I'm a college graduate, travelling to a new job,' I said. 'I lost my voucher, that's why I was on the train. But I'm not in a hurry. It looks as if you could do with some office help—'

'Huh. Now, where did I put that unauthorised travel form—?'

A roach scuttled out from under a pile of papers and dropped from the edge of the desk onto my lap. It made me jump in disgust. It made Nosey jump too. Next moment she dived back into the cap, the bug struggling in her jaws. The farmer manager pulled open a drawer, made another disgusted noise and shook three roaches from the document he took out. I moved my elbow, to hide the battle that was jerking my cap around 'How can I live like this?' he muttered 'It's making me ill.'

I saw two more bugs, horrible shiny brown things, crawling over an ink-stamp, and I realised the papers were *infested*. All was quiet in the cap. Then Nosey peeped out, and before I could guess what she was going to do, she had jumped up onto the desk, and grabbed another bug—

It vanished in seconds, and she grabbed another.

Mr Ismail couldn't see the carnage: it was hidden from

him by piles of paper. I was lucky he hadn't heard the crunching of Nosey's jaws. He gave me a sarcastic scowl, spread the form and took up a pen.

'A college graduate, eh? How old are you?'

'I look younger than my age.'

'Name? Sector? Settlement number? Date of birth? What were you doing on that train? Where were you running from? You should be ashamed of—'

Mr Ismail fell silent, staring at the desk top. Nosey had been working her way back to his side of the desk, and had just emerged in full view, a kicking roach in her jaws. Was she already *bigger* than when we arrived here? Yes, I thought she was. The bug disappeared incredibly fast. I held my breath.

The farm manager seemed frozen in astonishment. Both of us watched in silence as Nosey zoomed to and fro, committing bugicide after bugicide. She ran to the edge of the desk and crouched there, her long nose quivering; and I saw that the bugs on the floor had grown bold. They were ignoring the light and noise, and crawling around in the open, bold as rats. It was horrible.

Nosey wasted no time. She swarmed down a leg of the desk and went after them, moving fast. She was invincible, a killing machine beyond compare.

'Are the bugs a problem here?' I asked, innocently.

The manager couldn't take his eyes off Nosey. 'Poison doesn't touch them,' he growled. 'The cold doesn't kill them. They have evolved, faster than we can. Did you know, there are no poisons left *in the world* that will kill wilderness roaches? And every winter they move indoors. We freeze or we have them everywhere. In our food, in our clothes. I wake up in my bed, they are on my face. I stir my soup, there's a roach in the spoon. Imagine, eh? All so we can produce the beautiful furs, that the freight trains take away. Hmm ... What kind of animal is that? A mutie?'

'No, no!' I was thinking fast. 'Of course not! It's a new kind of factory-animal. Bugs are very smart these days, they avoid traps and poisons, so this little factory-animal has been developed. I'm an apprentice exterminator. I'm travelling north to join my officer, but I lost my travel voucher, as I told you—'

The ruthless slaughter on the office floor continued. Mr Ismail had a strange expression, of wonder and longing ...

'Look,' I said. 'I'm in trouble, you have a problem. Maybe we could come to some agreement?'

He looked at me hard. 'Are you are offering to sell government property, little girl?'

'Not at all,' I said. 'I meant you could hire us.'

The man's eyes narrowed, and he rubbed his dirty, bristly chin. He reminded me of Kolya the Nail Collector. He could kill me and feed me to the dogs: keep everything, and he'd probably never get caught. But most people aren't *really* wicked. I thought there was a good chance he'd rather do business.

'You could hire us,' I repeated. 'Listen, you see, what's happened to me is ... I was robbed, and lost my rail voucher. That's how I ended up jumping the goods train. I don't want money, I just want to join up with my officer again. If you'll trade me supplies for my journey, or, or a voucher if you can issue one, I could stay here, say a week. By that time you'd be free from bugs and roaches. She ... I mean, the factory-animal bug-killer, eats the nests and eggs too. We guarantee a year's protection if we have full access to the infested area.'

'Hm.'

'Then I could come back this way with my officer, and he could give you a regular contract.'

'I've never heard of travelling exterminators,' said Mr Ismail. 'I would have to see your papers.'

'They were stolen too. If you're not interested, you'd better just call someone to come and take me back to the ... the exterminators college. With my bug-killer.'

'Not so hasty, not so hasty—'

For a few moments we watched Nosey at her heroic hunting.

'You'd stay a week? You don't ... You don't notice the, er, smell?'

I looked surprised. 'What smell?'

It was a cunning stroke. Mr Ismail must have lived with the appalling stink for years: people don't get to change their jobs in the Settlements. He must hate seeing people wad their handkerchiefs and back away from him. He smiled warmly.

'It's natural when we're preparing the skins; it's quite wholesome really. But some people find the smell a little bit offensive—'

Then I had another piece of bad luck. Just when he was wavering, something on the desk started to buzz. Mr Ismail unearthed a black intercom box, put on the headphones and listened with a frown—

'You wait here. Something has come up. I won't be long.'

'Give us half an hour,' I boasted, 'and your office will be bug-free for a year.'

I heard him turn a key in the lock, jumped down from my chair, grabbed my knapsack and knelt there hugging it. There was a small window in the wall behind the desk. Was it big enough for me to squeeze through? I'd have to get it open without making much noise ... Nosey came scampering up, and hopped onto my knees. She was bigger again, but her eyes were still tiny and dim. I realised she didn't need eyes very much. She was all nose – and bug-munching teeth. I thought she had very good hearing too, from the way she darted straight for the slightest rustle of bug activity.

She must be able to filter out the smells she didn't need and concentrate on the tasty ones, because the fur-farm stink didn't seem to bother her. She was lucky: I was trying not to think about it, but that guff was *pulverising*.

She scrambled up the front of my dress and pressed her round, bullet head against my throat. When I caught her and held her, she took my nose between her little naked paws. I thought she was going to bite me: but she only wanted to touch noses. I wished I'd never thought her eyes looked weird, or that she was a kind of rat. She was the second of my magic Lindquist companions, a warrior and a conqueror, as brave as my darling Nivvy.

'You saved us, Nosey. You were terrific. But now we have to get out of here, and you have to get back into the nutshell—'

I was not convinced that Mr Ismail had bought my story. I didn't know what I was going to do for supplies, but the first priority was to get away, fast. If Mr Ismail decided Nosey was a mutie, she was *dead* ... If he decided to lock me up and send for the police, it was all over. I let Nosey run onto my shoulder, and quickly got out the nutshell. It had filled out some more, the wrinkles fading as the skin swelled up. It would turn from brown, through red, to yellow: and their cycle would be over ... The kits were all right, they hadn't been hurt when Mr Ismail threw the bag down. But they were huddled into a tight knot of little bodies, looking scared.

'You must be wondering what's going on,' I whispered, trying to sound soothing and calm. 'We're at a fur-farm. This is where they keep factory-animals, not real animals like you, and grow them into material for luxury clothes. You probably won't believe this, but they *make* it cold, in the winter fashion season, in the cities, so that they can wear furs—'

It was magical the way the kits relaxed at the sound of my voice. It made me feel so powerful, as if everything was going to be all right. Nosey scrambled down my arm. I thought she wanted to get back into the shell, so I didn't grab her. I opened the shield, keeping up a soft murmur so the kits didn't panic. 'We'll find somewhere to hide. It'll be dangerous but it will be worth it. I'll need a few days to find my way around, but I'm a good thief. I'm going to look for a sled, and some furs, and—'

I was used to smells. But if that fancy lady on the calendar knew how this place *stank*, I wondered, would she still want to wear her sables?

The door opened quietly, and Nosey dropped to the floor. I wailed, and grabbed for her. But she was gone, and the nutshell was on the floor, wide-open.

'We're not ready yet—' I gasped, desperately scrabbling it out of sight. 'A few more minutes. I have to run a check—'

I'd got the nutshell closed, with five kits safe inside: but too late. Mr Ismail had seen them. He took me by the elbows, and put me aside. I didn't struggle, I knew it was all over if I started to struggle: I had to talk my way out of this.

'Ah!' he cried. 'What do you have there? I thought so! Stolen fur-bearer kits!'

'No!' I shouted, desperately. Theft of factory animals was a very serious crime. 'Not fur-bearers! Exterminators! Bureau ... Bureau of Extermination property!'

The door of the office was standing open. Nosey had disappeared, and I was done for. Mr Ismail's grip on my arms turned me into a child again. He kept hold of me with one hand, shoved the nutshell back into my knapsack and gathered it up. Then he hustled me out of the office, locking both doors behind us, and shouting for assistance. A young man, in another of those shaggy brown and grey fur coats, came hurrying over.

'What is it, boss? Trouble?'

'Fur-bearers!' hissed Mr Ismail, excitedly. 'Bright brown ones, very fine, alive! I have five of them. The biggest escaped, it's in my office.'

'They're *not* fur-bearers!' I wailed. 'They're bug-eating exterminators, I have a licence for them and you'll be in trouble if you take them—!'

'What d'you want me to do?' said the guard, ignoring me.

'You be still,' said Mr Ismail, giving me a shake. 'Find the missing kit,' he told the guard. 'We can't have it roaming around loose. Get the staff checking every building. But search quietly. We have a visitor on the premises, remember ... But first, fetch Sultan for me!'

The younger man nodded and opened a gate in the wire mesh dog pen. He beat his way through the mass of yammering animals, and got a chain around the throat of a big one. Mr Ismail took the chain from him and hauled me and the dog, both, along to one of the big sheds. He shoved me inside, got down on one knee, grabbed the dog's ruff and pointed to me.

'*On guard*, Sultan. Don't move, girl, or he'll have your throat. I'm not joking!'

He slammed the door and left me there.

I was in despair. I was going to end up somewhere worse than New Dawn now, but I didn't care about that. The Lindquists! If I had lost them, oh, if I had lost them! I forced myself to stand still. The dog sat on its haunches on the earth floor and stared at me. It was not as big as I had imagined dogs to be, but it was big enough. Its mouth was hanging open: a long pink mouth, with the tongue lolling out between teeth like jagged white knives. I tried half a step forward.

Sultan curled his lip and made a low, menacing noise. I didn't dare go any further. A weapon, I thought. I need a weapon. I tried to look round, without taking my eyes off the dog. The shed was big and shadowy, lit by a few white tubes strung across the far away ceiling. There were packing cases stacked against the walls. I could read what it said on some of them. *Dog Skins, Grade 1; Dog Skins, Grade 2* ... In front of the cases on the left hand wall – almost within my reach – stood a metal rack with furs stretched on it: not silky black fur, like the kind the calendar lady wore, but rough and murky brown, like the guards' coats. They still had the shape of the animal that had borne them: four legs and a tail. Looking from the dog in front of me to those headless skins, I could easily see the connection. On the floor under the rack I spotted a gleaming metal bar.

Sultan watched me with an unwavering cold gaze. He's fur stock, I told myself. He's basically clothes, growing. He isn't trained to kill ... This didn't make much difference to my courage. To be killed by something that wasn't even animal seemed a hideous kind of death, like being killed by a ghost. Or a giant roach.

What could I do? I talked to the Lindquists, and my voice soothed them. Was that magic? Had it passed from Mama to me? Would it work on this brute? I was desperate enough to try. 'Sultan? You don't owe these people any loyalty—' I made my voice gentle, crooning, kindly. 'Look, those are *dog skins*. They send the fancy furs to the city, but they wear dog skins themselves. You know they do, you see them in their dog-skins every day. I bet you think they only take the weaklings, but it's going to happen to you. They'll chop your head and paws off, your flesh will be fed to your brothers and sisters—' I didn't think it mattered what I said, it was my voice that counted, but trying to scare him made me feel better. 'You think the humans here care about you? They keep you locked up, they keep you in chains, all they see is a big factory animal, just a *fur-bearer*—'

The dog pricked its ears. I thought it was listening, it was fascinated by the crooning sound. I slid my foot sideways. I just needed to reach that rail of skins, and shove it hard. Once Sultan was down, entangled in the furs, I would grab that bar and club him over the head . . . 'They'll come for you one morning. They'll probably give you a special meal, to fool you. Then they'll pull your teeth, stretch you out on the rack, and *skin you while you're still alive*, and the other dogs will gather round. The ones that hated you because you were Mr Ismail's favourite, they'll be snapping for bits of your flesh—' Sultan seemed to be taking this horrific future in: I hoped it was making him sweat, because I had cold dews and sick shivers running down my spine. I slid my other foot, I leapt sideways. I grabbed; I shoved with all my strength.

Sultan was on the floor, buried in a mess of partly-cured dog hides. I flung myself on the metal bar . . . but it wasn't a loose bar! It was bolted into concrete blocks. It was one of the floor-runners that the racks were meant to slide along.

If I could reach the packing cases before he was free, at least I could climb out of reach. But when I jumped up, my right leg, my bad leg, buckled. I barely managed to keep on my feet, holding a half-cured dog hide as a shield as I backed away—

'I'm telling you the truth—' I gasped. 'They're going to skin you—!'

The dog no longer seemed impressed. It came on, its front legs braced and the thick ruff standing up behind its head. Trained or not, it looked murderous. But something was happening behind Sultan, something very bizarre. There was a fresh, lengthening hummock in the earth floor. It was *moving fast*. It had come in under the door, it was zooming along like a mobile, miniature earthquake—

The hummock exploded. Sultan yelped, and leapt into the air. There was something dangling from one of his back paws. It was *Nosey,* twice as big as she had been in Mr Ismail's office. Sultan snapped dementedly at his own foot. Nosey let go, but instantly fastened her teeth again, in the tendon of the dog's heel. She had no fear! Sultan howled and danced in circles. I scrambled up the packing cases, and crawled along the top of them to the doorway. There was a gap between the wooden door and the frame, big enough for me to slip my hand through. I groped, and fumbled, and found the end of the bolt. I started to tug on it, but then I realised—

'Nosey!' I yelled.

She knew my voice. She came straight to me, clambering up the cases. Her paws had changed. They were broad and flat, like pink shovels with heavy, curving claws; her pelt was dark grey velvet. Sultan jumped and jumped, furious because he couldn't reach us. 'Nosey,' I gasped, 'I think I can open the door, but then I'll have to get down, and he's going to come right after me, barking his head off. *I have to find the kits.* Can you help?'

I knew my Mama's magic would have an answer.

Nosey sniffed at me, her bleary eyes lost in the velvet fur. There was a drop of blood on her twitching nose, but I'm sure it was Sultan's. She was now about the size of a man's hand, but it was still a mystery where she'd put all those roaches. She must have eaten twenty times her own weight. But then the mystery was solved, right in front of my eyes ... The Lindquist sat back and *grew*. She grew: her fur stuck out and thickened into pointed barbs. I saw her eyes grow brighter, and cheekier. She almost seemed to be laughing silently. Then she rolled herself up, dropped from the packing cases and landed on the floor, a solid mass of blackthorn spines, all pointing outward.

Sultan was beside himself, yelping and dancing around this strange object. He tried to bite it and leapt backwards, pawing at his mouth ... I tugged the bolt, and shoved the door. It came open. I dropped and ran for it.

I had to hope that Nosey could look out for herself.

It was morning now, a raw, grey, grizzly dawn, the kind of before-winter weather I hated. The snow was turning into slush. There were no fur-coated guards in sight. The dogs in the pen yelped and barked at me, but they'd been making a racket anyway: nobody came running. Mr

Ismail's office door was open. The room was empty, my knapsack and my coat were gone.

Between the dog pen and the sheds where Mr Ismail's office stood, a narrow alley led to another yard. I guessed that must be the way to the fur-farm itself. He thinks they're fur-bearers, I thought: he'll have taken them to the fur-farm.

The other yard was bigger, surrounded by grey, blank buildings with rows of small windows high up. The foul smell was even stronger. I saw a pair of fur-coated guards with rifles on their backs walking briskly out from between two buildings, heads down, scanning the concrete in front of them. I dodged through a pair of tall double doors that were standing ajar, found another door unlocked inside the lobby, and I was inside the fur-processing factory. There were some people in dark, close overalls with grubby white caps, tending the machines. But they were at the other end of the huge space: they didn't notice me.

The windows were too high to give much light. White tubes on the walls gave out a faint heat. The pens, or cages, were in three rows, with aisles between them, and moving trays under them that carried the slurry away. In the first row the pens were like tanks. Tiny things squirmed over the white tubes along the insides. I had never seen live factory-animals before, and I saw why Mr Ismail had thought I was carrying fur-bearers. The tiny things were covered in thick, black fur. I stared at them, and had strange thoughts about my Mama's magic. But these 'kits' had no heads or feet that I could see, and barely any bellies. They weren't animals. They were sheets of moving, fur-covered skin: clothes, growing, with no purpose or feelings of their own. Oh, if my kits had been put in one of these tanks! If they had already been somehow changed into things like this! I looked in all the tanks, sick with dread, and saw no bright brown. Only black and white; rust-red and blue-grey.

In the other two rows the fur-bearers started getting bigger. Still no sign of my Lindquists. I hurried on through. In a second huge room the air was icy cold, and here some of the furs were huge: almost ready to be killed – if they had ever been really alive. You could see how awful it would be if one of these creatures were to breed, somehow, with a wild animal like my Nivvy. Think of a sheet of mobile fur, big as a bedspread, armed with fierce teeth, brave and cunning and always hungry. Imagine an army of them, roaming the wilderness—

Beyond the cold room I was in the processing sector. Here there were long sinks, where it seemed as if the furs were scraped and washed in different treatments. But the machines were silent, and there were no workers about. Everything was cold, and dirty. Maybe the farm would have been stinking whatever anyone did, but nobody was even trying to keep things clean. Stacks of raw furs festered, waiting to be treated. Piles of stinking waste had just been shoved into the corners.

I didn't see Mr Ismail anywhere, but in a room labelled Specialist Hand Washing, on a shelf under a sink, as if they'd been hurriedly hidden, I found my knapsack, and Storm's jacket. The knapsack was fastened up. The nutshell was inside, and so was the nailbox, with the labcase. I'd hidden the map and the compass in the lining of Storm's jacket before I jumped on the train: they were still there, too. Finally I opened the nutshell, and my kits were there, scared but alive.

I felt like crying, I felt like praying. I'd hardly set out on the journey and already I'd broken nearly all Mama's rules. But the magic had saved me—

Then I heard voices. There were people coming down the corridor.

I backed into the shadows, and hid myself as best I could, ducking down behind a stack of unwashed furs. They smelled worse than anything. The door opened and someone looked in. I saw the silhouette of two figures, looking in.

I heard Mr Ismail's voice. 'Nothing to look at in there,' he said. 'See? Just a disused Washing Room.'

The other man – it must be the visitor who had called Mr Ismail away when he was dealing with me – muttered a question. Mr Ismail muttered back. I wondered if he was trying to explain why his workers and guards were all running around searching the factory floors, as if they'd lost something small and mobile—

The door closed and the footsteps retreated. I stayed where I was, crouched in the stinking gloom, hugging my treasure. I must be going crazy with fear, because I thought I had recognised that second voice! But it couldn't be. It *couldn't* be—

I waited to see if anything else would happen. But nothing did. Finally I put on Storm's coat, shrugged the knapsack onto my shoulders and started trying to find my way out. Further into the neglected back rooms of the fur-farm, I spotted a broken window, mended badly with cardboard and sticky tape. I ripped out the cardboard, put Storm's jacket over the shards of glass and climbed out, onto open ground. There was a double fence not far away, both sides capped in rolls of barbed wire. But it looked as neglected as the rest of this place, and there weren't any guards in sight. I crossed a bare field of slush, found a place where the base of the inner fence had come loose and wriggled under it. The outer fence was more solid. I headed left, away from the railway line, down the corridor between two walls of wire. I set off at an awkward jogtrot, my best pace: looking for a spot where I could climb. But the guard dogs were out, loose between the two fences: and something told me, even when I saw them in the distance, that I wasn't going to deal with them the way Nosey and I had dealt with Sultan. These dogs were different, silent and efficient. I could see ahead of me a fence-post that had come adrift, leaning at a crazy angle. I remembered when I had been able to run like the wind . . .

I reached it. I fell against it with a vicious stitch in my side. The biggest of the dogs had caught up. It didn't even growl. It lowered its massive head. I saw the saliva dripping from its jaws as it gathered itself to spring—

—and something came barrelling along, between the dogs' feet. A creature stranger than any factory animal, a scurrying ball of barbs. Nosey had found me. The pack jumped and yelped. The lead dog forgot me for a crucial half minute, as this extraordinary thing popped up in front of him. Maybe he'd been trained to feed on human flesh, but he still backed off, bewildered, from the sting of Nosey's spines. I scrambled up the fence-post. My Lindquist uncurled herself, and trotted cheerfully after me. I fell down in the slush on the other side, and lay there, trembling.

An hour or so later I had found a place to hide. It was an old packing case, hidden in a stand of bare willows, on the waste ground at the end of the railway platform, where heaps of fur-farm junk, cardboard, torn skins and other rubbish trailed off into the empty plain. I dragged some

121

filthy sacking inside, and some rotten furs. I knew I couldn't go any further. I was dead tired, and my weak knee had suffered badly in all the running and climbing. It wouldn't carry me any further. At least Nosey and I would be warm while we waited for the dogs to sniff us out.

But I couldn't rest, not yet. At dusk I left my precious knapsack in the packing case with Nosey, slipped down to the railway spur, dropped onto the ballast and crept along beside the track, back to the platform yard. There was something I had to know. When I'd been hiding in the Hand Washing room, I had heard a voice and seen a silhouette I thought I'd recognised. It was crazy, but I had to make sure I was wrong.

A half-solid sleet was streaming down from the leaden sky. The dogs in the pen were quiet. Two armed guards in the dog-fur coats lurked in a shed doorway: I saw the tiny burning coals of smoking cigarettes in their cupped hands. There was no one else about. I crept into the narrow alley behind Mr Ismail's office. Light fell, dirty and yellow, from the window. I could just manage to see inside.

Mr Ismail was sitting at the littered desk. He wasn't alone; he was talking to someone. They had a bottle between them, and shot glasses. The Farm Manager's words ran into each other. He was feeling sorry for himself, and probably he was drunk. But I was interested in the other man.

'Isawthemwithmyowneyes, *brightbrowns.* Youdon'tknowthefurbusiness, or you'd know, that's worth … Andthisgirlinstrangeuniform. What's it mean, eh? Wherewasshetakingthem? An'whatwasthatotherthing?'

The other man filled Mr Ismail's glass again, and murmured.

'You'reright', agreed Mr Ismail, dolefully.'IfImakeare-port strangegoingson, it all comes back on me. I'mtoblame. Muties, they'll say. No, no, I'mkeepingquiet, muchobliged toyou foryouradvice—'

The second man raised his glass, and tipped back his round, bristle-cut grey head. I saw his face. The groove between his eyes, the arched brows, that long nose, the expression of his mouth. I could not be mistaken.

It was *Yagin*.

I dropped to the ground, and crouched there, sleet in my face, hugging my knees, stunned. What could it mean? What was Yagin doing here?

Was he looking for me—?

7

Lagomorpha

I stayed in my packing case because I had no choice.
When I crawled back in there after I'd seen Yagin,
soaked and frozen and black with soot from the railway
line, I really thought I would be dead before morning. I'd
be chewed up by the dogs, the Lindquist kits would be in a
tank in the fur-bearers shed, and Nosey might have escaped
but she would be left all alone . . . But nothing happened.

After two days, I had to believe that Yagin – if I had
really seen him, if I hadn't dreamed the whole thing – must
have convinced Mr Ismail to forget the mystery fur-
bearers, and pretend he'd never seen the runaway girl in
strange uniform . . . But why would Yagin do that? If he
was chasing me, didn't that mean he wanted to catch me? If
he had tracked me down to the fur-farm, didn't that mean
he knew about Mama's treasure, and he wanted to take it
from me, the same as the bandits who had burned our hut
down? He knew I had the Lindquists; Mr Ismail had told
him. But how much did he know? Did he know more than
I did? I lay in my stinking nest, listening for the dogs,
putting together what I knew, and trying to make sense of
it all.

The way they changed and grew was so strange I had to

124

call it magic. But I thought I understood what the Lindquists *were*, now. I had remembered the names of the Orders. I remembered how my Mama had told me that Nivvy was a *real wild animal*. So ... there were no wild animals left (or hardly any), but there were these kits, that could *grow* into wild animals, the way fur-bearer kits grew into huge sheets of fur. But if that's what the Lindquists were, why were they a secret? Why shouldn't I take them to the Fitness Police – who were supposed to kill muties, but look after the true wild creatures . . . ? I could say, 'You think my Mama was a criminal, you think she did something terrible, but she's NOT. Look! Here's the marvel that she's been keeping safely, after she was dumped in the wilderness; all these years—'

I thought about it, and I thought about it. But I knew there was something wrong. It couldn't be that simple. Mama had said, when you have no one to turn to, look deep into your own heart. So I looked, and I found that though I longed to trust someone, *I did not trust Yagin.* No matter what he'd done for me I didn't trust him. I would keep faith with my Mama. I would do what she had planned to do. Somehow, all by myself, I would get the kits across the frozen sea, to the city where the sun always shines, and until then I would tell nobody, *nobody*.

Nosey foraged for herself: there were plenty of bugs. The kits did not need anything. Luckily it wasn't very cold, even at night, because I didn't dare to light a candle. I ate the remains of the food Katerina had given me, and tried to rest. The worst thing was having hardly any water.

On the third day I began to get over my fear and exhaustion.

I used the railway track as a kind of open-air secret passage, to get deep inside the fur-farm without meeting

125

any dogs or fences. I found my way into food and housekeeping stores: I found an unlocked shed of winter equipment and stole a small sledge, and a bivvy tent . . . The thieving was in ways harder than at New Dawn, because I wasn't an insider; but in ways much easier. The fur-farm guards and workers were a pushover compared to the New Dawn wardens. They didn't lock things up, even though there were notices everywhere saying they were supposed to. They didn't keep records. They didn't know what they had, so they weren't going to know the rations I took were missing. The plunder made me miss my school friends, even Rose: and it made me remember how Rain had died, which was miserable. But thinking of what to steal and how to steal it occupied my mind, leaving less room for depressing thoughts.

I felt like Mama in the Settlement: safe in the place of greatest danger.

Like me, Nosey was most active at dusk. When I returned from one of my expeditions she'd come trundling out of the dark, snuffling and grunting, and climb into my lap (I was glad I had my thick uniform skirt, to protect me from the prickles). She'd stand up with her paws on my chest, to give me kisses with her wet, berry-nose. She got fat as butter from feasting on roaches . . . unfortunately she also picked up a horde of fleas. But I was soon just as verminous, so we matched. I never undressed, of course, and I never washed. I got used to being filthy.

During the day we stayed in the packing case, unless I had to visit my latrine hole. I'd stolen a whetstone: I used it to rub the rust from my sledge's runners (most of what I'd stolen was in poor condition). I was making myself a hat as well, to replace Storm's fleecy cap which I'd left in Mr Ismail's office. I had not been able to find needles or thread, so I was trying to stick fur scraps together, skin to skin, with glue. It was a messy business. While I worked, Nosey would snuffle around after snacks, often coming over to touch my hands with her nose and make sure I was still there. The kits played in the nutshell, or sat watching us. I rarely opened the shield, in case there came a moment when I had to grab everything and run. They didn't seem to mind. They were lively and content, and had almost reached full size.

I told my family we were not wasting time. 'We're waiting for the weather,' I said. 'It's much easier to travel in the ice and snow, and the cold is not an enemy if you're prepared. Wait and see. You'll like it when you can ride on the sledge.'

It was as if the years at New Dawn had been a nightmare. I was safe again in Mama's care, getting ready to follow the route we'd planned long ago, snuggled together on winter nights, in our cupboard-bed. The dreams I'd had then had been a lot different from the filthy, smelly reality, and yet I was happy.

I started training Nosey to eat the same food as me, because she wouldn't be able to find bugs when the ground was frozen. She liked jerky, very much! She didn't like 'con' cheese, but she'd munch dried tomatoes or bread.

I thought she would be with me for a long time, all the way to the frozen sea and the city, and after that. I thought she would live as long as my Nivvy: but I was wrong. On the fifth day after our adventure with Mr Ismail she was out of sorts. I thought maybe she'd eaten too much. When I came back from my foraging I found her lying uncurled in our fur-and-sacking nest, shivering. Then I was worried, so I lit a candle for warmth (I tried to make sure no light could escape). I saw she'd grown again, and she was losing her spines, they were changing back into fur. But her whole body was shaking, and she whimpered when I tried to lift her. All I could do was kneel by her, stroking her and talking gently, and feeding her drops of bottled water. As the night passed she changed again, from this large, hairy shape to stranger forms, and then she started getting smaller fast, shuddering in a fever of change—

She knew me, all the way through. She would still touch her nose to my hand, and grip my finger with her claws. By the time she died she was a tiny thing, the same dim-eyed creature I'd met when we were riding on the freight train. I didn't cry, though it hurt very much to lose her. She had been so brave, and clever, and funny. I held her in my hand, the way I'd held her when she was little. I told the kits she was gone, then I kissed her velvet fur and laid her down. I burrowed into my smelly heap of furs and fell asleep myself.

When I woke there was a crackling rime of ice over my bedding. Winter is here, I thought. I must leave soon. In Nosey's part of the nest there was nothing left but a slim, dry, tapered pellet, the length of my fingernail.

'A Lindquist cocoon,' I whispered, remembering my lessons.

I told the kits, and they looked at me solemnly: almost as if they understood. It was so *strange*. An animal that turns into other animals, and then withers into a little roll of powder. What can you call that but magic? I was almost afraid to touch Nosey's remains, and I wondered if this had happened to Nivvy? I couldn't remember if Mama had let me see him dead . . . I did what I had to do. I took out the nailbox, unfolded the white case and prepared myself with my gloves, my mask, and a prayer. I collected the cocoon, put it in a fresh tube and sealed the tube with the colour that meant *Insectivora*. I could hear Mama's voice in my mind, saying, *Be careful you don't mix them up at this stage. We can sort it out if you do, but it's better if they're not mixed up.* There were six colours. There should be eight . . .

I wondered what had happened to the ones that had been 'lost'?

I wondered what it all meant, and I thought of Yagin the guard with longing. Could he answer my questions? *Was* he the person Mama had sent to help me?

All I could do was trust my Mama, and guard the treasure with my life.

I spent that day packing, and eating: stoking up the fire inside. I let the kits out for an adventure, as a treat. Once we were crossing the snow it would be far too cold for them to come out of their nest. I didn't let them off my lap, but they didn't mind that. They were full-sized now, but still small enough that I was a wide territory. I tried to pick out which was Nivvy, but they all seemed the same: mischevious, inquisitive, affectionate and bold. At night they got back into the nutshell, and I slept with it hugged in my arms.

When I woke there'd been a real, heavy fall of snow. It had drifted into the packing case, covering me: my furs were frozen stiff and caked white. I lay there, breathing air purified by the cold, and feeling a great change. No more half-measures: this was winter.

The fur-farm was no place for me anymore. No matter how careless the guards were they'd surely see my tracks in the snow, and the workers would be more careful about locking doors. I crawled out of my smelly nest, ate some jerky and drank some tepid water: I kept a water bottle inside my clothes at night, so it didn't freeze. Then I tucked the nutshell into my (stolen) overshirt, and fastened a belt around my waist. I put on Storm's jacket, my home-made hat and some stolen gloves that were too big. The sledge was already loaded: it was time to go.

I was pulling uphill at first, over rough ground, trying to keep to cover and convinced that someone back at the farm would spot me and let the dogs out. But when I stopped and looked back the farm was already out of sight. So was the railway track. I was alone in the white emptiness, the way I had always longed to be—

The plain opened, and I found my rhythm.

I wasn't cold. I'd stolen good clothes, including some waterproof overall trousers which I wore over my school drawers and under my dress. Actually, when I was sledge-pulling I was always far too warm, and had to wear my coat flapping open. I kept going for a *long* time, that first day. The snow was fresh and smooth but already frozen hard, and good to walk on. I'd use the compass to pick out something north of me, a boulder or a stand of reeds, and make for it. When I reached my mark I'd stop and pick out another. Soon I realised I could line up two marks with the compass, and then I could keep going for longer without having to check my course.

I didn't think about the hundreds of miles. I just marched, on and on under a clear sky, hypnotised by the emptiness: until the ache in my shoulders vanished, and my legs seemed to swing, unevenly but strongly, of their own accord. Every so often I'd stop, sit on the sledge and eat something, and then I'd open the nutshell to reassure the kits. They pushed at the shield with their little paws and noses: they knew there was something exciting going on. But I didn't let them out. It was far too cold.

Once a flight of small birds crossed overhead: I saw no other sign of life. I watched the sun's steady fall on my left-hand side, and kept the dark line of the forest ahead. How far away it was, farther than I had ever dreamed. How long would it take me to reach that friendly darkness? Weeks? The sky changed colour, from blue to turquoise, the sun went down in red-gold clouds: a silver moon rose, nearly full, almost as bright as daylight on the snow, and I kept going.

But I walked more and more slowly. Finally I shrugged off the sled harness. The sky was like an enormous bell, deepest blue overhead, shading through green to lilac above the horizon. The moon made violet shadows in the whiteness. I walked away from the sled with my head tipped back, counting the pinpricks of stars, and as I watched a veil of shimmering silver was shaken down over the blue. Curtains of light, first pink, then green and gold, swept across the sky and then drew back, to show a huge ring of bright golden light. It was the aurora borealis.

Mama had said that long ago, you could only see the mystic lights if you were so far north the sun never rose in winter. She said our world had changed in other ways besides the coldness. The envelope of particles out in space, that made this beautiful show, reached down further from the Poles, in our time. But I had lived under a cloud of smog every winter. I'd never seen this before. I had never seen anything so beautiful, or so immense. I stood there, alone with majesty, and forgot about everything. I forgot the cold, my chafed shoulders; forgot my trek, forgot the Lindquists, even forgot my Mama—

When the aurora faded at last, I saw something whiter than the snow, sitting on a rock a little distance away; like a fallen star. I went over there, my boots going crunch, squeak in the utter silence. It was an animal. He waited, and let me come up to him, fearless as a Lindquist. His fur was white, his face was long but not pointed, and he had a gentle expression. He had his long ears laid back, but when I was close he raised them, so they stood tall above his head. He sat up on his big back legs, his front paws placed neatly together, and watched me with quiet dark eyes.

'Are you a *mutie*?' I said. But I was sure he couldn't be.

His ears turned, swivelling towards the sound of my voice.

'Are you a real wild animal?'

The white fur shaded to blue-grey on his flanks. His amazing ears – they seemed half the length of his body – were pure white, tipped with sable. In the beauty of the moonlight, I thought he looked like a prince of peace.

'If you were a Lindquist,' I said, 'You would be the one called Ears. The Lagomorph who runs like the wind and hides in plain sight.'

I sat on the snow beside his rock, and we shared some bread and 'con' cheese. His front teeth were like sharp-edged chisels, but I wasn't afraid he would bite, and he had no fear of me at all. The stars shone down, and the snow hissed with bright, fierce coldness, but he wasn't afraid of the cold, and he didn't need shelter. I started to think I would tame him and take him with me, and he would teach me how to live in the beautiful emptiness. But as if he'd read my mind, he suddenly dropped down from the rock and shot away, leaving a trail of prints like splashes of indigo—

Then he stopped, and looked back.

'Goodbye!' I shouted. 'And thank you!'

I think he was the only true wild animal I ever saw.

I went back to my sledge, and pitched my bivvy-tent. It

was hard work getting the tent up, finding everything I needed in the bundles, and stowing it all inside. By the time it was done I was very, very tired. I thought how hard it would be to do this all alone, every night, and nearly cried. But I had the kits, and they comforted me.

I slept with the nutshell inside my covers.

I woke late, still extremely tired. By the time I got going the sun was past noon. I kept marching, heading north, into the pure white ... Sometimes I felt I was walking in my childhood dreams. Sometimes it was just hard slog. My prince of peace could run like the wind and sleep under the stars: I couldn't. Every night, I had to pitch the tent. Every morning, I had to pack the sled. All day there was no sound but the crunch of my boots and the *scwish, scwish*, of the iron runners. Sometimes I tried singing, or talking to the kits aloud. But soon I'd lapse back into a trance of strangeness, a white, waking dream.

I did my best to travel light. Half a candle burned in the bivvy warmed it enough for the whole night. I ate little and often, and sucked frozen snow to save my bottled water. I felt frightened (all the time!), but I felt strong ...

On the fourth day I started to lose my nerve. I had supplies for a month, but I couldn't walk for that long. My weak leg already had a slow-burning ache that I tried to ignore. I was looking for a caravan route, one of the bandit 'roads' that crossed the wilderness plain. There was one marked on Mama's map, which I had hoped to meet, but I was afraid I must have crossed it without noticing. Unless I met other travellers, and they gave me a ride, I would have to camp and stay put until my leg stopped hurting – or risk not being able to go on at all. But if I camped for long, I would run out of food, and then how would I survive—

On the fifth day I spotted a clump of tiny cones off to

the north west, barely visible against the sky. I knew at once what they were, because there were no natural hills on this plain. Those cones marked a big waste tip, a relic of long ago, when there were still cities outdoors. When I narrowed my eyes I couldn't see any smoke yet, or any vehicles or tracks, but I could see the wheeling motes of gulls.

'Come on, kits. See over there! *Dumps*! We're saved!'

By the time I reached them, the cones had grown to monstrous size. They loomed over me, snow-shouldered, pocked with dark hollows, steaming where heat from toxic stuff underground was rising. Long ago, some city or town had stood near here, and sent its waste out to the tip in giant dumpsters. Now only the rubbish heaps remained. I dragged the sled in among them, and sat on my strapped bundles, trying to spot a likely seam. I meant to stay here until other travellers arrived, and try my luck as a dump-hunter. You could not find food on the dumps, (there might be canned stuff, but it wouldn't be safe to eat); but there were rich pickings of other kinds. The bandits found things here that they traded for Settlements Commission supplies.

I took out the nutshell and opened it. 'I'll be careful,' I promised the kits. 'I know dumps are dangerous. But we *need* things. I need a hat, my home-made one stinks. We need something to use for a stove, and some fuel. And we need tradegoods, to buy more food. Look at the gulls. They wouldn't waste their time if there was nothing but toxic waste here.'

Five pointed faces peered out at me: I thought they looked disapproving. Maybe they were right, and I was just a fool for plunder, but we *did* need things. The great cold had hardly begun, and we were running out of candles. We had to have fuel soon, and something we could use for a stove, or we'd perish.

'All right, come with me,' I told them. 'To make sure I don't do anything stupid.'

I left the sled, tucked the nutshell into my overshirt, and climbed a steep slope, until I found a hopeful break where old layers had been opened up by a dump-slip. First I picked up a strip of metal, rust free, with a sharp edge, that made a great digging tool. Then I spotted the sheen of steel and dug out a big saucepan, with no handle but otherwise perfect, complete with its lid! If I could find some fuel, I had a stove ... I looked for the brown stain of tailings. If I could have a sack of coal waste, what luxury! (I didn't think about how I'd pull the extra weight.)

I didn't notice the other children until they were right in front of me. There were two of them, a girl and a boy. The girl was younger: she had long black curly hair, a green dress under a fleece-lined, embroidered coat, green trousers and thick felted boots. The boy was maybe fifteen, brown skinned, with slanting black eyes. He was dressed in black, but his clothes were equally fancy. He had fine red boots, and a red leather cap on his head. They were obviously scavenging, same as me, but they looked like a prince and a princess.

I stared, and they stared back. They didn't speak, so neither did I. I moved off further along the gulley. I knew what I looked like, and what I smelled like. I didn't want to hear their comments. But they must have some grown-ups with them. They must have transport. They hadn't walked here, dressed like that ...

I went on poking and digging, wondering how I could get a ride, until a big gull landed a few feet away from me and stood there, a patch of scarlet like blood on its wicked beak. I didn't like the look in its eye, so I threatened it with my digging stick: this turned out to be a big mistake. It raised its wings and lunged, striking me on the cheek. I hit back, but I missed, and suddenly there were gulls all round me.

I circled, swinging my weapon. The birds screamed and whirled, but they didn't fly away. They closed in, flailing their wings. I caught one of them a glancing blow. It wheeled and ejected a squirt of acid white bird-dirt that hit me across the eyes. I dropped my metal strip, and they moved in. They beat me round the head with their hard, heavy wings, so I didn't get a chance to wipe my blinded eyes or grab my weapon. I grabbed my steel saucepan – I had to abandon the lid – and began to scramble down the gulley. But the fancy children were there, heading up—

'Get back!' shouted the boy. 'They're massing down there!'

He was right. The cleft below was churning with wings.

'What'll we do?' gasped the girl.

'Backs to the wall,' I cried, yelling to be heard above the screams of the enemy. 'If we all three keep hitting at them, they'll give up.'

'No!' cried the boy. 'They're too smart! They'll bomb us with their dirt to blind us, and make us easy meat. We have to go up. Over the other side of the cone, we'll be safe once we're in sight of the trucks, they know about guns—'

We scrambled, in danger of causing a catastrophic dump-slip that would kill us anyway. I had to chuck my saucepan, but at least it hit one of the gulls and I think it broke a wing. We were about to pitch ourselves into a narrow fissure on the other side, when the girl yelled, 'Oh, no! Rats!'

There was a grey horde of them, swarming up from below. They'd seen that the gulls were attacking some major prey, and they'd come to share the feast.

'Up again! Retreat—!' shouted the boy.

'We can't!' I yelled. 'The gulls will pick us off! Forward! Charge!'

Gulls and rats had no fear of humans. They had learned to regard us as just a nuisance, unless we were carrying guns; or maybe prey. But we three stuck together, pelting them with any rubbish that came to hand: mud, metal, festering old rags. The gulls couldn't dive-bomb us once we were in the fissure, and the rats gave way before our onslaught—

Then suddenly, the enemy vanished.

'That was close!' said the boy. He flopped down on a pile of old bricks, taking off his red cap and wiping gull dirt from his face with a blue handkerchief. 'That was *close*! The Little Father was right, we shouldn't have come scavenging unarmed.'

'Would they have eaten us?' asked the pretty girl.

'Yes they would,' I said, 'I've heard of that happening.'

I looked down, and saw why the vermin had given up. I had found the bandit road. A swathe of ruts cut through the white plain, curving round the waste tips and heading for the horizon. There were six trucks parked together below us, and people moving around, men and women with rifles; and children too, all dressed in bright, flamboyant clothes, the kind of clothes you'd never see in a Prison Settlement.

'Where's your family parked?' asked the girl.

I shook my head. I wrapped Storm's filthy, ragged coat around my filthy, mud-coloured shirt, hugging the comforting outline of the magic nutshell, and walked away. I kept on walking, round the base of the cones, until I was back where I'd left my sled. At least it was still there. I sat on my smelly bundles, and put my head in my hands. 'I'm lucky to be alive,' I whispered. 'I know I am. You were right, I shouldn't have gone dump-hunting. But we're finished, kits. I can't ask for a lift. I *can't*—'

'Who are you talking to?'

The two fancy children had followed me. It was the girl who'd spoken.

'To myself,' I said. 'You do that, when you're travelling alone.'

'Where are you from?' asked the boy.

I shrugged. 'Nowhere, really.'

'We're with the caravan,' said the girl. 'But you're not one of us. We'd know you. Where are you going? There isn't anywhere. It's all empty land around here.'

'I'm heading north.'

'D'you want a ride?' said the boy. 'My name's Satin.'

'I'm Emerald,' said the girl. 'We're heading north too. We've got trucks.'

'Sloe,' I said. 'I saw the trucks.' I swallowed my pride. 'Yes, I need a ride. But I haven't any money and I don't have anything to trade.'

They smiled. 'You don't need money,' Satin assured me. 'You'd better come and meet the Little Father.'

'Your father?' I said, doubtfully. I knew how disgusting I looked, and I imagined these children must have a father like a king.

'Come on,' said Emerald. 'He'll pretend he doesn't want you, and say we've no room: but don't worry, we'll persuade him.'

'Little Father' was a big man, with thick, dark hair curling to his shoulders, and a thick, dark beard. Among the brightly dressed people he was drab, because he wore an over-coat made of sacking and tied with rope round the middle. But there was richer clothing under the dirty outer layer, and his hair was sleekly cut and combed. When we children came up he was sitting with some other men at a folding table, by a very big long truck. The table had been picnic furniture for a stylish city patio once; it looked strange in the snow. I saw the gold rings on his big fingers, as he listened to Satin's story and stroked his beard. I knew he was a bandit, but he looked kingly. He came to have a look at me: and quickly backed off, pulling out a handkerchief.

'Faugh. She smells like rancid meat.'

'*Please*,' coaxed Emerald. 'She saved our lives, truly, and she's healthy.'

Little Father went back to the table, and fetched a cup of hot water from the tea kettle. He sopped his handkerchief in it and rubbed at my cheek. I stood there, feeling terribly embarrassed, desperate to be accepted.

'Oh, hohoho,' said the big man, smiling with a flash of teeth in the dark of his beard. 'How long has this princess been lying on the midden, eh? Peel off the crust and she's a little white loaf, with eyes like black cherries.'

'She's strong and hearty,' promised Satin. 'And she has spirit.'

I didn't like being described as if I couldn't speak for myself, but I kept my mouth shut. Emerald and Satin seemed to know what they were doing.

'Hm,' said the Little Father. 'Walk about, my dear. Just walk about a little.'

Then I knew he'd seen my limp. I walked about, the men

139

and women of the caravan gathering, watching me. I tried to move as normally as possible.

'What a shame. That's permanent, I can tell. It spoils her.'

'Oh *please*,' cried Emerald, clasping her hands under her chin, and batting her eyelashes shamelessly, as if she was about three years old. 'For your baby Emmy?'

Little Father laughed, and cuffed her gently around the head. 'You'll have me taking in every stray in the north. Augh, go on, have Baba heat some water, see if she can peel off that stinking crust. Oh, and *burn* her clothes. We have plenty.'

Emerald took me to the back of the truck. The tailgate was open. Inside it was like a treasure cave of colours: curtains and bright blankets hanging on the walls, rugs on the floor. There was a stove with a chimney, and an old woman sat beside it, knitting. She made a big fuss, but she did what Little Father wanted, shutting the tailgate to give me privacy. I had to sit in a cut-down barrel of hot water, while the old lady scoured me with a scrubbing brush, and washed the grease and fur-farm muck out of my hair. It took three changes of water, but the water was *hot* and she used real, sweet soap. I hadn't been so clean since I was a baby. She tut-tutted at the cut on my cheek I'd got in our fight with the gulls. She put ointment on it and fitted the edges together, very carefully, with two clean paper-plasters.

I was given underwear and clothes, several layers of skirts, leggings to go underneath, a new jacket and felted boots. Baba even tried to put a ribbon in my hair, but it was still New Dawn short, so she had to give up that idea.

My top skirt was red, with sprigs of flowers. I loved it.

Satin and Emerald had been guarding my sledge from the

other children. When I came out, wearing my new clothes and with my face and hands pale as milk, Satin cheered and tossed his red cap in the air.

'Now we'll have a bonfire!' said Emerald.

I felt a pang when I saw my New Dawn uniform go. A lot of my life went up in those smoky, greasy flames. Not just the part that held Rain and Rose, and so many bad memories, but the schoolroom hut in the Settlement, and Mr Snory. The pride of getting good marks, the thrill of thinking I had won a chance in life. And I would miss Storm's jacket . . . Emerald and Satin had wanted to put my filthy knapsack on the bonfire too, but I'd refused. Baba had washed it instead. The kits were safe. I'd managed to slip them into the nailbox, along with my map and the compass, when the knapsack was emptied. I'd told Baba it was where I kept clean cloths for when I got my period: she understood how a girl would cling to that.

But I wondered how long I'd be able to keep any of my secrets—

'How do I pay for my ride?' I asked, 'Is there work I can do?'

'Little Father's rich,' said Satin. 'He's generous, he likes giving.'

'We work around the camp,' explained Emerald, because she could see I wasn't happy about being a beggar. 'It's not hard, but there's plenty to do.'

When the bonfire had died down it was dark. The truck where I'd been bathed was Little Father's own. He lived in a room at the front, behind the driving cab. Emerald and Satin lived in the back, with Baba to look after them, and that was where I would travel. The other children drifted off, the old woman called us indoors. She served us bowls of hot kasha porridge, with syrup and cream trailed over the top, which we ate sitting by the stove on a silky warm rug. Then we talked, and played (Emerald and Satin had a box of toys and puzzles) until Baba said we must go to sleep. She'd made up a bed for me, in one of the bunks that were hidden by the curtains that hung around the walls.

I waited till the truck was quiet, except for the old woman's rhythmic snores. The big tailgate was fastened up, but there was a little door in it, covered by a felt curtain, that was only bolted, not locked. I slipped down, barefoot, wrapped in a blanket, into the freezing night, and went to my sledge. It was still standing where we'd left it, by the embers of the bonfire, but all my bundles were gone. Anything of use had been taken into the general stores, and the rest thrown away ... When I'd planned to hitch a ride, I hadn't imagined anything like this. I had thought I would still be in charge of my own destiny. Now my clothes weren't even my own. I felt very strange.

'Do you want to keep it?' said a soft voice beside me.

Satin had followed me. He sat down on the sledge.

'I don't know what to do,' I said, 'You people are too generous.'

There was a long silence.

'Don't worry,' said the boy, at last, 'We understand, Emerald and me. We'll keep your sled, Little Father won't notice. Then you'll know you can get away.' He touched my shoulder, shyly. 'It's good to promise yourself that. Even if it isn't true.'

The day after I joined the caravan the weather broke up. The clouds had been thick and angry when we started off, but nobody had cared. When the storm broke, the trucks drove straight through it. We got up onto the upper tier of bunks and sat there safe and warm, while a blinding, whirling whiteness scoured the double-glass windows in the side of our speeding haven.

'If we were out there,' said Emerald, grimly, 'We'd be dead.'

I didn't think of the weather. I thought about hiding in plain sight, like the wild animal I had called my prince of peace. To survive without a home, in the wilderness, you must be able to take shelter on the open ground ... I decided that falling in with Emerald and Satin was the best thing that could have happened to me. I wasn't dressed like Sloe, I didn't behave like Sloe. I was part of Little Father's family. No one could mistake me for a lone fugitive with a secret!

I didn't have any trouble hiding the kits, or keeping my nailbox safe. The Little Father never came poking around in the back of the truck: it was our territory. And old Baba was half-blind, while Emerald and Satin never tried to pry. I kept my knapsack in my bunk, but whenever we stopped to do business, or to camp, I would carry the nutshell with me. Sometimes – not every day, but often – I would manage to slip away, between sunset and dusk, when the camp was at its busiest. I would walk off into the snow, and then I'd be able to open the shell and talk to them.

And be Sloe again, for a short while, alone in the cold immensity.

Emerald and Satin didn't like me doing this. They were afraid Little Father would notice my 'wandering' and he'd be angry. They seemed to love and fear their Dadda about equally (I supposed their mother was dead or taken away: I never asked about her). But they sympathised, especially Satin, so they protected my strange ways.

Our trucks kept to the ice-rutted road, but whenever we were moving there were outriders patrolling the waste, on powerful heavy-duty motor sleds. Nomadic life was supposed to be illegal, because it counted as 'unauthorised travel', but of course these scouts were watching out for rival bandits, not the law. The Settlements Commission (Mama had told me this) didn't really care what happened in the wilderness, as long as the people didn't try to get into the cities. Emerald and Satin and I, and the kids from the other trucks, would hang around when the scouts came in at dusk, to report to the Little Father. We were fascinated by the motor sleds, and the swaggering young men with their long rifles and tall boots.

One night, they brought in Yagin.

I had been accepted easily by the other kids, though I couldn't even talk to some of them: they spoke a different language in some of the trucks, an old bandit language from long ago. We were all playing football in the dark, when we heard the scouts' sleds. We'd stuck rag and oil torches into the snow, and were running around our shadows, yelling and squealing, and losing the ball. We abandoned the game and gathered near Little Father's picnic table. One of the scouts was riding a motor sledge that we hadn't seen before, and there was a stranger walking with them, between two of our young men. The grown-ups had gathered too. An actual stranger was rare – bandits all seemed to know each other. Whoever we met, someone in our caravan was a cousin, or knew a connection. I saw that the man was Yagin, and this time I wasn't even shocked. I just felt doomed. Of course he had found me again. He would always find me—

Things looked bad. He was walking free, chatting confidently to the young men. They had guns trained on him, but that meant nothing: it was normal bandit manners. I didn't know if I should just run for it, or stay and try to look innocent. I didn't look like Sloe! He might not recognise me—

I needn't have bothered with the 'looking innocent'. I watched him take off his cap, in respect for the bandit king. I watched him being invited to sit down at the table, like an honoured guest ... and soon I heard him telling Little Father that he was looking for a girl. A ward of the state, who had run away from the New Dawn College. Black eyes, dark hair, white skin, rather tall: about *so* high ... (he measured me, setting his hand in the air); a tendency to limp with the right leg. There was a generous reward for her safe return, and he would share it with anyone who could give him information—

'So you're a bounty-hunter,' rumbled Little Father, stroking his beard. 'What crime has she committed, the little snow-bunting?'

'*Serious* crimes,' declared my so-called guardian angel. 'Sedition, subversion, and poisoning the minds of her fellow students. It is a dangerous offence against the Settlements Commission to give her any assistance.'

'Well, that's very bad,' said Little Father. 'And how much is she worth?'

I saw Yagin bring out a black purse: I saw the rough-made gold coins of the wilderness spilling onto the table-top. He was a bold man! Didn't he know that the bandit king could just have him killed, and keep the lot? But something in the way Little Father looked at Yagin, and in the feeling of the crowd, told me that wasn't going to happen. My guardian-angel seemed to have put a spell on them ...

I walked slowly backwards, out of the gaggle of children. I knew where my sledge was. It travelled hooked up on the side of the truck, with other equipment: skis and sticks, shovels and brooms. I thought I could get it down alone. I had the nutshell with me. I would have to sneak into the back of the truck to get my knapsack, and maybe get some food ... I crept past old Baba, who was dozing by the stove, and collected the knapsack. I was quietly, quietly opening a food locker, when I heard Emerald's voice right behind me, and jumped a mile—

'Sloe?' She stroked my cheek, and squeezed my hand.

'It's all right, Sloe. Little Father's sending him away.'

'I don't believe you,' I croaked.

'Come up and see.'

We climbed the ladder to the second tier, the row of bunks that nobody slept in, and peered out through the double-glass windows. Yagin was still there. I couldn't hear what was being said, but I saw Little Father shake the gold back into the black purse, and toss it across the table. My mouth dropped open. Yagin started arguing, Little Father laughed. Yagin got angry. He waved his arms. The crowd stirred ominously, the scouts raised their long rifles. But Little Father did not give the order—

Yagin took his purse, and left on his sled, pursued by warning volleys.

'They won't shoot him,' said Emerald, in a matter of fact tone. 'He wasn't in uniform, but he's the police. You can always tell. But he'd better not come back.'

I didn't often get close to Little Father. When Emerald and Satin spent time with their Dadda I stayed discreetly out of the way. Instinct made me afraid of someone who had so much power over my fate. But after the Yagin incident I went to him, first chance I got. '*Thank you*,' I said, and I curtseyed and kissed his hand, the way I'd seen his own

146

people do when the Little Father had granted them a special favour.

His big hand smelt of herbal soap, it was soft and strong, with hairs growing over the knuckles. He laughed, and raised me up: smoothed his big thumb over the place where my cheek had been cut, and nodded in satisfaction.

It was mending well, I wouldn't have a scar.

'Little snow-bunting,' he rumbled. 'You're a good girl.'

Sometimes we thundered along at a terrific pace. Sometimes we camped for days, for no good reason. I wasn't worried. There were months and months of winter ahead. We were heading north, despite all the halts, much faster than I could have managed on my own. We three helped Baba with the chores, we played together, and sometimes played with the children from the other trucks. I found out that Emerald and Satin weren't Little Father's own children. Quite a few of the kids with the caravan were strays like me, that the bandits had taken in along the road. I thought this was very kind. I told Satin I wished more people in the Settlements knew that the bandits could be kind as well as ruthless. He shrugged, and said coolly, 'I suppose they are as kind as most people in the world.' I wondered why he wasn't more grateful.

We were friends, but Emerald and Satin often puzzled me. Of course I didn't tell them my secrets, and they never talked about what had happened to their families. That seemed all right. It was best to live in the present. But there was something empty about them. They had no purpose in life, no dreams beyond keeping warm and having nice food: and secretly I pitied them, although they were so rich.

The bandit tribes agreed with my Mama: winter is the

time for travel. We were heading for a great meeting, the winter fair: where there would be feasting and trading and a big exchange of news. My map stayed in my knapsack with my compass. I didn't want anyone to know I had things like that. But I had a good idea where this fair would take place, and I'd decided that's where I would leave the caravan. It would be time for me to start heading west, to reach the narrowest point of the narrow sea. I wished I could pay Little Father something. But the back of our truck, behind the curtains and under the hangings, was stuffed with bales and boxes, and I had seen his contempt for a purse of Settlements Commission gold. I had nothing except the map and compass, and my Lindquists. I just hoped that one day I would find my Mama again, and we would trace Little Father, and make some return for all his kindness.

One night, safe in my curtained bunk, I took out the nutshell to say goodnight to the kits, and noticed that the shell had crumpled a little, and started shading back from yellow to brown. The kits were curled up. They raised their heads very sleepily, and blinked at me. I said goodnight, and shut the shell, and lay down, very shaken.

'It's for the best,' I whispered to myself. 'It won't be forever.'

I didn't get a chance to check them the next day. When I opened the shell to say good night again, they were dead.

I lay and cried, without a sound. I thought of that night in my Mama's hut, when they had played on the lumpy mattress. The freight car, our big adventure at the fur-farm, the smelly packing case where we'd lived with Nosey ... Most of all, our crossing of the snow ... I had never been lonely, never once. I was supposed to be the guardian, but I would be lost without them—

I had no family now, no companions. I would just be carrying a box of seeds.

I harvested the cocoons, returning the powdered seed to the fresh tubes: which I put away carefully in the base of the lab case. I tried to behave as if nothing had happened, and failed miserably ... But it was easy to get away with being sad. We were getting close to the big meet. Other streams of vehicles were moving with us now, converging from other roads. Everyone was busy: there was no time for play. Baba spent hours polishing Little Father's brass and silver goods, work she didn't trust to anyone else. Emerald and Satin had been set to make lists of the contents of those mysterious bales. There were more guns about, and we children were kept inside the trucks: no more games of football.

The meet was held in a natural arena, a flat space surrounded by rising ground, at the crossing of several winter roads. Our caravan arrived at night, and Baba had been ordered to keep the tailgate bolted, which was frustrating. We peered through the second tier windows, and listened to the snarl of strange engines, the grind of big snow-tyres, the hubub of a crowd; while Baba sat below with her knitting. I was excited, though I was still mourning for the kits. Beyond the glare of lights, I thought I could see the darkness of the forest ... Emerald and Satin seemed downhearted. I thought it was because Little Father had forgotten them, on this big night. I felt guilty, because I was going to desert them too.

Instinct had told me that I should not say goodbye. Easy come, easy go. I'd been collecting food stores, the kind of stuff that wouldn't be missed, and I had my knapsack packed. I was debating with myself whether to take a pair of short skis. I didn't want to steal from my benefactors, but they had so much—

In the morning I dressed in my warmest clothes. Baba went to fetch our water herself, which was usually our chore, and reported that the temperature, according to the truck's outside thermometer, was twenty below. She washed us and combed us as if we were babies, and fed us our bowls of kasha porridge with a sentimental smile. I thought it was the thrill of the big meet that made the old lady seem a little strange.

I'd brought my knapsack to breakfast, instead of leaving it in my bunk. I was thinking of an excuse for taking it to the fair with me, when there was a banging on the tailgate. Baba unbolted the small door, and Little Father himself squeezed in, followed by two of his outriders, and some other men I didn't recognise.

'Yes,' said Little Father. 'Yes! Stand up, all three of you!'

We stood up. The back of the truck was full of bodies. The strange men peered at us, and one said, 'Let's see them in daylight.'

I looked at Satin. He shrugged. Emerald kept her eyes on the floor.

We got down. There was a group of children standing together; I noticed it was composed of all the caravan's strays. I was told to walk up and down, my limp attracted comment. One of the strange men looked inside my mouth, and felt the fat on me with hard fingers, while the winter fair proceeded merrily all around. I was so horrified, I did not notice that the same things were happening to Emerald and Satin. I thought I was being handed over to the bounty hunters after all, and didn't understand why these other children were watching. I was desperately hoping for a chance to run for it ... The men picked out me, and Emerald and Satin, and three others. The other strays were dismissed, and that's when the truth began to dawn on me. And I recalled, too late, little things people had said and done, that ought to have warned me—

The traders said Emerald was too young, and Satin had poor teeth. They argued even harder over the price Little Father asked for me. But he was adamant. My snow-bunting, he said, she's a college student. Skin like milk, eyes like black cherries, reads and writes like a scholar, you don't often find this kind of girl. You should have seen the money I've turned down for her.

In the end the haggling was over, and everyone seemed satisfied.

Emerald and Satin had their bundles of possessions, I had my knapsack. The other three, a boy and two girls, had their belongings too. I wasn't shocked at Little Father, I wasn't shocked at the men who bought me. I knew it was just business. I was *disgusted* with Emerald and Satin. They'd known all along that I didn't understand. They'd known when they offered me a ride, at the Dumps, that they were tradegoods, like the other bales and boxes in the back of Little Father's truck. They'd known that if I joined them, I would one day be sold like them, as a slave.

8

Rodentia

No one paid any attention as we were walked across the fairground, roped together with our hands tied. Above the white slopes that rose all around, through the throngs of people and vehicles, I caught glimpses of the forest margin. We had reached that black line which had been the fartherest limit of my world for as long as I could remember. But it looked as if I wasn't going to get any further.

We were taken to the slave-auction ground, where we saw the grown-up slaves huddled in a fenced-off pen. Our buyers got us registered for sale while we stood shivering. We'd been allowed to bring personal belongings, but not our coats. The auctioneers' office was a dark, shaggy-roofed hut on stilts: the kind of building the bandit tribes carried around with them, in pieces, on special trucks. I thought it looked like a big malevolent dark bird. The men who'd bought us from Little Father wanted us to be given special treatment, because we were high-class merchandise. But the auctioneers said there was only one holding-pen for children. We were taken into the back room of the hut, and our hands untied.

One of the auction men said, 'There, that's not so bad, is

it? Indoors, out of the cold. Bucket in the corner if you need it.' Then they left, with their lantern.

Heavy bars were shoved across the door, and a key was turned. The back room had no windows. The only light came through cracks between the rough logs of the walls. We could make out a confused mass of bodies, huddled at the far end. Someone down there whimpered, a wordless cry of misery.

'Who are you?' a cracked voice cried.

'Just children,' answered Satin. 'Here to be sold, like you—'

'*What have you got?*' came another voice, speaking the old bandit language. The bodies surged towards us out of the dark. It was like a tide of roaches with human flesh. I know I felt no pity ... I think none of us did. The six of us fought the slave-children off, with determined thumps and kicks. We were fresh and strong: they quickly gave up, and retreated. We got ourselves into a corner and sat on the dusty floor, with our possessions and Emerald, who was the youngest, in the middle. I wondered how long it would take for us to become like those others—

We couldn't see the bucket, but we could smell it.

'I n-need a wee,' whispered Emerald. 'Sloe, come with me?'

'You *knew*,' I hissed at Satin, '*You knew* we were going to be slaves! And you didn't even warn me! I thought you were my friends. You *betrayed* me!'

'You'd have been out in the storm, remember?' He acted surprised at my anger, 'You'd have been dead if we hadn't taken you to Little Father. It won't be so bad. It's better to be worth money than to be just a stray child. Trust me, I've tried it.'

'We didn't betray you,' cried Emerald. 'It wasn't like that! We knew Little Father might sell us, but, but he was nice to us. I was like his own little girl, and I had pretty things. It was nice. It might be n-nice again ... Tell her, Satin.'

'I thought you knew,' he said. 'We all thought you knew. We didn't talk about it, because we never do. What's the use in talking?'

I glared at him, and hoped he could see my expression. There'd been plenty of times he could have made sure I understood ... But Emerald and Satin didn't think the way I did. They did not belong to themselves. They did not *expect* to be free—

'Let's not fight,' said the other boy who'd been bought, whose name was Bakkial. 'Let's us stick together. We're all mates, let's stay that way.'

'I hope we get good masters,' said one of the girls, bravely. She was the biggest of us, a tall strong teenager. 'I don't mind working, for a good master.'

The six of us sat in silence, holding hands. Emerald and Satin weren't royalty now: we were all the same, the refuse of the world. We had no human value. We would be lucky to end up hard-working bondservants. There were worse fates.

'Little Father doesn't let his people keep grown-up slaves,' said Satin, in a flat voice. 'He says it's not worth it, they can never be trusted. They just pick up pretty-looking strays, treat them well and trade them as a sideline.'

'How long d'you think those other children have been here?' I wondered.

'Maybe they're the ones no one wanted to buy, at some other market—'

'*We'll* be sold before the end of the fair,' said the big girl, whose name was Tanya. 'We're good quality, anyone can see. So that's only ten days at the most.'

Ten days in here!

'I still need to have a wee,' said Emerald, unhappily.

'I do too,' said the third girl. She was younger than me, and she had long corn-gold braids; I couldn't remember her name—

I went with them, as a bodyguard. I was glad of the dark when we found the bucket, which stood in the middle of the room. It was nearly overflowing. Shadowy, dirty faces peered at us, groping hands tugged at our clothes, but we didn't have any real trouble, and came back to the corner safely. It was very cold. It was going to be a lot colder at night. If no one gave us blankets we might have to join that squirming heap of human roaches, just to stay alive. The idea made me feel sick.

I sat beside Satin and Emerald, my arms wrapped around my knapsack, trying to plan. Once I had been sold, I would find a way to escape. That much was clear. But how could I keep the Lindquists secret? I remembered being a new girl at New Dawn College. They'd taken everything I owned away from me, stripped me naked the moment I arrived. How long would I be able to hang onto my knapsack, if I was a slave? At least the kits were in their seed form. They wouldn't be frightened or hurt, whatever happened—

The kits . . . An idea rose in my desperate mind.

I heard my Mama's voice: *Strange things, marvellously strange things happen to the Lindquists, at full expression* . . . I remembered Nosey, the brave warrior who had rescued me at the fur-farm—

'Hey. What if I could get us out of here?'

'Don't be silly,' said Emerald. 'We've got no outdoor clothes.'

'It would be no good,' said Tanya. 'We're money in a locked box. We'd be caught and brought back. Money can't walk. It's hopeless.'

'We can't escape,' said Satin. 'Calm down, Sloe. It's not so bad.'

I didn't know what would happen if I tried to kindle the kits. I couldn't remember if there was a minimum time that they had to be left dormant. Maybe the process just wouldn't work, or the kits would die. But I had nothing else. 'I've got something in my knapsack,' I said. 'It's sort of magic. I could try to use it. But you all have to promise, whatever you see me do, you must never, never tell anyone—'

Five faces stared at me.

'Oh, that knapsack!' said Satin. 'Sloe's knapsack, that no one better touch!'

'Shut up, Satin,' said Tanya. 'Everyone watches their stuff.'

'Is the magic why the bounty hunter came after you?' asked Emerald.

'Yes. But I can't talk about it, and you mustn't tell.'

'We won't tell,' said Bakkial. 'Never.'

They formed a half-circle round me, in case the auction men came back or the slave children advanced again. I took out the labcase and opened it, put on my mask and gloves and silently prayed. There was very little light. I worked by touch and memory, as fast as I could. I kindled all the kits: I didn't know if they would grow if they weren't together. I wouldn't have known which Order to choose, anyway.

'What will happen?' breathed Satin, when I had finished and the nutshell was sealed again. 'Will a *Djinn* come to do your bidding?'

'I don't know what a *Djinn* is.'

'A powerful spirit. Magicians can make them obey.'

'Is it a bomb?' demanded Tanya excitedly. 'Is that round thing a *bomb*? You're crazy!'

'I'm not allowed to talk about it,' I said.

'How long will it take to work?' asked Bakkial.

We all peered towards the huddle of slave children. They were quiet now, but they knew we had stuff. They wouldn't leave us alone for very long.

'I think something should have happened by sunset.'

The cracks between the logs were grey knifeblades: the icy air came in, and the blurred noise of the fair, but you couldn't see out. We didn't talk much. We all had food and water in our bundles (I had all the supplies I'd stolen for my trek); but we didn't dare take anything out. We dozed a bit, leaning against each other, but always on the watch. Twice there was a surge from the other end, and twice we drove them back. After endless hours, there were footsteps outside the door. The lock rattled, the bars were taken down: the slave children pressed themselves against the back wall, like roaches disturbed by a light. An auction man came in with a lantern, and set a big steaming tub on the floor. 'Here's your porridge,' he said. 'Come on, don't be scared, eat up.' The children at the other end scuttled forward, scrabbling to get to the edge of the bowl, scooping up the hot porridge in their hands. There were no spoons. We stayed where we were.

'I'm not hungry,' muttered Satin.

'I am,' said Emerald, in a very small voice. 'But that doesn't look tasty.'

Another man came in and walked around with another lantern, like the 'ticket collector' in the freight car, checking on the state we were in, making sure the bodies that didn't move were still alive. He had a whip in his belt, but he didn't use it. He came up to me, and lifted my chin as if he was picking up a fold of cloth from a bale. 'Very nice,' he muttered. If we all got together, I thought, all of us children, we could overpower two men . . . But they knew we wouldn't try anything. We could overpower them, and then what could we do? Where would we go?

Soon the tub was empty. The men took it away, and the door was barred and locked again. The room was much darker now.

'It's time,' I whispered. 'Keep them off.'

My friends prepared to repel an attack. I took out food, (a chunk of con, and some dried berries) and the makeshift oil-lamp I'd made in my Mama's hut, the night the Mafia came. I had to have light for this part. I put the lamp together and filled it from the small jar of oil I'd sneaked out of the food locker in Little Father's truck. As soon as the light sprang up the slave-children came swarming: starved faces, hollow eyes, gleams of teeth, ragged clothes and half-naked limbs flashed out of the dark. Satin and Tanya and Bakkial drove them off: and I knelt in the circle of lamplight, my Mama's magic gift in my cupped hands. Like the girl in the fairytale, I opened up the shell. The kits were alive. They were at the doll's house stage: so tiny I was afraid to touch them, but perfect. They jumped towards me, pressing on the shield, and my heart welled up with love. I can't explain that feeling: how glad it made me, in this dirty, desperate place, just to see them again—

There was no time to think. I prayed that my choice should be right, and lifted out the liveliest. Then I sealed up the rest, while I held it in one hand, feeling the tiny tickle of its whiskers as it nibbled a scrap of con. Emerald and the girl with the corn-gold braids helped me to put everything away. The slave children hadn't seen what I had in the nutshell, but they must have felt that something strange was going on. They gave up the attack and did their roach-scuttle backwards, making the signs that wilderness children make against evil. I could feel the kit in my hand, like a tiny beating heart. It was already growing. I opened my fingers a little, to push some slivers of dried berry between them: a minute nose sniffed my finger, and the kit *bit* me, with the tiniest of teeth. I felt its tongue licking up the drop of blood.

Nivvy—?

My spine tingled. Mama had warned me Nivvy could be dangerous—

'More food,' I whispered, urgently. 'Small stuff, but keep it coming.'

They didn't ask questions. The girl with the corn-gold braids thrust dried berries into my free hand. Emerald dug slivers of chocolate off a block with her fingernail. The others kept watch. Within a very short time, all the food I'd taken out was gone, and the Lindquist kit had grown to the size of a small apple. It sat on my palm, feeding itself industriously on the last of Emerald's chocolate.

It wasn't Nivvy. Its fur was brown and white, its body soft and plump, its eyes like two red berries. It had round naked ears, little pink paws, chisel-teeth, and no tail.

'Will it grow into a dragon?' asked Emerald, hopefully.

I had a terrible feeling I'd let my secrets out for nothing.

'This might take a while,' I said. 'The magic needs time to work.'

My lamp was dying. I snuffed it out and packed it away. The room became utterly black. I lay down, facing the corner: making my body into a barrier so I could let the Lindquist run on the floor. The others settled round me.

Satin and Corn-braids took first watch, guarding the bundles and facing the twin dangers of the door and the slave children. Emerald curled up against my back: Tanya and Bakkial muttered to each other, and fell silent. I kept on feeding the kit, dipping into my food stores again and again, in a trance of cold tiredness. She kept vanishing into the blackness and coming back. Then I heard her gnawing at the logs. She's trying to break us out of jail, I thought. But it's going to take weeks. I reached out and stroked her with one finger, and discovered something that made me jump. Where there'd been *one* little animal, there seemed to be several ... My Lindquist had had babies.

The gnawing went on, and became a chorus.

I groped again, and found there were *more, and more—Impossible,* I muttered.

But I had always known the kits were magic ...

The black hours passed. I never truly slept, but everything ran together: the groping attacks of the slave children, the stink of that bucket, the cold: and the sound of gnawing. We hit the fumbling hands, and they went away. The Lindquists kept coming to me to be fed, and then hurrying back to their work. On and on. The touch of whiskery little noses, a scuffle behind me as the others fended off another attack; more food out of my pack, the weight of Emerald's head on my shoulder—

I woke hugging my knapsack. It felt emptier, and the blackness had turned grey. It was the cold that had woken me. The corner was a mass of sawdust. There was a gaping hole, easily big enough for my head and shoulders, gnawed through the log wall, and a seething carpet of small brown and white furry animals—

'Wake up! Everyone, grab your stuff! It's time to go!'

Satin was already awake, and staring at the horde.

Emerald lifted her head and peered through her tangled black curls, shivering. Bakkial woke with a start, and gasped, and crossed himself against the evil eye. The girl with the corn-gold braids said, in a scared, awed voice, 'What are those things? Are they muties?'

'No,' I said. 'I promise you they're not. They're very important, and I have to take them somewhere. I have to go north, but you can all come with me—'

Five faces stared at me, dirty and weary in the grey light—

'We'd die of cold,' whispered Emerald.

'But we won't be slaves . . . We won't head off straight away. It's a *fairground*. It'll be full of stuff we can steal, and people not paying attention. Come on!'

'I can't,' said Tanya, her eyes fixed on the Lindquists. 'I don't dare. I'm afraid. It isn't so bad here. I might get a good master—'

'We can't run away,' said Bakkial. 'Little Father would lose face, and be mad as fire. He'd hunt us down, and what would happen to us then—?'

'Who cares? They won't catch us if we go *now*—'

There was a low muttering from behind us. Then one of the slave children said clearly, bitterly. 'They're breaking out. They're getting away.'

Another voice took it up. Somebody started to bang on the floor. Soon they were all banging on the floor and chanting, *They're getting away, they're getting away, the pretty ones are getting away!* They didn't care that we were children like themselves. They were so sunk in misery that we were just the enemy . . . In another minute the auctioneers would come to see what the noise was about.

'*Please*—!' I begged. '*Please* don't make me leave you behind!'

161

'You have something important to do,' said Satin. 'You should do it.'

'Go on Sloe,' said Tanya. 'You're a good kid, but we'll be all right.'

The Lindquist horde was already pouring through the gap like a furry waterfall into the grey space beyond. 'I'll pay you back,' I wailed. 'One day, I promise—!'

There was tremendous rattling at the barred door, and the chanting rose to a shout as I dived through the hole—

I'd forgotten that the hut was on stilts. I fell two metres onto frozen snow and got to my knees. The Lindquist horde swarmed around me. But they were withering like dry leaves, only faster, they were shrivelling up: they were nothing but little grey pellets of dust. There was only one brown and white animal, with her tiny paw on my knee, looking up in total trust, her cranberry eyes like drops of shining blood.

There were trucks parked next to the hut on stilts. I could see the undersneaths of them, at my eye level. I scooped my Lindquist up, tucked her into the front of my clothes, and swarmed across the snow on my belly, dragging my knapsack with one hand: under one truck, then a dive and a roll under the next, and so on ... A couple of times I was nearly spotted, by people lighting fires under their engines to get them moving after the night: but nobody really saw me. I reached the end of the row, got to my feet and quickly walked away.

Somewhere behind me I could hear shouts and the sound of pounding feet. Maybe that was for me, but I didn't run. I buried myself in the crowd. I found a black waterproofed blanket that someone had draped over a parked motor sled to keep it from icing up. I wrapped myself in that, and my

162

bright clothes disappeared. I wandered between rows of flaring torches, turning pale in daylight. I lingered by the hiss of bonfires and braziers. An old woman cooking maize cobs gave me one for free. I tried staring at another man who was grilling dog meat, but he didn't give me anything. Once, I found a roost in a big stack of rape-seed oil drums, and felt safe enough to take my Lindquist out and stroke her. She was bigger than Nosey's small form, but not so big as spiny-Nosey. Her red eyes were rather strange, but she had a very gallant, cheery air. 'I know who you are,' I said. 'You are the Lindquist who becomes many, Order Rodentia. I called you Toothy, when I was a little girl.'

I stroked her and praised her, and gave her the last of my corn. I was slightly afraid that she would *become many* again, if anything threatened us. If anyone saw that happen we'd be in big trouble. She'd be killed with all her children, and so would I, probably. I tried to be very calm. I told her I was an expert thief and I'd soon collect supplies for the next stage of our journey—

It was about twenty-five, maybe thirty below. I wasn't dressed for the cold, and I was very tired and hungry, but I didn't know it. I thought I hadn't been doing anything: I'd just been sitting in that hut for a day and a night. Something dangerous happens when you get very tired and hungry, and it's really cold. You stop thinking straight – and you don't feel it coming over you. I decided to go back to Little Father's trucks, and steal my own sledge. I knew exactly where it was, hooked up on the side of the truck with the short skis and their poles—

I needed my sledge so I'd have somewhere to put the food I was going to steal. I'd given all the food in my knapsack to Toothy, when she was rescuing me from the slavers' hut. I needed to start the stealing soon. My teeth were chattering, the wind went through my raggy old blanket and my pretty clothes like a knife. Maybe it would be easier to steal from Little Father's tribe, because I knew everybody's habits—

It took me ages to find my way back. My head was swimmy, and it was getting hard to concentrate. At last I saw the trucks I recognised. Little Father must be at his picnic table, because everybody was gathered around there (unless they were off at the fair). It hurt me to see the familiar scene. I wanted so badly to climb through the felt-lined door in the tailgate, to sit by the stove in that cosy, colourful cave, and eat porridge with Emerald and Satin. Instead I walked round the back and took down my sledge. Nobody saw me. I slipped my shoulders into the harness, and wrapped the black blanket over my head again.

Then I decided I'd better see what was going on at the picnic table. I casually drifted to the edge of the crowd, and found a place where I could get a good view. Not too close, but with nothing in the way . . . I saw a group of four men in long, sweeping dark coats, standing in front of Little Father's table. I saw the coloured flashes on their collars, and the blazons on their sled-helmets.

Fitness Police!

That looks like trouble for Little Father, I thought. The Fitness Police were the only authority the bandits feared. They didn't just hunt for muties. They were entitled to search any vehicle, and confiscate the goods of anyone suspected of trading in factory animals, or transporting them without a licence. These were the worst crimes you could commit in the wilderness, aside from trying to get into a city—

I came out of my daze with a jolt. What if the Fitness Police were looking for *me*? What if they already knew

164

what had happened at the slavers' hut? I had to get away at once! Forget about stealing: I would head straight for the forest. I had my fine felted boots, my sledge, my blanket. I would find food and warmth and shelter somehow. My magic Lindquist would save me.

I walked away, trying not to hurry. I circled around the edge of the fair, until I came to a break in the ring of snowy slopes – where a road from the north entered the arena. The sky had been thick and low since daybreak: snow started to fall as I left the crowds behind. Before long, the great blot of the fair had been wiped out behind me. I was alone in a whirl of white.

I was so dazed, I thought that was a good thing—

They'll never find me now, I thought, as I headed into the blizzard. Soon I realised I'd lost the road. I took out my compass and found north instead, and kept on. The Lindquist was getting heavy. She was so heavy I had to hold her in my arms, with her head over my shoulder. Her fur had turned dark, and her whiskery face was chunky, her teeth were big long yellow chisels. At least she was keeping me warm.

'Are you going to get too big for me to carry?' I muttered. 'Right now, it would be good if *you* were big enough to carry *me*.'

I hoped she would not change too much. I remembered that Nosey had changed too much, and Nosey had died . . . My head was very swimmy. I should be in the forest by now, but it had melted away. When the wind parted the snow I saw only a tree here, a tree there, with starved and leafless branches. The trees were sick, like the tree I used to watch when I was at New Dawn. Mama had said that the forest would shelter us . . . I couldn't take another step. I sat on my sledge at the foot of one of the sick trees, with my blanket over my head and under my bum, and Toothy in my arms; the only warm patch in the world.

'The trees will shelter us, Toothy. We'll make a shelter of branches.'

I could see nothing but whirling powder, it was getting in my eyes.

'I'm very tired,' I said. 'I'll lie down.'

I curled up on the sledge and closed my eyes. Toothy climbed out of my arms. I heard the grind, grind of her teeth. She was attacking the sick tree! I tried to sit up, mumbling, 'No! It will shelter us!'

She just slapped her fat, flattened tail against the snow, and went on gnawing.

'Not enough to eat,' I muttered. 'Not enough to eat. I have no fire inside. Mustn't go to sleep. If I go to sleep I'll never wake up.'

The snow fell. I thought about Emerald and Satin, and Tanya and Bakkial, and the girl whose name I couldn't remember. I hoped they'd be sold together. Toothy kept on working, like a creature with an important plan. She was a very purposeful Lindquist, but her purpose was always the same. *Gnaw* ... The tree was not very thick in the trunk. She gnawed until it was near to breaking, then she stood on her hind legs and pushed. The torn wood screeched, and the tree fell down. She had made a house for us, a log cabin with only one log. She dug the snow and shovelled it over me and the sledge and the fallen tree together. I would be cosy and warm.

'Not enough to eat. No fire inside. Mustn't sleep without eating.'

But when she'd made the house and burrowed into it beside me, I couldn't help falling asleep. I hugged Toothy's warm body, with only my nose and a scrap of blanket peeping out of a breathing hole, and it was blissful.

I stayed asleep for a long time. First I was truly asleep, then I was in another state, where I knew I was drifting close to death. I wasn't cold. There was no difference between warm and cold. I was like a stove with only the faintest thread of red on the dial, and that faint thread was fading. I passed from there into a deep blackness, without dreams, without feeling.

I woke suddenly, all of a piece. I thought I was in the dormitory at college: soon the warden would come along with her jangling keys. But I could smell a wood fire. I opened my eyes enough to see I was lying on a bed piled with blankets, in a little room with a fire glowing in the open stove. There was a man sitting near it. He must have heard me move, because he turned to look at me.

It was Yagin.

9

Artiodactyla

He had looked round, but he hadn't seen that my eyes were open. He turned back to the fire. I was still dressed, except for the outermost layer of my pretty clothes. My red sprigged skirt, and the ruched blouse that went with it, were hanging over the back of a chair beside Yagin's chair, close to the stove. My boots stood on the floor, steaming. My knapsack was on a table that stood in the middle of the room, and Toothy was lying beside it on a clean white cloth. She had changed back to her soft, small brown-and-white form. She was on her side, her upper lips retracted from the brave stumps of her gnawing teeth. I could see that she was dead. I had distressed her, she had changed too much and this had killed her.

I wished she was not dead. I wished my Mama's magical creatures did not keep having to die to save me. I was supposed to be their guardian—

Yagin looked up. He didn't say anything. He came over to the bed with a steaming mug. I sipped the heavenly sweetness of fruit tea with honey in it. He's drugging me, I thought, and fell back into a deep asleep.

When I woke again my head was clear. It seemed to be

night: there was a lamp glowing on the table. Yagin was sitting by the stove reading a book, with a pair of spectacles on his nose. My red skirt and blouse lay at the foot of the bed. I got up, very quietly, and put them on. My boots were there too. I looked at the door of the room. It was bolted and barred, and sure to be locked as well. My sledge was propped against the wall, which was made of rough logs, like the slave-auction hut. My knapsack was still on the table. On the white cloth beside it, where Toothy's body had been, was a small grey cocoon. Yagin knows everything, I thought. He knows *everything* ... Oh, Mama, I'm sorry. I padded over in my socks and stood looking down at what had been Toothy, tears stinging my eyes.

'Are you going to harvest that?'

His hair had grown. It was rough as dog's fur, a mixture of black and grey. He looked healthier than he had looked at New Dawn College. His face was ruddy: his eyes had a light-coloured, penetrating gaze, and the crease between the brows that I remembered. I stared at him and said nothing. I was in his power and maybe I had nothing left to hide, but that didn't mean I was going to co-operate—

Yagin laughed. 'Come and eat.'

He had a pan of con stew bubbling on the stove. I realised I was terribly hungry, shrugged, and went to join him. He handed me a spoon, took another for himself and we ate, passing the pan between us, until the savoury mixture was all gone. I felt the warmth of it running through me, and hope returned.

What if I had been wrong, what if I could trust him after all?

'Who are you? *Why* have you been following me?'

'My name is Yagin,' he said. 'I am your guardian angel. I

am here to help you fulfil your quest. What more do you need to know? Nothing! That's plenty.'

'Where are we?'

'Safe in a cabin in the forest, as you see.'

'But there was no forest. The trees were sick.'

'The forest is sick at the margins where I found you, but now we are much further in. I brought you here. Don't be afraid, no one will find us here. There's a hell of a blizzard going on, it has been snowing for two days, it could snow for a week. I only just found you in time, girl. You're lucky to be alive.'

'You got me expelled,' I said. 'And you . . . you tracked me to the fur-farm.'

'If you hadn't been expelled,' said Yagin, 'You'd have ended up in the Box yourself, or worse. I think they'd have sent you to an insane asylum, since you're too young to go to prison. It's very difficult to get someone out of one of those places. If you are not crazy at the start they keep you in a rubber cell, they put poison in your veins until you are really crazy, then they throw away the key.'

I had thought about this, or something like it. I nodded warily.

'That's what would have happened to your mother,' said Yagin. 'When they took her from your Settlement, they put her in a secure hospital. But friends spirited her away from there, she's safe now. And I came to New Dawn, to watch over you.'

Mama was alive! Mama was safe! I don't know how I stopped myself from crying out. My head was spinning, but I just nodded again, straight-faced. He had given me hope at New Dawn, and that's all he'd given me now. Hope, and a whole lot of unanswered questions.

'You tried to buy me from Little Father.'

'Ha! You mean I tried to save you from being sold as a slave. You're lucky I stuck around. I've been looking for a chance to get you away from that nice, kindly child-thief of yours. That's how I came to find you in the snow.'

He got up and went to the table, opened my knapsack, and took out the nailbox. It was a shock to see him do that, even though I knew he knew about the Lindquists. I had to follow him to the table, I couldn't stop myself—

'You really must harvest that pellet. They shouldn't be exposed to the air for long, the DNA will deteriorate. So you grew another kit, eh? What a reckless girl you are. Didn't your mother tell you, never take a kit to second stage unless you are perfectly secure? You can't tell what will happen to a second stage Lindquist under stress! You're supposed to be keeping a secret, not playing games.'

He was letting me know that he knew Mama's secrets, to convince me that he was her friend: but something jarred: Something made me hold back.

'I needed them.'

I didn't know what to believe, but I was still the guardian. Without looking at him I took out the labcase. I opened it, put on gloves and a mask, transferred Toothy's remains to a fresh tube, and capped it. (Toothy's colour was green.)

'You know your job, I see,' said Yagin.

The praise warmed me, in spite of everything. I'd been alone with this mystery for so long, with only a child's knowledge of what it all meant: always afraid I was making terrible mistakes. Yagin reached into the knapsack again, and drew out the nutshell. It had filled out, and was turning from brown to red. I remembered with a shock that the kits were alive in there. He laughed at my expression, and turned the nut in his hand, running his finger along the seam. Nothing happened.

'See? They are safe from me. Only you can open the incubator, my dear Sloe. You, or your Mama. Now, shall we talk this over?'

Without a word, I went and got my chair. We sat down, on either side of the table. Yagin reached inside his jacket, brought out a folded card and handed it over. I found I was looking at coloured pictures of animals. They were not very good pictures, not much better than what a child might draw, but—

Yagin was watching me with a strange, intent, almost hungry look—

'Have you seen any of these almost-mythical creatures, Sloe?'

I recognised Nosey, in her spiky form, with the word *Hedgehog* printed next to her. Nivvy was called a *Weasel*. Toothy, in her 'many' form was a *Lemming*, but she had been a *Beaver* when she chewed down the sick tree. The animal I had met on the plain, a true wild creature, not made by my mother's magic, was a *Snow Hare*—

My mother's magic, the real wild animals—

'Where did you get this card from?'

'That? It's the official guide issued to the Fitness Police, so they can tell the true wild animals from muties. Usually the recruits have never seen the creatures they are supposed to protect, not even in pictures. The guide is considered sufficient.'

'But it isn't! I mean, that's got to be Nosey in her full sized form—' I pointed to the *Hedgehog*. 'But you can hardly tell that she has spikes instead of fur. And the *Beaver* looks the same size as a *Lemming*, which is completely wrong—'

Yagin drew in his breath, and his eyes shone.

I felt caught out, and angry with myself. However much he knew, I'd just told him even more. I shoved the card back at him.

'How did you get hold of that, if it's issued to the Police?'

'I stole it. You're in big trouble, little girl. The Fitness Police don't know for sure what you're carrying, but they're on your trail. It's only by keeping close to them that I've been able to protect you.' His eyes were still shining. 'So,' he added, staring at me as if I was something magical myself. 'They survived. And they are still viable.'

'Why would the Fitness Police have a guide that's no use?'

'There's a simple rule,' said Yagin, gravely. 'If you don't recognise the animal, it must be a mutie: kill it. If you think you recognise it, kill it anyway, because it may be tainted, who can tell?' He pointed his finger at me, and sighted along it. 'Shoot them and burn them! That's the way to keep nature pure!'

'But that doesn't make sense—!'

'Ha! Your Mama thought the same. That's how she ended up a convict.' Yagin tucked the picture card away, and leaned forward, arms folded on the table.

'Listen, little girl. The populations of wild animals have been in catastrophic decline for a hundred years or more. If you don't know what that means, it means there are very, very few of them left. It was our pollution, our monster farms; it was loss of habitat caused by human numbers; and then the great cold . . . The birds, the fishes, the flowers and trees and fungi are all in trouble too, but the wild mammals were maybe the worst off. So the government ordered that seedbanks should be made, DNA storehouses for all the diversity that we were losing. The idea was that the animals – and plants, and birds and all – could be saved that way, so that one day, when the climate improves, we could repopulate the earth. Your Mama and your Dadda, who were scientists at the Biological Institute, were the leaders of the team who developed the wild mammal seedbank. They made these amazing, wonderous creations we call the Lindquist kits. Do you know this story? Did she tell you?'

It was for telling me about her science that my Mama had been taken away.

I shrugged, and kept my face as blank as I could.

Yagin laughed. 'Well, I'll tell you again, anyway. Your Mama and your Dadda made the Lindquists. Then they discovered that the government had no intention of repopulating the world with wild things. The Fitness Police are really exterminators. The junior officers don't know it, but the senior officers know: the real plan is to get rid of the last of the wild mammals. Then human beings will have no competition for the scarce resources of our winter world. Nothing will live except for man, and his vermin, and the monster things we breed for use.'

'But then why did the government want the Lindquists?'

'Oh, the *seeds* are useful. The wild mammal genes have many properties that could be valuable in factory animals. The Lindquists kits were meant to be kept as insurance, or money in the bank, purely for industrial use. When your Mama and Dadda found out, they decided to smuggle the kits out of the Institute. They destroyed their records, destroyed everything but one set of kits ... which your Dadda was to take to another city, a more enlightened place. This was ten years ago, when things seemed to be changing. He believed he was doing what the good side of our government wanted, and that everyone would soon

174

know he was right. But that was not the view of the Police. He was arrested—'

I was still trying to keep my face blank, but maybe Yagin saw something there that made him pause. He began again, in a gentler tone.

'Your Dadda was caught, but he managed to destroy the kits before they could be taken from him. Your Mama was sent to the Settlements, with you, for the crime of being married to him. But no one suspected how closely she had been involved, and no one knew there was a duplicate set. I was their close friend, and I always suspected the truth. I knew your Mama: how gentle she seems, how bold she is in her soul. But I didn't know where she had been taken, and I didn't dare try to find out, in case I drew suspicion onto her. The wilderness is a vast place, and there are many, many prison Settlements ... So the years passed, your Mama patiently waiting, I suppose, for the chance to take the Lindquists to safety. Until one day a little girl was sent to New Dawn, and a new episode of the story began.'

I didn't want to talk about New Dawn.

'So, what happens now?' I asked.

'You've given me a great deal of trouble,' said Yagin sternly. 'But I forgive you. What happens now is that we wait until the storm is over, and then I take you, with the kits, north to the frozen sea, avoiding our pursuers. We make the crossing, and deliver them, as your Mama intended, to the city where the sun always shines.'

'All right.'

He looked at me suspiciously. I risked a timid smile, and he grinned.

'Good! That's agreed, then. The incubator is live,' he added, in a strangely wistful tone. 'I can tell by the colour. Will you let me see them, eh?'

I thought of the Principal's office, at New Dawn. I knew his whole story could be another cruel trick. But I needed him to believe I trusted him: so I opened the shell. The kits had grown. They were about the size of the top joint of my thumb. Five little pointed faces peeped over the parapet of their nest: five pairs of tiny berry-black eyes lit up, when they knew I was there. Yagin said nothing, he just watched, riveted and fascinated, as the kits gained confidence and scrambled out, one by one. They came trundling over to me, on their little stripey bow-legged limbs.

'Why are they called Lindquists? Mama never told me that.'

'It's the name of a great scientist of long ago,' said Yagin, softly, his eyes fixed on the kits. 'She was the one who worked out that mutations – the natural, tiny changes whereby animals evolve – can be stored in the genome, and then revealed all at once, at the flick a genetic switch, which can be attuned to stress … You know that every animal holds a tiny instruction set, written in the DNA of each of its cells? Each of your Lindquists holds several *different* instruction kits: the DNA instruction sets for a whole big family, or Order, of wild mammals.'

I nodded, hearing my mother's voice in my mind, my Mama telling little Rosita the magic words: *Insectivora, Lagomorpha, Rodentia, Artiodactyla, Chiroptera, Carnivora.*

'The marine mammals were lost—'

Yagin gave me a sharp look, and cleared his throat. 'Hrrmph, indeed. Well, I was saying: these little primitives –' He gestured at the kits: they darted away from shadow of his hand. '– are recreated from an early stage of mammal evolution. Their name is Haramiya. The real creatures lived in the Mesozoic, two hundred and fifty

176

million years ago. We sow the DNA spores in a little very special nutrient gel—'

New-treat, I thought—

'Which produces these little things. To develop to the second stage, a different type animal for each Order, they need to eat normally, and to have contact with their surrogate mother. All the other species can be induced to express in the laboratory, or they may be revealed by stress . . .'

'They can change very strangely,' I said, thinking of Toothy.

'So I believe,' said Yagin, giving me that hungry look again. 'Though I have never seen it. The compressed genomes are full of tricks. Nobody but your Mama knows how it was done, but there's a little something from the fungi and slime-moulds, for astonishing speed of growth. Something from the insects, for the metamorphosis – the shape-changing. Oh, a lot of clever tricks! The Rodentia,' he tapped Toothy's green-capped tube, 'as I remember, has something from the aphids. The type animal, which is a Lemming, is actually born pregnant, so she can quickly establish numbers: that's going to be necessary, for the ecology of predator and prey. That must be something to see!' He raised his eyebrow, looking at me: but I wasn't going to tell him anything I didn't have to.

'But then they aren't really the same as the wild animals.'

Yagin shrugged. 'Of course, the foreign additions would be snipped out of their genes before the breeding populations were reared, for release into the wild. That was the plan. To your Mama and Dadda, the clever tricks were not important. Just a means to an end, that they meant to throw away—'

The groove between his brows was suddenly sharper and

deeper. The kits shot into a huddle, and I hoped Yagin didn't guess that this meant I was scared—

'If you want them,' I said. 'Why don't you just take them?'

'Because they are yours!' The scary tension went out of him, and he laughed. 'Didn't she tell you? Then watch this. This is very entertaining, it's a party-trick.'

He reached for the labcase. I was shocked to the core when he actually touched my Mama's magic case, but I didn't protest. Briskly, he covered his mouth and nose with a mask, slicked gloves onto his hands, and made up a dish of Toothy starter, his big hands very neat with the tiny glassware. Then he took my wrist, used the sharp lip of a dropper to scrape my skin and put the skin scraping in another tiny dish, with a dab of nutrient. He shook the dishes gently.

'What are you doing?'

'Oooh, just watch, little girl.'

When he was satisfied that something was happening he used his gloved fingertips to push the two dishes around the tabletop, chuckling through his mask. I saw how the mixture in one dish *moved*, trying to get near to the mixture in the other. Wherever Yagin put the kit dish, the starter climbed the side of the glass, as if it was alive: trying to get near to ... to the dish with *me* in it.

'It's imprinting,' said Yagin, 'Imprinting at the level of the genes. The chemical bases themselves, they think you are their mother. Or life itself! Every cell of every Lindquist would die for you, as the cells of your own body would gladly die to save your life.' He stripped off his gloves and mask, and began to clean the dishes. 'On your side, well human emotions are more complex. But you are fond of them?'

The kits were still in a frightened huddle. I set my hand down beside them, and let them scramble into my palm, put them back in the nutshell and sealed it.

'I think you know a lot,' I said, 'but you don't understand much.'

'Now I've offended you. She will have taught you to see spiritual beauty in the way the Lindquists love you, and you love them. I'm sure she did. Manya always had to drag in something spiritual. The cold fact is, this bond between the kits and their keeper was engineered, it is just a chemical trick, for their protection.'

My mother's name was Maria. I had never heard anyone call her *Manya,* that I remembered, but the nickname stirred something in me. Lost memories—

'I like Mama's way of seeing things better.'

He roared with laughter. 'Of course you do! But you're going to trust me, anyway? You won't try to run away again?'

I suddenly thought that he'd probably been drinking. When I looked around I saw the bottle, a tall thin bottle standing on the floor by his chair, uncorked, half full of clear liquid. I would bet there were others somewhere. I glanced at the door of the hut, and then wished I'd controlled my eyes. Yagin wasn't as drunk as all that. He was smiling as if he could read my mind.

'Well, well, no hurry. I have been waiting for this since you and your Mama were sent to Siberia. I can wait a little longer for your trust—'

' "Siberia"? We were sent to a Wilderness Settlement.'

He leaned over and picked up his bottle, and offered it to me. I shook my head. 'Siberia? Once it was a cold place far away, where people who offended the government were sent to freeze and starve. Now it's Siberia everywhere. The whole world has been sent to Siberia, we're all in Siberia.'

He knocked back a large gulp of vodka and heaved a sigh. 'No hurry. We're stuck here for a while. You can't go anywhere until the storm has blown itself out, and before then I will persuade you that I'm your friend.'

I didn't want to go on talking to him. I got up and went to the window, and pushed the curtain aside. It was double-glass, proving that this hut had once belonged to someone rich. I could hear the storm buffeting the log walls: all I could see was a whirling blank. I watched the snow while Yagin stared at the stove, nursing his vodka bottle. There was something he hadn't told me, but it was obvious. The Lindquists were *valuable*, extremely valuable, like gold and jewels. Maybe the Fitness Police would destroy them, but other people would want to get hold of them and use those clever tricks my Mama and Dadda had invented – to make new factory animals, to do all sorts of things. If Yagin had saved my life, if he had been following me to protect me all this time, wasn't it just because I was valuable too? He'd just shown me how important I was, to anyone who wanted to develop the kits.

But I longed to trust him.

There was only one room in the cabin, and one bed. It had a mattress that rustled, and smelled of something dusty and sweet. I slept there. Yagin slept on the floor, on blankets spread over a heap of brushwood that he'd brought in from the woodstore. He had a stack of canned food, and a supply of vodka. He wouldn't let me go outside at all. He fetched fuel from a woodstore, and filled the cooking pan with packed snow, to melt for fresh water. There was a privy bucket in a closet he called 'the bathroom': Yagin would go out into the blizzard to empty it. Whenever he went outside he would lock the door behind him, and lock it and bar it again when he came back. He kept the key on a string around his neck. I spent my time reading – he had some books with him, in his big pack. I put the nailbox away in my knapsack, and he seemed to accept that he wasn't going to see the kits again.

He started sewing me a jacket and a cap, out of doubled blanket and some thick oil-cloth stuff he'd found in the cabin. He was very handy at sewing.

On the day we first saw a gleam of daylight through our window, he went out to fill the snow pan and was gone a long time. He came back saying the wind had dropped and the barometer on his sledge was set fair. We might leave, tomorrow or the next day. I said, 'That's good!' But Yagin didn't look happy. The crease between his brows looked as if it had been gouged with a chisel.

I was looking at the Fitness Police guide, which Yagin liked to leave around, in the hope of getting me to talk about the Lindquists again. His big hand came down over my shoulder, and touched the page—

'*Artiodactyla*,' he said. 'The even-number toe-walkers.'

I remembered my Mama trying to teach me that difficult word—

'Digitigrade is another name for those families,' said Yagin, sitting down. '*Finger-walkers*, but toes or fingers, it's all the same. The five-fingered limb: it's something all of us mammals share. A shrew, a mole, a monkey; an ape, a beaver, a man: we all have paws of the same design. The cattle-families adopted mutations that made them lose some of their fingers and toes, because that proved useful for running. Look at the bones. You can see the underlying pattern and how the pattern has shifted. They are walking on their toe-nails, which we call their hooves—'

He picked up my hand and folded down the thumb, and then the two outer fingers, against my palm.

'*Artilodactyla* means even toed, it could be two or four. In the more developed species it's usually two toes, though you can often see the other two, tucked away. Imagine a great hippopotamus on tiptoe, in a ballet skirt.'

I didn't know what a hippo-potamus was.

'A water horse,' said Yagin. 'Smooth skinned, very fat. They used to live in rivers. You won't find them on that card. They are long gone, gone forever.'

He dropped my hand, took the cooking pan to the stove and sat there.

'The true horse is called *Perissodactyla*, odd-toed, and that could be three or one, but the developed horse runs on one toe, which has become a hard-rinded hoof. There is no Lindquist for the horse: the wild horses of Europe were lost, at the last moment. They never trotted onto the DNA ark. Maybe it doesn't matter. They had vanished from the New World, for unknown reasons, until the Spanish took them back. Horses are like a folksong, weaving in and out of human history, disappearing here, reappearing there . . .'

He poked the melting snow in the pan in a dissatisfied way. 'What a *poverty* of life there is now. If this was the old days I would go hunting, in the still after the storm. I would bring back a brace of hares, or a fat young deer.'

'How can you want to kill them, if you want to help me keep them alive?'

'Because I'm an animal myself,' said Yagin, baring his teeth. 'A tertiary consumer. I am designed to eat the weaker kinds, until I am eaten myself, by death, who is always

182

stronger. That's natural predation, little girl. It does no harm.'

Yagin was a strange man. He explained things I was hungry to know, and then he'd say something that made me hate him, as if on purpose. Deliberately, I went to sit by the stove, poured a glass of vodka and handed it to him.

'Which way do we go, when we leave here? Do you have a map?'

He closed one eye, and smiled. 'Do you?'

I shrugged. I expected he'd searched my knapsack by now, some time when I was asleep. There was nothing I could do about that.

'You still don't trust me, do you?' He knocked back the spirit, scowled, and held out his glass again. 'It's a long way to the coast. Further than you can walk on that poor weak leg of yours, that's for sure.'

I poured more vodka. 'Does your sled have enough fuel to get us there?'

'My sled has no fuel at all,' said Yagin ruefully. 'I used it all searching for a stubborn little girl, when I found out that she had escaped from the slavers and run for it. But I know where there's a fuel dump. I can't take you there, it would be too risky. I'll fill up and then come back for you.' He emptied his glass. 'I know where these questions are leading. Get it into your head, every hand is against you out there. The slavers are looking for you, the Little Father is looking for you, the Fitness Police are looking for you. Promise me you won't try to make it on your own.'

'I solemnly promise. I will not try to make it on my own.'

Yagin sighed. 'Ah, those black eyes.' He reached over and took my chin between his finger and thumb. 'Your mother's very eyes. But when I go to fetch the fuel, I'll still lock you in!' He tossed his glass down. It didn't break, it just rolled on the plank floor. 'Time to eat. Let's see if I have anything besides that damned stew.'

There was nothing but con stew, and fruit tea with syrup. It was tasty food by my standards, but Yagin was clearly used to something different. He ate without appetite, I finished most of the can. Then he got me to try on my cap and jacket. The jacket needed a little more sewing. He worked on it until it was ready, then he sat drinking, in gloomy silence, until he stumbled to his bed on the floor. The stove burned low. I went and knelt beside him, and stared at his sleeping face.

Yagin knew so much. But if he was somebody I should trust, why didn't he tell me the one thing that would make me believe in him?

Who are you?

I wanted to fetch the photograph Mama had left for me out of my knapsack, but I didn't dare, in case he woke up. I tried to imagine him younger, but I couldn't see through the years. He was fast asleep, lying on his back and snoring. Carefully, I turned back the blanket, and the collar of his dingy shirt. At the base of his throat, on the right hand side, just where it ought to be, I found the delicate little tattoo, a circlet of feathery green leaves. It was the Chervil Ring, the mark of the Biologicial Institute. I'd seen it on raggy textbooks at New Dawn College. Mama had told me that Chervil is the first herb that the old-days people would plant, when they were making a new garden. It meant the renewal of life. Yagin had been a scientist at the Institute, like my Mama. That was obvious from the things he'd told me; and the things he knew.

184

Mama's tattoo had been defaced, when she was disgraced.

She had been betrayed by someone close to her. She had never told me that, exactly, but I'd always known it.

I tucked his shirt back, and the blanket. He didn't look like waking; he was out cold. I went to his big backpack, which stood by the wall, and undid the fastenings. I was looking for more information, and for things to steal. There were chocolate bars, and a map, which I set aside to transfer to my knapsack (the map might be better than mine.) Underneath the map were some folded clothes. A long black uniform coat, and a tunic with badges of rank. Of course. I saw in my mind's eyes the Fitness Police standing in front of Little Father's picnic table, and I knew, cold and hard, that Yagin had been one of those men ... He'd come alone at first, pretending to be a lone bounty hunter. When Little Father had refused to sell me, he'd come back with reinforcements.

I folded the coat, and put everything back the way it had been.

When the snowlight woke me in the morning, he was still snoring. I made up the stove and brewed some tea, using one of the packets of medicine Katerina had given me, the night the Mafia came. I stirred a lot of syrup into it to disguise the taste, then I woke him, and told him he needed a brew to cure his hangover. He grumbled, and muttered, and drank it down.

'You'll have to give me the key,' I said. 'I have to get wood for the stove, and snow for water, and I have to empty the privy bucket.'

'I will get up soon.'

'Your head aches, you feel ill. You drank too much

vodka, go back to sleep. We can wait another day. You can have my bed, and be comfortable.'

I helped him over to the bed. He gave me the key, and fell asleep.

I took out the nailbox, and opened the nutshell. When I broke the seal five identical kits looked up at me, making tiny purrs of delight. I looked at them for a long time, until I thought I *knew*. Then I picked her out, and fed her.

Yagin fell deeper into darkness as the hours passed, and I fed the Lindquist; and she grew. His skin turned pale and clammy, his breathing sank to a murmur. I had given him the whole packet of sleeping medicine, about ten doses. I knew Katerina's herbal mixtures could be very strong: I hoped I hadn't killed him. I didn't want to murder anyone, whatever wrong they'd done.

I'd decided to take the black uniform coat with me: it looked useful. I had it rolled up now, on the table, with all the food and extra blankets it would hold, and tied with rope. I'd packed my knapsack with more food, including Yagin's chocolate, and his map. I knew that if I'd asked him about the coat, he'd have had an answer. He'd say he'd been *disguised* as a Fitness Police officer, the same as he'd been disguised as a New Dawn College guard; so he could protect me. In my heart I faced the knowledge that I could be wrong. Yagin could be my true friend, and Mama's true friend; or even more than that.

But either you trust someone, or you just can't.

The treasure I was guarding had to come first. I couldn't take a chance.

I made up the stove. I had left him some food, and he had plenty of blankets. I put on the jacket he'd made for me, and the cap. He was alive when I left the hut: I thought his breathing was getting stronger. The new Lindquist trotted out into the snow ahead of me. She had grown to be about the size of the wild hare I had met on the snow plain. Her coat was reddish brown, and her back legs bigger than her front legs, though not by much. She still had *fingers*, thicker and stronger than fingers should be, but not solid like a hoof. She was walking on the splayed tips of them. I locked the door, and tossed the key away. The Lindquist nuzzled my hand and trotted away. I knew she wouldn't wander far. Yagin's motor sled was in the woodstore. I checked the gauge, in case he'd been lying, but it really didn't have any fuel. I found a big stone, and did as much damage as I could, anyway.

The moon was full. The deep snow gleamed, the trees looked as if they were cast in metal. It seemed like a hundred years since I'd hidden and watched while the Mafia torched our hut, at the start of this long journey – could it really be just two months? I sat on my sledge and waited ... When my new friend came back she was much bigger, the biggest animal I'd ever seen, with a thick grey coat and a long back. 'I think you are a reindeer,' I said. 'I saw you on that card. But I'll call you Toesy.' She bowed her head, and nibbled at my face while I rubbed her velvety antlers: her breath was warm and sweet.

We left the clearing, and entered the silent, silver forest.

10

Chiroptera

The track that led to the cabin had been buried deep by the blizzard, the skirts of the young trees on either side were drowned in snow. Toesy walked ahead; I struggled with the sledge, taking care to blot out her prints. It took hours to reach the road that I'd known must be somewhere near. At least it was obvious when we got there. The wind had cleared some of the surface down to the frozen ruts. I tried to make it look as though I'd headed north, then I dumped the sledge. I shoved it into a gulley just inside the trees, and kicked a mass of soft snow after it: that was the best I could do. I put my arms around Toesy's neck, and rubbed my cheek against her warm grey coat. 'We'll make it,' I said. 'I know we will.' I slung the blanket roll over her shoulders. When I tried to get on her back, she bent her knees of her own accord to make it easier. We left the road, heading west, and I let Toesy find our path.

We kept going for a long time, in the moonlight. At last I spotted a snow-cave that the blizzard had created, under the branches of one of the white-skirted trees: like the shelter that Toothy had made for me, only bigger. There was room for me and Toesy. I'd taken a groundsheet from Yagin's pack. I wrapped myself in that, and blankets, and the big black coat, and curled up against Toesy's flank, with the knapsack in my arms. I didn't sleep for a while, I just lay gazing at the stillness. The night air was like silver knives in my throat: the forest was as magical as I had ever dreamed.

Through the forest to the sea—

Next day I did a lot of falling off, and I always seemed to choose a place where the snow was hard and lumpy as a bed of stones. Toesy would stand over me and lick me with her long thick tongue, as I lay with my head ringing and nudge me into getting up if she thought I stayed down too long ... Nosey had been my naughty, funny friend. Toothy had been someone strange I didn't really under-stand. Toesy was like a mother to me. I felt very safe with her.

I got better at riding, and managed to stay on her back for hours at a time. Sometimes the trees were thick as grass in the summer wilderness, sometimes they were sparse; or dead and still standing, leaning against each other. Some-times we walked over frozen swamp, where everything was veiled in frosted lichen and moss. Sometimes there were clear, shining rides that seemed as if they must be the roads in an ancient city. I never looked at the kits: I was afraid to let the cold touch them. I thought about my Mama, and about Yagin, and tried not to think of the lonely vastness that stretched out all around. The forest was beautiful, but it was frightening. We would keep going far into the moonlit nights, because Toesy never seemed to tire, and only stop where I saw a place to make a snow shelter. Then I'd light a candle, stick it in the snow or on a branch if there was a convenient one, and try to study my maps. There were no Settlements in the forest, but it was crossed by several bandit routes and trails, like the one we'd left behind. If we kept on heading west, we would strike the big Settlements Commission supply road, that Mama had shown me long ago was the way to reach the sea ... I thought it would take us maybe ten days to reach this. Then we should turn north again: but we'd have to keep out of sight. There would be vehicles moving on the big road: supply trains for the Settlements; bandit caravans. And I couldn't exactly hide Toesy inside my coat.

Almost a hundred miles through the forest to the big road, then another hundred miles to the sea. I kept measuring the distance – with my fingers, with a piece of string – and comparing it to the scale on the side of the map. I couldn't make it less.

Toesy found her own food: she ate the moss from the trees, and from the ground whenever the wind had scoured the snow away. I was going to run out of canned stew and chocolate before long (I never tried to light a fire, I kept the food from freezing by sleeping with it inside my bed-clothes). But when we got to the big road, there'd be places with supplies. I would hide Toesy, and go thieving.

We crossed trails, and once passed a deserted factory-farm, with big fences, but we never saw anything moving. When the sun was as high as it would get, on the sixth day (I thought it was the sixth: it's very easy to lose track when you're travelling alone), we were crossing an upland break in the forest. Toesy seemed uneasy, and I felt the same way: we didn't like being in the open. I noticed a line of black poles, like straight ink strokes, over to the west, that must be snow-markers on a stretch of road. I burrowed in my layers for the maps, feeling worried. We shouldn't be anywhere near a marked road ... Toesy gave a start that almost threw me. Then I heard what she must have heard: a high-pitched, insect whine. Three tiny black dots came zooming into view, from the direction of those ink marks.

Motor sleds!

I locked my fists in Toesy's thick coat, and tugged to make her turn around 'Run, Toesy—! Back to the trees!'

I hoped it was only the outriders from a caravan like Little Father's. They must have seen Toesy, but they'd soon give up when we got into the thickets. Why would bandits chase a mutie? Toesy picked up her pace, stretching out her legs. I clung on, lying flat, trying to keep my knees tight against her sides. My backbone was jolting its way out of the top of my head, my teeth were jammed together—

We plunged into a shallow bare valley, where Toesy floundered shoulder-deep in soft drifts, but the trees were nearer, and I thought we had a chance. Then I heard the insect whine *ahead*, and another black speeding mark, like a fly skimming over the whiteness, came hurtling to intercept us. I tried to push Toesy onward with my fists and knees, screaming at her. The blanket roll went flying. It was gone, too bad—

'Get past him Toesy! Get past him—!'

The sled cut a great sweep, sending up a silver wave of snow, and stopped. I saw the rider reach behind him for the rifle on his back. I urged Toesy, desperately, but something was happening to her: she staggered. There were shudders and surges, like explosions inside her . . . I felt a shock, like something big and invisible rushing by, and I was in the snow, on my back. The man had left his sled. He had fired once and missed. He was coming closer. He was dressed in a dark uniform, with high boots and a shiny sled helmet, but without a coat.

I wondered where he had hidden his rifle and his helmet,

when we were in the cabin. I should have known he would never give up.

Toesy's face appeared, looking down into mine. She had changed. She was lower at the shoulder, but much more massive. Her antlers had gone. Instead, a pair of murderous curved tusks rose from her snout. But her motherly eyes were the same. She wouldn't let me get up. She shoved me back down and stood over me, her forelegs splayed and her great head lowered.

'Sloe! Get away from the beast—'

'*Traitor*! Leave us alone!'

'I'm trying to help you,' Yagin yelled back. 'God knows I hate to do this, but I have to. Get out of the way!'

He was staring at Toesy: I could feel his awe and wonder.

'Don't kill her!' I begged. 'How can you bear to kill her! *Please*!'

'My men have seen her. I've no choice.'

I beat at Toesy with my fists, 'Run, Toesy! Go!' I struggled to get up, but my right knee wouldn't bear me, and it was too late. Toesy had made up her mind. She was moving, thundering, charging, in ridge-backed bristling fury, her great head down like a battering ram. I heard Yagin give a cry that sounded like a wail of despair, and his rifle cracked once more.

When the three men came up, Toesy was lying on the snow in a huge splash and trail of scarlet blood. Yagin had brought a fuel can from his sled, and was tossing the stinking liquid over her body. He hadn't come near me. He knew I couldn't escape: I couldn't even get up. The Fitness Police officers jumped off their sleds (two of them were doubled up, sharing one); and gawped. They were young-ish, with well-fed, innocent-looking, indoor faces.

'What *is* that thing, Sir?' asked one of them, saluting.

'Mutie,' declared Yagin, with authority. 'A man-eater. Very dangerous. It was dragging her off to its den.' He tossed a match, and the mass of hide and hair and flesh that had been my Toesy began to burn. Yagin stared into the ugly flames.

'The girl's lucky we saw what was happening, and reached her in time.'

'I don't understand how she got this far, Sir,' said another of the young men, 'We're nearly seventy miles from the cabin where she left you.'

'There's a lot you don't understand about this business,' said Yagin. 'She has confederates, of course. And we'll have to track them down, too.'

He strode over to me. I was sick to think I'd ever been close to trusting him, but I was glad I hated him so much. It saved me from crying in front of them.

'This young woman is the daughter of two enemies of our fragile Environment,' announced Yagin. 'One of whom has successfully defected, helped by other dangerous criminals. That's why I was keeping her under covert surveillance at her school, and why I've pursued her, alone, since she went on the run. I *didn't ask for reinforcements*, but you three have been hmm, a great help. Her crimes are many.'

'Yes Sir,' said the three young officers, in chorus.

'There's the fact that she ran, and the mysterious torching of her mother's hut. She also disgraced herself at the school, caused damage at a fur-farm, and has been involved in the child-slave trade; and finally she tried to poison me.'

He stooped. Before I knew what to expect he had picked

193

me up in his arms. 'Let's get her back to the cruiser, before she tries any more tricks.'

Yagin and his men had used a lot of fuel chasing Tosey, and two of the sleds were burdened with extra weight. We moved slowly, in close formation. I think Yagin's men were afraid of meeting more 'Man-Eating Muties'. It was after dark when we reached the place where they'd left their snowcruiser: at a 'fuel dump' on the big road that I'd seen from the ridge. It was the road I'd been heading for, Wilderness Supply Road 808; I had misjudged the distance, or else the maps were wrong. The fuel for official vehicles was kept in a blockhouse, heavily guarded behind tall fences. Next door to it was a long grey shed, with a salt-gritted parking lot. The snow-cruiser was there, alongside several battered, gaudy-painted trucks that were not official transport. The young officers took down the tailgate, rode the sleds into the back and locked it again. I stood shivering, cold and stiff after the long ride, looking at the lying claim on the side, *Fitness Police: Protecting Your Fragile Environment*.

They'd had a long search: for Yagin after he'd gone off looking for me on his own; and then for me, through the forest. Yagin decided they should get something to eat and drink in the shed, which was a restaurant, before they set off again.

'What about the girl?' asked one of his men. 'We take her in with us?'

'No,' said Yagin. He pointed at the other trucks. 'Can't you see this is bandit territory? I don't want her making contact with the riff-raff inside.'

The officer who'd spoken looked sorry for me, but he nodded. The three younger men were very respectful of

194

Yagin. Yagin roughly 'helped' me up into the cab, and into the drivers' sleeping compartment. His men were standing watching. 'You stay here,' said Yagin loudly. It was the first time he'd spoken to me since we left Toesy burning in the snow. Then he leaned close and muttered, 'We had an accident in the blizzard, so there's a *badly cracked window*. But I can't help that!'

I wouldn't look at him. He pulled the metal shutter across, and locked me in.

The sleeping compartment was like a cupboard-bed with a very low ceiling, and small thick windows on either side. There was a spiderweb crack in one of them, and the frame around it was bent out of shape. I could see the flares of the parking lot, and white blurred heaps of ruined buildings: the 'fuel dump' was in the middle of an abandoned town. I took off my knapsack and hugged it on my knees. I was glad that Yagin was alive. The thought of having murdered someone had been giving me the horrors.

Why hadn't he taken the knapsack from me?

He needed me as well as the kits because the Lindquists were 'imprinted'. But if he wanted to be sure I wouldn't try to escape, all he had to do was keep hold of the knapsack. Maybe he didn't want the junior officers to know what it contained. Or maybe he really was playing a double game. I rolled over and traced the outline of the spiderweb, feeling the sharp edges. I thought about the way Yagin had talked in the cabin, and the very different way he talked in front of his men. What if he'd killed my Toesy to protect the secret of the Lindquists? What if he had left me in here to give me a chance to escape . . . ? But I had nothing except my knapsack. If I got out of this locked box, either Yagin would find me again at once, or I'd be dead before morning.

Mama always used to say: *Guards aren't needed in the wilderness.* Yagin didn't need to guard me. He didn't care if I 'escaped' again and again. He had me on a string. He knew where I was going, he could always track me down. The cold and the emptiness controlled me, but Yagin *frightened* me. The mysterious way he behaved, the way he looked at me, the way he talked—

I lay down, still hugging the knapsack. The mattress felt incredibly soft. I thought of the kits. Toesy had died unharvested, but the Artiodactyla Lindquist was still safe. They were all still safe . . . But they were prisoners, like me. Wild animals, turned into powder and locked up in little tubes. I tried to picture them, one by one. Artiodactyla, big and strong. Nosey the bug-eater; Ears, the beautiful snow-prince; Toothy with all her children; my darling fierce little Nivvy. And the last Lindquist, Chiroptera, a little furry animal with wings. I wish I had wings now, I thought.

Once there was a little girl called Rosita, who used to play at being the magic creatures. It was her secret, even Mama didn't know. She liked being Chiroptera, the most strange and unusual one. She'd hold out the skirts of her dress, and flit around the bare, drab prison hut, saying cheeeep! Cheeep! Sometimes she'd keep her eyes shut . . . Although she could never understand how saying *cheeeep* helped you to find your way in the dark, she kept trying.

I sat up. I felt as if Rosita had joined me. A naughty, defiant little girl, with her own ideas about everything . . . 'I am *not* helpless!' I whispered. 'I *won't* give up.'

I measured the cracked window with my forearm. It wasn't big, but it was big enough. Then I quickly ransacked the bed box. I found a pair of gloves, a bottle of tea, and a stale pack of sliced black bread. The mattress had a blanket and a light thermal quilt (Fitness Police slept in style). I rolled the bedding up and strapped it on the outside of my knapsack, and stuffed the other things into my pockets. The parking lot was dark and deserted. I lay back and kicked the window with my left foot, until the cracked pane fell out. No one came running to see what the noise was: I wriggled through the hole, dropped, and scooted, limping hard, to the shelter of the bunkers full of rubbish that stood against the end wall of the shack.

It had been cold in the cruiser. It was a *very* cold night outdoors. I heard a rustling behind me, and peered into the shadows, surprised that even rats could be moving. Children's faces, filthy, blue-shaded, pinched with cold, peered back at me. They'd seen me escape from the police van. They didn't speak, and neither did I.

Silently, they burrowed out of sight.

I remembered what Satin had said: better to be a slave, than to be a stray child in the wilderness. That's what will happen to me, I thought. Either Yagin will catch me again, or I will become one of the lost. I wanted my Mama, more than I had ever wanted her ... But I wasn't alone. Rosita was with me. *Cheeeep* ... I whispered, and spread my arms, a little girl pretending to have wings.

I drank half the sweet tea in the bottle, ate two slices of the black bread, and left the rest for the stray children. I watched the restaurant doors, flapping my arms and whispering *cheeeep* occasionally. Maybe I was going a little mad, but it seemed to help. Before long two people came out alone, talking and laughing. The woman had an embroidered scarf. As she fastened up her coat I glimpsed a belt decorated with gold coins, and a swinging red and

197

yellow skirt. The man had scuffed but flashy red boots. Bandit tribesfolk, I thought. My kind of people.

I ambled over to them, hiding the limp as best I could, and looking confident.

(*Cheeep* . . . I'm a strange and unusual wild creature—)

'Hey, you two. Can you give me a lift?'

Disaster struck. The woman peered at me, with slanting dark eyes like Satin's in a brown face with rosy cheeks, and I *knew* her. She was from the caravan. She knew me too, at once. 'It's Little Father's snow-bunting,' she exclaimed. 'What's all this? You're the kid who escaped from the slavers' holding pen, and then the god-awful mutie police came asking questions about you. Little Father was mad as fire!'

'It shows how little you know about Little Father's business,' I said. 'That was the third time I've been sold this year. I was supposed to hide until the end of the fair, and get picked up again on the road. But those devils of mutie police picked me up, instead; for no reason. I've just got free of them. Where's the rest of the caravan?'

The man laughed. 'Oh my God, a scam. Trust the Little Father!'

'You're a bold kid,' said the woman who had recognised me. 'We're on our way to join them now. If you're sure that's what you want, you can come along.'

My friends were called Yulia and Aliek. Yulia had stayed on at the end of the fair with her boyfriend, now Aliek was taking her back to her family. They would meet Little Father's trucks at Rocket Town – another abandoned town, where the bandits liked to gather in the winter. Rocket Town was in completely the wrong direction for me, but I could double back: I just wanted to get away from Yagin.

Their cab was warm, and full of colour: painted panels, scarves and shawls and dangling ornaments. We caught up on the caravan gossip (and it was easy to behave confidently: I was *Chiroptera*: I was flying, strange and free). Soon Yulia decided she was peckish, though they'd eaten. She cooked boiled sausage, on a hotplate up on the bedshelf. We ate it with real mustard, washed down with vodka-laced fruit tea. I don't know what was in the 'meat', but I had never tasted anything so greasy and delicious. The snow-tired truck bulldozed majestically through the little drifts, and swerved around the big ones, while the walls of grimy snow on either side of the road zoomed by, looming up in the light of our great headlamps, falling away again into darkness.

'We should be in Rocket Town by tomorrow noon,' said Aliek. 'We'll take you right to Little Father, I know where he camps.'

'Oh, there's no need,' I said casually. 'Drop me anywhere, I'll find him.'

Aliek, who was driving, glanced at Yulia with a crooked smile.

'Little snow-bunting,' said Yulia, kindly, 'We don't blame you for trying it on but you're a runaway slave. Are you *sure* you want to be taken to Rocket Town?'

Every hand will be against me, I thought. I am finished. I forgot about being Chiroptera.

'No,' I said, coming down to earth hard. 'I don't.'

I was sitting between them, I couldn't reach either of the doors, and anyway Aliek drove fast, even over ice in the dark. They looked at each other over my head.

'So, where do you really want to go?' asked Aliek, calmly.

'I want to go north, to the frozen sea. I . . . I was trying to get there, when I got collected by the Little Father. My mother had escaped from a prison Settlement, and crossed the sea. I was trying to join her.'

The road plunged just then, as if straight into the centre of the earth. We went down into darkness. Aliek hit some smooth ice and rode into a magnificent skid.

'Drive into it! Drive into it!' shouted Yulia. 'Don't brake! Change gear!'

The big truck buried its armoured muzzle in a wall of rock-hard drift. Aliek laughed, put it into reverse, and it did the same wild gyration backwards: except now we were missing one bank of headlights.

'Back seat driver,' he shouted. 'Get into the back seat, or drive yourself!'

'You know my night vision is no good!'

Then Aliek stopped the engine, and the silence of the cold, cold night out there gathered around us. 'We'll catch hell if Little Father finds out,' he remarked, after some moments' thought. 'But we could take her to the Depot. It isn't so far.'

'Why should he find out?' said Yulia. '*I'm* not going to tell him.'

I fell asleep. Yulia woke me up, and coaxed me onto the bedshelf. I lay curled up with my back to the cab, and dreamed of flying. In the grey dawn Aliek shook me awake, and put a mug of very hot, bitter-sweet dark liquid into my hands. Yulia was driving.

'What is this?'

'It's called *coffee*. It's very good, and rare as hens. It will wake you up.'

I got into the front seat again. There was no sign of the forest, no high walls of frozen snow, only a flat, wind-scoured heathland in every direction. We drove for another hour, until we reached a wide pan of concrete, swept bare by the wind. There was a row of sheds. Around them, piled up anyhow, partly buried in snow, partly stripped naked, there were heaps and heaps and heaps of different sized boxes.

'Where are we?'

'This is the Depot,' said Yulia. 'The Commission Supply trucks come here. Folks say it used to be an airstrip, but there are no planes any more. There've been no planes for years and years. No fuel they can use, or no parts, or something. Now the trucks just unload for no reason. Caravans come here, to see if there's anything useful.'

She pointed over the ramparts of boxes.

'The narrow sea is that way. Not far, about a mile, I think.'

'You go to the Observatory,' said Aliek. 'That's where people meet, who are going to cross. Don't try it on your own! It's very dangerous.'

'Are there guards?'

Aliek shrugged. 'No need. Who cares if you cross, it's still the Wilderness on the other side, unless you have city papers.'

'There used to be guards in the Observatory,' said Yulia. 'But not any more.' She gave me a hug, and tucked a greasy paper parcel into my pocket. 'Good luck, little snow-bunting. Enjoy your freedom.'

Aliek opened the cab door and let me down, tossing my jacket after me. 'Don't cross alone! Wait for other people, they'll turn up. People like you!'

I stood looking up at their smiling, weather-worn, carefree faces.

'Come with me. I . . . I have something like city papers. I can get you in. You can be free too, and live in comfort, and not be outlaws—'

Yulia laughed. 'We are free already.'

Their truck had looked big when it was beside me, racketing and shuddering. It looked very small before it disappeared, but I was much smaller. I was freezing, in my pretty clothes. I picked up my jacket and put it on. It had been lying on the floor of the cab, and the folds were stiff with rime. My leg was stiff too. I didn't have wings anymore. *Chiroptera*, the furry animal who flies, needs a lot of energy, and I suddenly had none. I hobbled over to the nearest boxes and sat down to rub my knee. I wondered if I could even walk as far as the sea. And what then?

What then?

The boxes were stamped WS, for Wilderness Settlements, with a Brigade, a Sector and number. Long ago they'd been sealed with sticky tape, but it had withered and fallen away. They looked oddly familiar. I pried open the lid of the nearest one, wondering what I would find. Maybe I should search this 'Depot' for useful supplies—

It was full of nails.

I put my head in my hands, and cried.

I cried for my Mama, and all the years she'd been chained to that workshop bench, all those hours of useless toil under the red rat-eye. For the magic that couldn't save me from loneliness or helplessness. For the countless lives wasted, so that the cities could stay warm and bright. I cried for everything hateful about my world, and everyone who had struggled and hoped and *tried*, and finally failed—

Then I got up and set off, limping and very stiff in the cold morning, to see if I could find this mysterious 'Observatory'.

11

Carnivora

There was only one building. It stood on a headland, at the furtherest point of a wide bay, where the white waste of the heath met the pale sky. It had a domed roof, and windows all around; the double-glass crusted over with snow. It must have been a look-out, or maybe a weather station, when people still lived on this coast. In front of it a concrete path – partly blocked by drifts – cut through the low, reddish cliffs, down to the shore. I had never seen the sea before. But all I could think, as I stood there, was that the lumpy grey ice that stretched to the horizon looked like ugly walking.

The door was on the landward side, in shelter. When I knocked the snow off it, I found it was fastened with a padlock and chain. But it was only a Settlements Commission sort of chain. I hit it with a rock until it snapped. There was a short, shadowy passageway, with old framed photographs of ships on the walls, and then the main room, about twice the size of Mama's hut. Dim light came through the veiled windows. The dome, high overhead, was made in sections that looked as if they were supposed to move. There was a gallery around the base of it, reached by a wrought-iron staircase. There was a stove, with a stack of wood (I was very glad to see that), and bunks around the walls, with cupboards under them. Some of the bunks had tattered mattresses. A child's mitten, covered in dust, lay on the dusty floor.

'Mama?' I whispered. I felt her presence so strongly. It was as if we had agreed to meet here: but where was she?

I lit a fire with one of my last precious matches, ate half the boiled sausage Yulia had given to me, and drank some of my remaining water. Gradually warmth crept into me, and a little courage. I began opening the cupboards. In the first one I tried, I found a cardboard box full of pots and pans. 'That's *good*!', I muttered, trying to be positive. The next cupboard held canned food that looked quite fresh, a coil of rope, and a lamp that was also a stove, with a supply of little blocks of fuel. A heap of slick, folded fabric proved, when I pulled it out, to be an inflatable bivvy tent.

I knelt there with my mouth open, dazzled by this plunder.

I was saved!

I went back to the stove, took the nutshell out of my knapsack, and opened it for the first time since the morning before Toesy died. The four remaining kits were at their full size. They looked up at me, bright-eyed. 'Hi,' I said. 'I'm sorry I haven't been talking to you. Toesy and I ran into trouble, and Yagin caught me again. But I got away and everything's all right now. We're in a good place, just where we're supposed to be, and we've got everything we need for the last part of the trek.'

I looked in the other cupboards, and found a good box of matches in one of them, and a few very rusty, swollen tins in another. There were two trapdoors set in the floor. When I pulled up the larger one I saw a ladder going down into darkness. A gust of deadly cold rose up: it was a cellar, cut into the frozen earth. I decided to leave that for another time. The smaller trapdoor had only a shallow space under it, that held a dark-covered exercise book, and a pencil. I opened the book, and found dated entries, like a diary—

19th December ... Ice gauge reading satisfies our guide at last. We embark on the sea crossing tomorrow.

I didn't have a guide. Where did the guides come from?

16th March ... Blizzard continues, but we must leave tomorrow, or we won't have enough supplies. Smaller sledge lost when crossing the bay, a blow ... Pray for us. Saskia Lensky, Jacob Lensky, Shastha Sigratha, Victorine Sigratha (aged eight)

That one scared me, but some were even worse.

12th February ... Little Ekaterina died today. She will join her brother. How terrible to leave our babies on this desolate shore. We leave as soon as Papa's feet are better, walking gives him great pain—

Some of the entries were in faded ink, some in pencil. They went back for years. All of them the last messages of people like me, who had reached this far in their desperate escape from the Settlements, or some other kind of trouble. Though Mama had never told me about this place, and it wasn't marked on her map, there was no doubt I was where she had planned to be ... The supplies I'd found must have been spares, excess baggage left by some other party of fugitives—

7th March ... We will leave as soon as Manya has recovered from her fever. The season is late, but Vadim says the ice will still be good for two more weeks ...

Could that *Manya* have been my Mama? There was no year-date, but it was one of the last entries. She had been ill ... Oh, but she'd been here!

I told myself I couldn't be sure. But the hope I'd been

clinging to since I left New Dawn had never burned so strongly.

I took a pan outside and packed it with snow for fresh water, and put a mugful of it to heat for some tea. Then I spread my stolen quilt and blanket by the stove, and settled there with a tin of jam and a spoon, and the nutshell open so I could have the kits for company. They pushed their paws and noses against the shield, but I wasn't going to let them out. I didn't feel as secure as all that.

I was very tired. My arms and legs were aching. I sipped hot berry-tea, and turned the pages of the record-book. There were charts and useful tips, but I wished so many people hadn't reached here, and then died. Especially the children . . .

I started awake.

The room was dark and cold. I grabbed the nutshell and sealed it, shocked that I'd fallen asleep and left it open, and fed the stove until the fire burned brightly again. There had better be more wood somewhere . . . But what was that? I had glimpsed something moving, out of the corner of my eye. There was something white, moving creepily slowly across the floor. Oh, no, please, not a ghost. Was that a child's white hand, groping out from the trapdoor that led to the cellar . . . ? I grabbed a burning stick from the stove, and held it up.

The white thing was the package of boiled sausage. It was moving because it was being dragged away by a huge grey rat. I yelled and threw my torch . . . and then had to run after it, stamping out sparks. Then I heard a rattling, rolling sound behind me. I spun around to see two more rats, making off with the nutshell! I swooped on them, grabbed the shell and stuffed it into the front of my blouse, snatched another burning stick from the stove—

A carpet of little red eyes glinted back at me. The floor was swarming with rats. For a moment I was paralysed. Then I ran around in a frenzy, screaming and beating at them with my torch. Very soon they had all vanished, into cracks and holes I couldn't see. Unfortunately, they would surely be back.

Rats! I *hated* rats. I couldn't stay here. But I had nowhere else to go.

There was only one thing to do. I retreated to the wrought-iron staircase with my quilt and blanket, and the knapsack, and the rescued sausage. I had solemnly promised myself, after Toesy, that I was not going to take another kit to second stage. But I hadn't reckoned on rats. I opened the shell, and the shield. Three of the little ancestor creatures were burrowed deep in their nest. The fourth was sitting up, bright-eyed, very interested in all the excitement . . . The kits still looked identical – but I was beginning to feel the hidden differences.

'Mama said I should be very careful about growing you, Mr Carnivora. She said you could be dangerous. But that's for the rats to worry about.'

I took him out, sealed the others away, and gave him some of the rescued sausage, torn into tiny scraps. He liked that a lot.

I spent the rest of the night on the stairs, wrapped in my quilt and blanket, alternately dozing, and feeding my new Lindquist. When the grey dawn came he was looking very like the animal I'd found on the doormat, all those years ago. I took him with me when I went in search of more plunder. I needed fuel, and much more important, I needed a sled. I could not carry everything I needed. I wasn't strong enough, even if I could have found a pack for it.

I tried the cellar first. There was nothing down there

except empty boxes. Three of the walls were frozen earth. The fourth had been blocked off by sheets of metal. I lifted my lamp, wondering if they could be useful, and saw a cross had been drawn there, maybe in charcoal; the wilderness sign against evil. Then I understood. You can't dig graves, in the winter. I stood for a moment, thinking of the dead.

'Come on Nivvy. This is not for us. We shouldn't be here.'

The cupboards in the gallery held old broken pieces of scientific equipment: nothing I could use. I wrapped myself up and went outside. It was another calm day, but fiercely cold. 'I hope this good weather lasts,' I said to Nivvy, who was tucked inside my blouse and jacket. Had anyone else been here this winter? I didn't think so: the last entries in the book seemed to be older than that. I kicked around in the new snow, looking for footprints, but I couldn't really tell if any were recent. The woodpile was beside the door. There were no trees on the heath, it was all scavenged timber. One of the pieces caught my eye. I pulled it out and stood it up: a flexible board, about as wide as the length of my arm, and almost as tall as me.

'Nivvy! This is our sled! All it needs is some holes, for fastening the harness and roping things down—' Something glinted, out on the heath. I looked again, and it was gone, but I was sure I'd seen a flash of light, like a reflection on glass—

But rats love woodpiles. Just as I was searching for that glint of a reflection, a great big daddy-rat, disturbed by my poking, came jumping out, right in my face. I fell backwards, and a slender, russet brown body leapt from my jacket. The rat disappeared, with Nivvy in pursuit. There was a terrific squealing and scuffling, then a small, sleek head popped out from among the timbers: bright eyes, round ears, and a fierce, bloodied grin. Nivvy licked my fingers, chirruped and dived out of sight. He quickly reappeared dragging the daddy-rat. He laid the body in front of me, smoothed his whiskers modestly with his front paws, and vanished again. Another terrific scuffle, and another rat was carried out. He repeated this process once more, and then he seemed satisfied. He took a few token bites, and rippled up to my shoulder, purring and nuzzling my ear.

My Nivvy was back! My dearest, first companion.

That night I built a good fire, and cooked up a can of con stew. Of course the rats soon gathered, but we were ready, and Nivvy wreaked havoc. I had found a shovel in the woodpile, which I used to move the casualties. I built a triumphal pyramid outside in the snow, and counted twenty-seven corpses ... I thought of Yagin, and almost wished that strange man had been there to see the joyous slaughter. A little rampant predation, he would have said, never does nature any harm.

After that the rats didn't bother me. I found a metal spike in one of the planks on the woodpile, heated it red-hot and used it to punch holes in my flexible board. I made a sledge harness, with shoulder-padding from scavenged bunk-mattress. I packed my supplies, and repacked them. I memorised the notes and charts in the diary-book. No one came, nothing moved on the heath or the frozen sea. The weather stayed fine and calm, I ate well, and slept well. Nivvy rarely left my shoulder, except when he was ratting. I played with him and talked to him, the way I had done when I was four years old. At night (I slept by the stove: I didn't fancy those rat-gnawed bunks) I would wake, with Mama's

210

nutshell hugged in my arms and Nivvy in the crook of my shoulder, and think I was a little girl again, in the cupboard-bed with my Mama: dreaming of the great journey we would make, to the shores of the frozen sea.

I felt watched, all the time. But I thought it was my imagination.

Or maybe the ghosts, or my Mama; thinking of me far away—

On the fourth day I packed my sled and dragged it down the cliff path. There was a bank of frozen shingle, clotted with snow, and then the ice. I stood with the sled at my feet, staring. Yulia and Aliek had said wait for company. But what if nobody came? Anyway, I couldn't wait, because of Yagin ... I was rested. I had everything I needed. Except maybe the courage to set out alone. It was about sixty miles across the strait. According to the diary-book, I should be prepared for at least ten marches, ten days and nights on the ice. I thought of being out there all alone. The ice failing: me waking up in the freezing water, my knapsack sinking, nobody to help me—

'This is our trial run,' I said to Nivvy. 'Across the bay, and back overland.'

It took me several hours to cross the bay: including a stop in the middle, when I practiced putting up my tent, made myself some tea, ate a meal and packed everything up again. I was tired but pleased with myelf when I reached the western shore. There was no path here, but the cliffs were much more broken. I hauled and struggled, cursing the rocks and the sudden drifts. Eventually I reached the heath again, drenched in sweat. I set off for home at once. It's best not to stop when you're over-heated, you'll get a chill. There was a tingling like invisible messages in the frozen air, and on the east and western margins of the sky stood two pillars of light, unimaginably tall, shading from pink to green. A great silver arc unfolded between them, the point of the curve seeming to dip into the sea. I had not seen the northern lights since the time I met the wild snow-hare, on the plain beyond the fur-farm.

'That's got to be a good omen!'

Nivvy made a grumbling noise, from the warmth of my greasy, dirty layers. I gazed until the magic faded. How beautiful the winter world is, I thought. In spite of everything. Then I realised I could still see lights in the sky, dull yellowish lights, that seemed to be coming from the ground ... I heard a murmur, *a human voice*. I could see nothing, but sound travels far on cold dry air. I slipped off the sledge harness and crept toward the skyline.

I was looking down into a valley, a shallow rift in the heath. In the bottom there was a big, sleek black vehicle with caterpillar treads. I'd seen the light of its headlamps. Beside it stood a group of men. Two of them were wearing sheeny, square-shouldered dark coats, and sable hats: they had a look of power, but they didn't look like officials. The word that came to my mind was *Mafia*. The men with them were rougher, and carrying guns. Except for one, who was in uniform, a tunic with collar flashes, a peaked cap and high boots. It was Yagin, of course.

He wasn't carrying a gun, but he had a shiny pole in his hand. As I watched, he folded this shiny pole up on itself ... I had seen a telescope at New Dawn.

It was *Yagin* who had been watching me—

He was telling the Mafia men something: explaining something. One of them beckoned, and an armed man came up, carrying a flat case. Yagin took it, looked inside, and nodded. I couldn't hear a word. But I'd seen enough.

I shot backwards, and rolled to the bottom of the slope, getting a mouthful of snow. 'It's Yagin!' I gasped, thrusting my arms into the sledge harness. 'He's been here all along, he's been watching us! He's sold us to the Mafia! We've got to go, straight away, anywhere, we've got to get out of here—!'

I set off at a frantic pace over the iron-hard, uneven ground, the sled bouncing and jarring. I was lucky I didn't break an ankle. Suddenly the desperation to rush went out of me. What was I going to do? Where was I running to? I let the harness slip from my shoulders, and sat on my roped bundles. The cold sparkle of the snow glittered between my feet, every broken and jumbled flake distinct.

Yagin is here. The words drummed in my head.

I had realised he must know about the Observatory. I'd been expecting him to turn up ... But this place, so silent and lonely, had put me off my guard. He had sold me to the Mafia, I was sure of that. But why here? Why not before? And why had he been watching me, when he could have just grabbed me? Don't try to understand him, I told myself. Just think. Think of a way out ... Yagin had been in uniform. That told me he was still playing his double game, even now. His men might be near. Could that help me, somehow?

I had everything I needed; I could set off right now across the ice. But I would be on foot. My enemies would come after me on motor sleds ...

A soft growl made me start. Nivvy had slipped out of my jacket, and I'd let him go; I knew he wouldn't stray. I looked around and saw that my Nivvy had become a bigger animal, the same sinuous body but much stronger and longer, with thick dark hair, a snarling muzzle. A pair of evil yellow eyes gazed at me with anxious love, a paw with claws like razor-sharp meathooks lay on on my arm—

'Nivvy—?'

He jumped up, and rubbed his face against my cheek. The air was full of his stink. Nivvy excited was always quite strong, this was much stronger. I hugged him, feeling the formidable muscle under his fur. I must keep calm! If I got scared he would go into that cascade of change, and die like Nosey.

'Nivvy, I've got a sort of plan. Come on! Back to the Observatory!'

I marched, under the stars, Nivvy bounding beside me. When I finally reached the point where I could see the Observatory, I found out I'd been right about the Fitness Police. The snowcruiser was there. They hadn't been able to get it onto the headland: it was parked on the heath, its security lights glowing, lighting up that lying promise blazoned on its side. *Protecting Your Fragile Environment.* Yagin had been here on his own, with his telescope. But the young officers had caught up with him. Had he sent for them, by radio or something? Or had they come without instructions – and nearly caught him at his double-dealing?

There were lights inside the Observatory too. The police would have found the proud entry I'd made in the diary-book this morning. *Trial Run* ... Now they were waiting for me to return.

I had planned to come back here and hide: hide and watch them search for me, and steal what I needed, the same way as I had done at the fur-farm. Now things would move faster than that.

Nivvy's nose bumped against my hand.

'Let's find the sleds,' I said.

I jogged down the slope. I knew I couldn't be seen or heard from inside, not unless I went and knocked on one of the snowy windows, but when I got closer I moved very cautiously. The three motorsleds were in a row by the woodpile. I left my laden sled at the top of the cliff path, and crept back. I chose the one with the fullest fuel gauge. One of the young officers had left his rifle in the sled: I decided I would take that too. Then I opened the engine housing on the others, pulled at whatever would pull, opened the fuel caps and quietly, carefully, tipped them over into the snow. We made two trips to the shore: first I took the laden sled, then I went back for the motor sled. It was a slow, awkward business getting it down the path, kicking it with one foot, while trying not to make a sound. When it was done, I was shaking.

I realised I hadn't eaten for hours. I forced myself to stop, and get that fire inside burning. The stars burned down on me as I sat there in the icy dark, on my bundles, and ate a jar of con and pickled peppers, and a chocolate bar. And by my side my magic guardian kept watch. His teeth were daggers, his tufted ears turned this way and that, alert for any danger; his coat was richly dappled. His eyes were still full of love. I licked oil and herbs from my fingers, and tied the board-sled on behind the motor sled ... I'd need it when the fuel ran out, and anyway I didn't have time to transfer everything. I hugged my Nivvy, burying my hands in his beautiful soft ruff. 'This is it. Here we go.' He jumped up beside me. I turned the key, gripped the steering bar and away we went. The whine of the engine sounded horribly loud.

North. What other direction could there be? All my life, north had been the dream, the way to freedom. I felt sick with excitement, and clutched the steering bar with a manic grip. We shot out of the mouth of the bay, onto the open sea. The stars shone in the black sky, the sled bucked and bounced, leaping over the frozen crests where I would have stumbled and toiled. It was as if I was flying—

Suddenly I *was* flying. I was in the air, the stars cartwheeling. I landed with a crash, on my bum, and collapsed in mortal terror, praying for luck I didn't deserve, while Nivvy sniffed anxiously at my face. I got up slowly, testing my arms and legs, and retrieved my cap. The knapsack was still on my back: I took it off, and checked the kits. They were all right, just scared. They looked up at me in bewilderment. 'It was a little accident,' I whispered. 'Nothing serious. It won't happen again.'

The motorsled was on its side. I righted it and turned the key: it started.

I hobbled over to fetch the wooden sled, collected my scattered gear, counted the bundles, and packed everything securely. I slung the rifle over my shoulder and knotted the sledge harness where it had snapped. 'So that's how easy it is,' I muttered. 'That's how easy it is to wreck everything, and die.' Fear gripped me. It was a long, cold time – only minutes, but long ones – before I could convince myself to get on the sled and start again. I found out how to use the steering bar – don't clutch it, hold it gently – and how to use the brakes. I found a pace that wasn't too fast and wasn't too slow, and kept an eye on the little dials that lit up all by themselves in the dark. I could recognise the compass, and the fuel gauge, and there was a clock, and a thing that might be measuring distance ... Nivvy pressed himself against my shins, his chin on my knee, and we flew north by the stars, until my hands wouldn't grip on the bar. Why are my hands getting so clumsy, I wondered, vaguely annoyed—

I slackened my speed, we glided to a halt. Fear opened up and swallowed me, but I forced myself to do what would take the fear away. Hug Nivvy, feel his warm breath and his rough tongue. Bury my frozen face in his beautiful soft fur. Drink water and *eat something sweet*, quickly. Unpack the tent, inflate it, drag everything you need inside, crawl inside with this big Nivvy who is still Nivvy.

I filled my stove with fuel, lit it and heated a can of stew. Nivvy wouldn't touch it, so I ate it all myself, and lay down wrapped in my quilt. Never do that again! Never let the fire inside burn low! Your brain will stop working, you'll do something stupid, you'll die, and it will all have been for nothing ... It was a long time since I'd taken any of my clothes off; they were stuck to me with grease and dirt. Somewhere under this filth is Sloe, still dressed in the pretty clothes that Little Father gave her.

I must sleep.

When I woke, the sky outside my tent was brilliant blue, and the sun felt warm. Nivvy wasn't with me. There was no sign of land anywhere. I was alone in the white emptiness, and it was as magical as I had ever dreamed ... Only where was I? When I checked the mileage on the sled, it seemed to say I had covered forty miles. Nearly two thirds! But the fuel gauge said I was soon going to be walking. I took out the nutshell and ate a can of cold stew, talking to the kits and reading the notes I'd made about the route. Nivvy must have gone looking for something to eat. I wished I'd thought of bringing along some frozen rats. Could I cut a hole in the ice and catch a fish? But the thought of a hole in the ice made the fear rise up. I must remember the fear was just under the surface, and do nothing to wake it. I must keep telling myself that this strait was narrow, and that people like me crossed it all the time.

Another twenty miles, except it wasn't quite that simple. There were currents where the sea rarely froze past the brash, the broken soup stage; and other places where the ice was liable to crunch up into ridges, *sastrugi*, like a nest of vipers, and I would break my legs trying to get through.

'NIVVY—!'

I shaded my eyes. I couldn't see him, but the ice was deceptive. It had lumps and blue towers that you thought were the size of a fist, then you'd realise they were tall as houses. He could be close by, and out of sight . . . I looked all around again, and saw a black dot, coming out the south. The fear washed over me, and vanished as if it had never been. I had no time to be afraid now. I stuffed everything really precious inside my clothes, slung the knapsack on my back, stripped out the bivvy tent and stowed everything in about two minutes flat. I shouted again for Nivvy, but for once in his life he didn't come to me . . . Go then, I thought. Stay away, don't come near. And if you see me taken, live whatever life you can. I tied the wooden sled behind the motorsled, jumped on board and turned the key, and immediately felt hopeful again, because I was moving—

When I looked back, grim reality returned. The devil was gaining on me fast. I couldn't win this race. He knew how to use a motorsled and I didn't. He could fly. If I hit rough ice I would have to slow right down or—

I was flying again.

I lay on my side, my head spinning. I had smashed into a huge lump of ice; I couldn't work out how I hadn't seen that coming. The sled lay in a crumpled heap, my gear was scattered. I heard the whine of the other engine suddenly cut off. I heard, with my ear to the ice, the crunch of his boots, and I saw the rifle within reach of my hand. I rolled over, grabbed it, and struggled to my knees.

'Don't come any closer!'

Yagin was not close at all: he was about twenty metres away. He put his hands in the air. 'Sloe! You haven't enough fuel!'

'I can walk.'

'I have fuel here. I brought it for you.'

I kept the rifle trained on him while he stooped, reached into his sled and brought out a can. He walked towards me, steadily, holding it up. He was hypnotising me ... Then I realised he was *wading*. He was crossing a wide river of brash, which I had crossed without knowing it. My hands started to shake.

'You're on their side. You want to destroy the Lindquists.'

'I'm trying to save them ... Sloe, listen to me. I'm a Fitness Officer, but I've been working for another cause all along. I had myself put in charge of the hunt for you so nobody else would get the job. I could have handed you over time and again. I've had you in my hands and helped you to escape—

'Yes, and I know why. The other cause you serve is *Yagin*. You sold me to the Mafia. I saw you with them, on the heath, taking their money—

'They aren't the Mafia,' said Yagin. 'They are just powerful businessmen. I convinced them I had to gain your trust or you would destroy the kits. I had it all figured out: how I could do my deal, and still get you safe to your mother. I told them it was better to let you run, with me using my powers as a Police Officer to stay close, until you

219

were on the last lap. I was going to take you across the ice. That tent you're using, and the supplies, I brought here, for us—'

I could never have pulled the trigger, even if I'd known how to use a rifle.

'If you hadn't run away from the cabin, that's the way it would have been. But you ran, and my trusting young men found me, and that made things more difficult—'

He walked up and took the rifle from me, and tossed the weapon into that river of mashed ice, where it sank out of sight. I had *longed* to trust him—

'Now give me the knapsack, and let me explain—'

'NO!'

I fought him, but it was useless. He peeled the knapsack off my back.

'You traitor! You *traitor*!'

'You have to die, that's the only thing that works. They know something about the imprinting. They want you, as part of the package, and I'm not going to let that happen. So you die, trying to escape. I save the goods, and that's the end of the hunt. Don't you see, Sloe? I tell them I saw you drown—'

He had pulled out the nailbox. He had the labcase in his hands. He ripped it open, and stared at me.

'*Where are they*?'

I shook my head, backing away from him. I could hear thunder, I thought it was the sound of my world falling apart. But there was something else, a message, a thin, fine, secret singing that seemed meant for me alone ... Yagin, his fist full of doll's house glassware, turned to look behind him, and cursed—

My mind wasn't putting things together. I saw the snowcruiser, and only dimly realised that the thunder in my head was the rumble of its tracks. But the other vehicle, the big black shiny one, was speeding up, getting closer—

Yagin dropped everything and started to run, waving his arms.

'Stupid boys! Damned fools! Stop! You can't! The ice won't—'

The cruiser stopped by Yagin's sled. The young officers got down. They started running, saw the brash, and then one of them yelled, and pointed.

Nivvy had come back.

He was a four-legged beast, but taller than a man. He came galloping out from behind a blue tower, moving with such power and beauty I could only stare, seeing the Nivvy I loved still there, in that fearsome majesty. He reared up, I saw the appalling gape of his fanged jaws. I saw the Fitness Police rifles levelled. They screamed at each other in terror. 'Run!' I wailed. 'Nivvy! Run! Get away!'

But the bond we had wasn't like that. I couldn't tell the Lindquists what to do, any more than you can tell the cells of your own body not to save your life if they can. Nivvy, king of the snows indeed, charged at Yagin. Red fire spat across the ice . . . But my message was coming clearer now. I felt it through my body, an invisible zigzag lightning, as the fault line spread, the flaw opened. A monstrously huge, jagged table of ice reared up, and flopped down again with a cracking, rending groan. The whole frozen sea seemed to shift, and shrug, making a chasm in which the cruiser and the Mafia-type vehicle were both engulfed. It took the policemen down with it. The shock wave reached Yagin, he fell backwards into the open lane of night-blue, killing cold. I saw him rise up. I saw him swim, arm over arm, to the place where the cruiser had disappeared. He called his men's names, then he vanished. I thought he had gone. But he appeared again, sounding up right beside me. He rose almost to his waist, groping in the front of his tunic with a grey-white hand. On my knees, I reached out to him—

'Take my hand!'

His eyes held mine. He pushed something into my palm: cold, smooth slivers of ice. 'Pinnipeds,' he said. 'Cetecea.'

The gulf swallowed him.

I was holding two fragile glass tubes, with colour-coded caps. I stowed them inside my clothes. Everything else – the knapsack, the labcase, the stored remains of Nosey and Toothy – had vanished. I limped over the Nivvy and knelt beside him, and stroked his wicked, wedge-shaped head, his bloodied fur. He was bleeding, but I didn't try to find the wounds: there was nothing I could do. I just stayed there, while his body shuddered through change after change. When he was small again I picked him up. He was still alive, but limp as a rag. He made his little chrring noise in protest: but I wasn't going to leave him behind. There was too much I'd had to leave behind. I packed what I could salvage onto the wooden sled, and we walked on, under the low arc of the winter sun, which was still shining, bright in a cloudless sky.

I stopped often, to check my compass, and Nivvy was always still alive: but no more than that. We camped when the sun went down, and got up and did the same again the next day. The day after that, we reached the place the diary-book called Rescue Island, and I was saved.

Rescue Island wasn't natural. It was a big block of concrete, floating in the ice and anchored to the sea bed. It had been an oil rig when people still got oil from under the sea, instead of growing it. It had been converted into a place where the people of the city I was heading for dealt with fugitives from across the ice. Being an asylum-seeker isn't much fun. I was asked a lot of questions, and not everybody was sympathetic when I refused to answer some of them. Not everyone understood how shaken up I was. I stank pretty badly, and I wouldn't let them undress me: I suppose that didn't help, either. But they didn't take Nivvy away, and they didn't search me. They just put me in the secure hospital, with a bathroom I could use, and gave me some clean clothes. One day a woman came to my room. She was middle-aged, thin and stern. She wore a white coat with the Chervil Ring embossed on the buttons, and she'd brought a tray of shiny instruments.

'Sloe, will you let me examine, er, Nivvy?'

'Are you going to kill him?'

'No.'

She laid out her instruments, and I let her take Nivvy from me, though he protested. She looked him over, and measure him: checked his teeth, and shone a kind of ray-thing through him so she could see his insides. Finally she took a scraping from his mouth, and looked at it through her microscope. The room got very still.

At last she raised her head and stared at me with shining eyes. 'This is incredible. And you are? Tell me your name again,—'

So I told her my true name, the name I had never spoken to anyone since I was four years old, and hardly knew it was mine. She went away, and came back with a phone. I spoke to my Mama, for the first time in nearly four years. I heard her voice and I said 'Mama I'm on Rescue Island, does that mean I'm safe? Is it safe?' She told me afterwards that I wouldn't say anything more, I just kept asking that question. But she knew it was me. She knew it was me . . . When Mama had told me it was safe, I took out the nutshell, and the seed-tubes I'd hidden inside my clothes, when I saw Yagin coming on the ice.

Insectivora, *Lagomorpha*, *Rodentia*, *Artiodactyla*, *Chiroptera*, and the two new ones *Pinnipeds* and *Cetecea*. And of course *Carnivora*, whose living type-form was sitting up on my shoulder now, fascinated by these strange events.

The kits were dead. They had come to the natural end of their miniature lives in the first days I'd spent on Rescue Island. But nothing was lost, because the seeds were safe. I had brought them through.

They call it 'the city where the sun always shines' because of the solar panels, which collect sunlight so efficiently that the city doesn't need any other power source. Inside it was just like any other city, only rather small. You could walk across it: and people usually did walk, everywhere. My mother's house was in a square with a beautiful garden in the middle: and every house had its own garden in front of it, too. Walking up to her front door was like walking into a specially flowery grove in a green and blossoming wood. There were roses and violets and snowdrops all in bloom at once: and every rose bush had flowers of ten or fifteen different colours. Birds sang, and there was a little stream, singing back at them.

Mama hadn't been able to come to Rescue Island. Things were really changing, but some important people in our country still regarded Mama as a dangerous rebel, and she must not leave the city of refuge. She was standing at the door. My beautiful Mama was just the same as I remembered her. I had been a child when we parted. Now I was taller than my Mama, I would soon be fourteen, and I had done so many bad things . . . I looked at her; she looked at me: we didn't speak. Then she hugged me, and I hugged her back. Nivvy, who had to be carried in a little case around the city, started to chrr indignantly: so I got him out, and gave him to Mama. He went beserk with joy, rippling all over her, sniffing her and licking her, holding her face with his paws. Mama began to laugh, and cry, at the same time; and so did I.

We went indoors, to a pretty room with rugs, and pictures, and a wide window looking out on the garden. We sat on Mama's sofa, holding each other's hands.

I had talked to her on the phone, after that first mad time, but there was so much I hadn't been able to say. Suddenly it all came bursting out. Every worst thing I'd done. How I'd boasted about her science-teaching, and Madam Principal's yellow cake. Rose and the thieving, Rain and how I'd let him go in the Box and die. All the bewildering things Yagin had told me . . . at New Dawn, and afterwards. How I'd told Mama I understood about the Lindquists, when I didn't, and I'd had no idea what they meant, and I'd almost lost them in a stinking fur-factory. Leaving Satin and Emerald and the others with the slavers, and how Toothy became many, and Toesy died. And Yulia and Aliek who had helped me when they knew I was a runaway, and they'd probably got into bad trouble with a bandit boss. And the northern lights, and the silver forest, and the wild ride across the ice—

Nivvy got bored, and went exploring.

Mama told me parts of her story too. We sat there for I don't know how long, repeating ourselves, interrupting each other, the lost years all unfurling, and folding around us, until we were bound together again, as if we'd never been apart.

Mama said that after she'd been smuggled out, and reached this city, people had tried hard to get permission for me to join her. But nobody had known how bad things were at New Dawn, so they hadn't wanted to try anything extreme like kidnapping me ... They hadn't known about the Lindquists. Mama had told no one, not a soul. She'd been betrayed once, she wasn't going to risk it again. The kits were done for, if any word of their existence got to the wrong people. Nobody at New Dawn had told me anything, of course. Nobody had told me that my Mama had escaped, or even whether she was alive or dead. Except for Yagin and his mysterious promise, about the spring being a dangerous time—

'Mama?' I asked. 'What made Yagin do what he did—?'

I knew his real name now, but he was still 'Yagin' to me.

She shook her head. 'I suppose he wanted to survive, although he didn't like the price he had to pay. He'd been a scientist at the Biological Institute. When the government took over the Institute and made it just a branch of the Fitness Police, he had the choice of losing everything, or going along with that ... He chose to become an Intelligence Officer for the Fitness Police: but he kept in touch with the other side, too, although of course he wasn't trusted. That's how he knew I was safe. I'm sure it's true he'd guessed I had a set of kits, and he knew they hadn't been found. When you turned up at New Dawn, he saw his chance to get hold of a fabulous treasure. But he still wanted to save your life.'

I nodded. I believed now that Yagin had never meant to kill me, on the ice. He had meant to rob me, to take the kits and let me go.

'That's what I meant,' I said. 'That's what I don't understand. The way he felt about me, the things he did.' I hesitated. 'For a while, I thought ... I thought he might be my Dadda. That my Dadda had escaped, and you had sent

226

him to help me, but it was a secret so he couldn't tell me who he was—'

'Your Dadda is dead.'

'I know,' I whispered. 'They told me, at Rescue Island—'

'Rosita . . . I mean, Sloe. I keep calling you both: which do you like?'

'I don't know.' But then I did. 'Call me Sloe, it's my name.'

She touched my cheek. 'All right, Sloe. It suits you, my dauntless winter flower. Listen, I will tell you a story. It's a grown-up story, are you ready for that?'

I nodded.

Mama looked away from me, out into the garden. 'Well, it starts more than ten years ago. There were three scientists, working together at the Biological Institute. Two of them were married to each other, and had a baby girl. A very naughty, clever little baby girl, who used to make me tear my hair out. But the three were all close friends . . . When your Dadda and I found out what the government planned to do with the wild mammal Lindquists, we decided to take action. We made two sets of the kits, then we destroyed all our work, leaving not a trace to show how it was done. That was when the marine mammal kits disappeared, and we were very afraid this must mean there was a traitor. Your Dadda tried to take his kits to safety anyway. He was arrested. As you know, it's a very serious crime to move factory animals without a license. Taking the Lindquists was much, much worse, and I knew there was hardly a hope. But I thought I knew who had betrayed us. I went to him, and he—'

'This was "Yagin".'

'Yes . . . Maybe I should say he was married, but to someone he didn't love. To a very highly placed official's

227

daughter, in fact.' Mama drew a deep breath. 'That's the way life was ... if you wanted to get on in the world. Well, he was drunk that night. He told me he had always loved me, and he said if I would be his mistress, he would use his influence to save your Dadda's life. I laughed at him. I said I didn't believe he'd do anything to save Pyotr, however I humiliated myself. I went away, and I never saw him again ... I don't know what power he had, really. I will never know if I signed your Dadda's death warrant.'

Nivvy came trotting back, and curled himself in Mama's lap.

'I think he really loved you,' I said, after a long silence. 'And whatever he had done, at the very end he chose to make amends. I think that's what matters most.'

Mama looked at me, with a strange smile.

'You've grown into a fine young woman, my little girl.'

I held her hands, and we cried again, although we were so happy. For my Dadda, and for Yagin too. For all the losses of the winter world: for everyone twisted and broken by the cold, and for the chances that would not return, though spring would come again.

Returning . . .

The train drew up at a deserted platform in the middle of nowhere, and a young woman got down with her bags. There were no guards with her. No one left and no one came. The hut which might have been a ticket office looked as if it had the same splash of mud on its door as had been there for seventeen years. The blank, grassy plain of the summer wilderness stretched out to the rim of forest on every horizon.

Eventually the Community Tractor grumbled up. The driver got down and slung the young woman's bags into the cart – except for the knapsack she carried, that she wouldn't let him touch.

'You never sent me that postcard,' said Storm, with a slow smile.

'I forgot.'

They both got into the cab, and the tractor drove away.

For my Mama, returning to city life had been coming home. She had her work, she had friends, she loved her house and garden. She would never return to the city where I was born, though they'd have welcomed her as a distinguished scientist these days. But she was very happy indoors. I had not been able to get used to it. I missed the open air, the wildness, I missed dirt: I even missed the cold. I looked at Storm, and calculated he must be about twenty-four now. He hadn't changed much. He had the same slow smile, the same dry way of talking. I wondered what he thought of me? The city girl who came back outside, of her own free will: just when wilderness people were being allowed into the cities. He probably thought I was crazy.

'What are you going to do with yourself out here, eh?'

'I'm going to teach. Here, and other places.'

'A job with travel, that'll suit your habits.'

He started grinning slyly.

'What's so funny?'

'Oh, I was just thinking about you and Miss Malik. What're you going to do if you get stuck with a horrible pushy little girl who's twice as smart as you?'

'Teach her to be three times smarter. What about you? Are you still in the illegal internal import and export business, with Nicolai?'

'Partly ... Partly I'm a farmer. Got a land grant: it beats labour camp.'

'What do you grow?'

'Birch scrub and frozen swamp, at the moment. Few berries. I plan to diversify.' Storm looked at the knapsack I was holding in my lap. 'What's in there?'

'Seeds. From a seedbank. It's time to try planting them out again.'

'We could be partners.'

I didn't say yes and I didn't say no. I just smiled. I thought of the dresses that life wears, all folded down so small, and how I would shake them out and set them dancing, in all their brave, and funny, and marvellous diversity.

And the tractor rumbled on, through the flowers and grasses, under the empty, magical vastness of the wilderness sky.

Author's Note:
The Seedsavers

The greatest seedbank in the world is held in Leningrad, a city we now know by its older name of St Petersburg. In the Second World War, Leningrad was besieged for nine hundred days. Half a million people starved, but the curators of the seedbank barricaded themselves in, and defended their stocks – the hope of the future – from the starving citizens. When Allied soldiers finally entered the facility, they found the emaciated bodies of the botanists lying beside full sacks of potatoes, maize and wheat, a priceless genetic legacy for which they had given their lives. This is the story that gave me the idea for Sloe and her adventure. Susan Lindquist, whose name I've borrowed for the Lindquist kits, is a real person, and a Massachusetts Institute of Technology Biology professor. She really has worked out that there's a prion (a kind of protein) that can act like a genetic switch, controlling the expression of many tiny mutations, until they are all revealed at once. Of course the idea that you could build a compendium-genome, where several different species could be hidden and 'revealed' like that, is a complete fantasy. But the winter world that Sloe lives in could be ours. As you may know, a colder Europe may be one consequence of the phenomenon known as 'Global Warming'. The great Oceanic Current we call the Gulf Stream, or the North

Atlantic Drift, may switch into reverse, bringing cold water instead of warm water to the western seaboard of Europe, and causing land temperatures to drop sharply. You could, if you like, imagine that Sloe's journey starts somewhere to the east of Warsaw; she travels to the Baltic coast (a journey I have made myself, by way of roads still potholed in places by Second World War bombs), and the city where the sun always shines is across the sea in the south of Sweden ... somewhere around Malmö? But maybe not. You can imagine the adventure happening wherever you like. The Siberia I'm talking about in this story is not a place. Siberia is a state of mind.

Also by Ann Halam

Dr Franklin's Island

What's it like to see your best friend transformed into a bird in front of your eyes? What's it like to know it's your turn next?

On a tiny tropical island the palm fringed beaches hide a terrible secret. Beyond the azure waters and white sands is Dr Franklin's 'hospital'.

Miranda, Semi and Arnie, sole survivors of a plane crash, are about to become his next victims. He's been waiting for them. They're perfect specimens for his experiments in genetic engineering.

A horrifying, fascinating story of three friends who leave their human forms to become fish and fowl – nothing like it has ever been written before.

Taylor Five

What's it like to be 14 years old and know that you are a clone – 'a human photocopy'? Tay (or Taylor 5 as she is officially documented) is trying to come to terms with herself when her jungle home in Borneo is attacked by terrorists. She escapes with 'Uncle' a highly intelligent orang utan, and the bond forged between ape and girl on their perilous journey to safety proves to her once and for all that she is not an elaborate doll, but just an ordinary girl with an extraordinary life.

A moving and emotionally powerful read that raises some searching questions.